The Things We Said in Venice

KRISTIN ANDERSON

DEDICATION

This novel is dedicated to Shonna Vear Howenstine, Eva Hvingelby and Tracy Sires Dugan. You girls were there during key moments of my formative years, discovering the world along with me. Together, you instilled humor, a sense of adventure and a quest for romance into the foundation of my character. In other words, this is all your fault.

ACKNOWLEDGMENTS

Thank you Kirsten B. Thomas, Giovanna A. Muñoz, Jesse Wedmore, Melissa M. Segonds and Janita van Nes for taking the time to read early versions of this novel and provide valuable feedback that helped my characters and locations blossom. Additional thanks to Giovanna (Italian) and Janita (Dutch) for your translation work, which prevented me from butchering your native languages and Joanna Bouma for your help with our native language of English. Thanks to my son and husband for giving me the space and time behind the computer. And last but certainly not least, to author Francis Guenette, who aided me during a particularly nasty bout of writer's block by responding to the following request: Give me three elements for a short story along with a genre of your choice. Her answer: *A suitcase, a stranger and a train. Love story.* Clearly, this story wasn't satisfied being short. Let the fun begin!

PART ONE: GRAND EUROPEAN TOUR

Chapter 1
Sarah

While the locals shuffle carefully over the snow-slicked sidewalks, Sarah runs like a mad woman toward the Belluno station. *I will not miss this one*, she chants in time to the distant, yet steady clickety-clack of the train's metal wheels gliding over tracks. She picks up her pace, the icy air burning her nostrils, the straps of her pack chafing her shoulders despite her thick winter layers.

She cuts through the abandoned village park, her laborious movements at odds with the utter stillness as Belluno train station finally pops into view. As she slows her pace, her body relays physical complaints to her mind: the surprising weight of her backpack cutting into her shoulders, the ache of ice-cold air in her lungs, the burning sensation of snowflakes on her cheeks.

When she comes to a standstill, a rush of heat explodes through her body. Moments later, perspiration builds beneath her thick winter layers, cooling her down. Damp curls form a blanket of cold around her neck. She shakes her head involuntarily as the first shiver crawls up her spine.

As means of distraction, Sarah people watches, though the pickings are slim—a thickly built woman holding the hand of a stout, large-eared boy, presumably her son, and an older, clean-shaven man in military uniform. All three sport dry hair.

By the time the train pulls into the station and Sarah hears the familiar hiss of the doors opening, her teeth are chattering. She finds a free place in the third railcar and finally unstraps the cumbersome backpack, setting it in the seat beside her. The whistle sounds and the train is about to take off, but it doesn't. There is some sort of commotion. The doors open and close again. She can hear two men talking, perhaps the conductor and a male passenger. Although she can't make out the words, one voice is laced with tension and a bit too loud. The other voice, which she assumes belongs to the conductor, remains calm.

Back home, she would need to know why the doors had to open once more and what these men are discussing. But in the past four weeks of free-wheeling through western Europe on her own, she has adjusted her way of responding to things beyond her control. She has learned to let go. It is so different from how she acts at home that she has given her newfound skill a name: *European Style Detachment.*

Her feet and hands begin to return to body temperature as the train finally leaves the station. She leans into her large backpack and closes her eyes. She feels a slight pulsing in her subconscious, like an alarm clock going off in the neighboring hotel room; something you hear, but can choose to ignore. Except that she can't. Something's not right. It could be that slightly angry conversation she overheard, or it could be that the bag she is leaning into doesn't smell like her bag. It has the faint scent of cinnamon and musk tinged with sweat; the scent of a man.

Sarah straightens in her seat, scrutinizing the travel backpack as one might scrutinize a naked stranger you have unwittingly brought into your bed—curiosity tempered with fear. It is black like hers. It has the white North Face logo of her bag and the same rainbow strap she put on it to differentiate her black bag from all the other black bags of the world. But isn't the strap in a different place? And come to think of it, it felt heavier than her bag when she was sprinting to the train station.

Maybe it smells so manly from being in the pile of luggage where she stashed it while she grabbed a brioche at the café. Or, it could have been shuffled around in the compartment beneath the shuttle bus from Cortina to Belluno; cologne from a man's bag spilling on hers.

I'm being ridiculous, she tells herself. But she unbuckles the exterior straps anyway and peers into the top compartment.

"Oh my God!" Sarah exclaims as she shuffles through the doppelganger of her bag. Several passengers turn toward her momentarily and then look away, exemplifying *European Style Detachment*. At the top of the backpack is a photography magazine written in what she thinks must be German. She pushes aside the magazine, revealing an impressive stash of Cote d'Or chocolate bars in their distinctive red and gold cardboard wrappers, cloth handkerchiefs in a Ziploc bag, a leather-bound journal, water, men's plaid underwear size XL, slacks, long sleeve shirts, pants and thick woolen socks. On the inside tag of the top compartment is a name written in black permanent marker: Fokke van der Veld. She stops her search and pushes the bag away in shock. How the hell did this happen?

It has stopped snowing outside and sun reflects off the whitened fields, punching into the window. Sarah reaches automatically into the side pocket for her sunglasses, but of course they're not there. Her mother is in a thick pea coat, wearing Sarah's missing sunglasses and deathly blue lipstick that promises to make her forthcoming tirade all the graver:

What are you going to do now Sarah? You should have taken your time in Cortina d'Ampezzo to make sure you had your own bag! Your passport, your money, your iPad. Everything is in that bag! You could be mistaken for a terrorist and thrown in prison for traveling without identification.

The locals say Cortina, not Cortina d'Ampezzo, Sarah counters. As a school counselor, she is well aware it's abnormal to be seeing visions of her mother in her head, not to mention silently conversing with her. But as usual, mom's got a point. Sarah thinks about Italian corruption, envisions a musty 17th century prison cell with a mangy rat family in one corner and instruments of torture in the other. She stands suddenly, wanting to take action; wanting her mom to shut up. She has thirty euros in her jacket pocket along with the train ticket and the address of the hotel in Treviso where she will be staying. That's at least something. But how on earth is she going to get her bag back? And who the hell is Fokke van der Veld?

Chapter 2
Fokke

Fokke van der Veld doesn't like pink. At least not until they arrive in Cortina late in the afternoon in time to see the chiseled pink granite of the Italian Dolomites glowing on the horizon. And that's before the sunset starts doing its thing. Even though his photographic memory has already archived his surroundings, he blows through at least a gig of memory as he clicks away at the view of light playing across snow-dusted mountains; granite shapeshifting through a thousand permutations of pink: magenta-pink, pinky-orange, burnt pink umber, marigold pink; a mountain range formed 240 million years ago putting on a spectacular show of nature in this moment.

These aren't exactly thoughts to share with his old fraternity brothers, but that's the beauty of this trip; even after all these years, they don't need a lot of words to communicate with one another.

"Fucking amazing," Jan comments. Peter nods in agreement.

"Exactly," Fokke smiles. "Barometer?"

"Mind blowing. But let's hit the bar before it snows. It's got to be about -2 celsius out here." Barry Townsend, also known as Barometer, is sensitive to both altitude and temperature, heralds from Australia, and at six feet two inches, or 1.8 meters, is the shortest man in the group.

It begins to snow. They huddle together on the deck of the lodge as Fokke stretches his long arm up in the air and takes a selfie of the four of them, catching the last glimpses of the Dolomites before darkness descends.

Tomorrow they will be hiking in the Dolomites, or perhaps skiing if this weather keeps up. Fokke isn't sure how this is going to work out for Barry, seeing as he's so weather sensitive. In the cold winters of Amsterdam twenty years ago when they were all at university together, he had the uncanny ability to predict the outside temperature within half a degree — hence the nickname Barometer.

He isn't as worried about the other guys. Jan van Buuren and Peter Admiraal are built like their Dutch ancestors: tall men with thick torsos, broad backs and endurance in their beefy legs designed to remain steady at sea or eke out a living in the frigid landscape of The Netherlands. Peter has added a few kilos to his bulk that isn't muscle, but is still in decent enough shape due to chasing around his four kids. Jan has aged well, except that the golden chick-magnet curls of his youth have given way to a bald head.

Fokke is tall and lean, striated with muscle stretching skyward to the tune of 6 feet 6 inches, or just under two meters. His straw-hued curls are a bit salted, but he is in peak shape at forty-two years old. In fact, life is pretty sweet as long as he doesn't think about women; especially one named Jackie. Which reminds him, he needs to try Grappa, a regional distilled spirit made out of the grape skins left over from the winemaking process — a ninety proof fiery kind of spirit that is sure to burn any thoughts of women or their offspring right out of his head.

Peter tries his best to talk about something besides his kids, but he's at it again. Fokke wants to be happy for his friend, to listen openly about the trials and successes of the four little ones, not to let his own old issues get in the way, but even though it's been over a year, it's coming to the surface all over again. It had been easier on the train. He could occasionally glance out the window to center himself. But here in the bar, facing each other, it's harder. Peter must see something in his face, because he abruptly changes the subject, which is reason enough to order another round of Grappa.

Jan talks about his law practice and shares a few sordid yet entertaining details about his clients. Barry, being a dentist, has little to say about his clients, but can't shut up about his wife Genevieve and their five-year-old daughter.

Fokke doesn't want to talk about Jackie, which means that everyone else wants to talk about her — the female white elephant in the Italian ski lodge. The story might be entertaining in a heart breaking way for a moment or two if they were watching some screwed up Dutch reality show. But this is his real life. So instead of telling them about the white elephant in the room who was supposedly pregnant with his child—a child he wanted and loved before it was even born — he tells them instead about his latest stint in Cambodia writing about the ancient Buddhist Temple of Angkor Wat.

Although travel writers are as abundant as micro plastics in the ocean, Fokke is of the rare, decently-paid variety who has made a name for himself. He has the perfect job to escape his problems, which he has been doing successfully for the last fourteen months. But seeing these guys and hearing them talk about their families, their wives — brings it all back. Grappa.

Barometer seems to be taking liquid measurements and analyzing pressure, because he keeps drinking right along with Fokke in silent solidarity, waiting for that perfectly calculated moment to pop the question. Fokke should have remembered how that wily little Australian guy could loosen his tongue while drinking him under the table.

"So I think we should talk about she who cannot be named," Barry intones in the same gentle dentist voice he might use to tell a patient that the root canal is not optional — which would probably be less painful than talking about Jackie. So they talk about her, and keep on drinking.

***

Fokke is cold and alone. He huddles by the ashes of the fire, even though it has burned out long ago. He stirs the gray ash, looking for an ember that might yet spring to life, but it is a field of powdery gray without a sign of the campfire that once heated the cold, dark space. He needs to look for wood, to find matches, but he cannot will himself to move.

He awakens from the dream suddenly, opening his eyes to find Jan prodding him awake before he moves on to the others. They are going to miss the shuttle to Sappada if they don't hurry. Four guys and one shower. Fokke opts out of the shower and packs in haste, though he manages to brush his teeth, pop two ibuprofen and purchase bottled water to fill the last empty spot in his backpack for the upcoming hike. They dump their bags at the checkout area and drink espresso standing like the Italians do. They order a few jam-filled doughnuts called ciambellas in the restaurant café, which take impossibly long to make the trip from behind the glass counter onto the white plates. The shuttle bus arrives. Fokke's backpack is not in the pile with the others, but before panic sets in, he sees it next to the luggage rack. They make too much noise for middle-aged men in a chic ski lodge, but they do not care. These four friends who share a twenty-year-old bond are about to make new memories to usher that bond into the future.

Chapter 3
Alexi

The cloudless Barcelona sky forms a blue backdrop behind La Sagrada Familia. Alexi uses her time in the line to read over her notes on the interiors once again. She takes out her phone and scrolls through the comments on her vlog, memorizing names and requests. She reads through her emails and chats amicably with a couple from Austria in front of her. The line is still crawling. Like everyone else, her neck is craned skyward, studying the spectacular church. Her anticipation grows as she finally reaches the entrance.

As she edges inside, the hushed murmurs of the crowd convey awe and wonder that mimics her own. The building is spacious, filled with light. Off-white columns rise skyward like trees. Flower-shaped stained-glass windows bathe the walls in gold, green and orange. The vaulted nave soars forty-five meters high. She has seen this sacred church in books, read about it online, but nothing could have prepared her for this moment.

After she's caught her breath and is fairly certain the flush in her cheeks has gone from crimson to an acceptable blush, she sets up the tripod, fussing with her hair before pushing record.

"Hi everyone. It's Alexi and its day nineteen of my tour. I'm finally inside La Sagrada Familia, the gorgeous church originally designed by architect Antonio Gaudi. He designed this building, knowing he would not live to see it finished. The construction started in 1882 and is still continuing today. It won't be finished until 2026 or later. I've visited over twenty cathedrals and churches in the last three weeks and nothing prepared me for La Sagrada Familia.

"I usually start my travel videos outside the cathedrals, but today, I wanted to do it differently and start inside. I have been speechless for the last fifteen minutes, but my voice is coming back to me and I want to share this with you." Out of respect, she keeps her voice low, which makes it husky, intimate. "This structure feels like an architectural forest—a collaboration between nature and man. If this temple were to be in the middle of a forest, rather than the middle of a city, one might think it grew from the earth." She pans the camera around, showing the walls, the windows, the naves. Nature and architecture cooperate as the sun brings the windows to life. She spends a few more minutes pointing out the interior details before she approaches the candle area, thankful that no other tourists are nearby.

"It's time for the candle lighting." The flames shimmer like the surface of the ocean under a full moon, but in fire hues. "The first candle goes to Evelyn in Ontario, Canada. This is for your brother, John, who passed away yesterday morning. Sending peace to you all the way from Barcelona, Evelyn."

She tucks a long lock of chestnut hair behind her ear as she lifts a matchstick to a lit candle, giving flame to another.

"The second candle is for the spirit of Antonio Gaudi, for his ability to think beyond the limits of his own mortality and leave us this treasured temple." The candle soars to life, the flame shining strong. Alexi pauses, taking a slow breath, creating space. "The third candle is for my mother. You would have been filled with peace standing within this sacred space." She gives the camera a slow smile she doesn't quite feel.

"Coming up next. The exterior of La Sagrada Familia! See you in a moment." After she turns off the recorder and breaks down the tripod she approaches the candles again. If ever there was a place for God to pay a visit, or answer a prayer, it is here. She lights a fourth candle, uttering a silent prayer of her own not meant for any camera or vlog post. She stares at the flickering sea of candles in front of her, willing the tears to come.

***

Alexi takes her time walking through the interior of La Sagrada Familia until she feels like she has absorbed some aspect of the energy of this space, as if it might heal her. She is not in the right frame of mind to give the outside tour, but then she remembers her followers, their questions, encouragement and comments.

Back outside, she is pleased to discover the slight chill in the air from an hour ago has worn off. She is perfectly comfortable in her capris and short-sleeved sweater. She sets up her video camera on her tripod, adjusts her sunglasses, practices what she wants to say; aware of the dates and details but not too scripted. She presses record.

"I'm now outside La Sagrada Familia. I don't know how much you can see through my video camera, but I'm going to zoom in," she explains. "This whole temple is a story about Christianity. I'm standing in front of the Nativity façade. Gaudi designed it to face east so that it would catch the first morning light through its windows." Her voice is soft, reverent as she gazes upward.

"There is so much going on here. So many figures, shapes. If it weren't for the natural sandstone colors, it would be even more overwhelming. This façade tells about the birth of Jesus, as well as his childhood and early adult years." Several tourists discreetly come to a standstill, listening in as she explains the story captured in sandstone.

She walks on, returning to the entry and angles the camera further skyward.

"The spiraling towers remind me of honeycomb, the undulating form beneath the windows of waves, the pillars here at the entrance of trees. Organic forms; organic architecture." She continues to narrate, explaining different aspects of the building in what she hopes will do it justice, without being too detailed.

She has now reached the stage in her vlog where she addresses some of the questions from her viewers. It's the scariest, most challenging part of her whole project.

"I want to tell you how much I appreciate all of your comments, besides Hugo from San Francisco. If you want someone with a lower cut shirt and tighter jeans, then go check out a Victoria's Secret catalog. I'm traveling and discovering life, not trying out for a beauty pageant.

"The rest of you. Wow. Your feedback is amazing. You enjoy the vlogs and the details about my visits, but you also want more about me. Yeah. I can do that, especially now that I'm in Barcelona."

She adjusts her rhinestone sunglasses, clears her throat. "This city is beautiful, the people friendly, but there is a strange duality here. The signs are both in Catalan and Spanish. Catalan is a unique language quite similar to Spanish that is only spoken in four provinces known as the Catalonia region of Spain. The history of Catalonia and the reason for a separate language within Spain is a bit complicated, but just Google it and you can get the scoop.

"So I'm like Barcelona. I have two languages within me; two cultures coming together. I'm not talking about actual languages, but rather a duality of personalities. Although friendly and comfortable in one-on-one situations, I'm actually quite shy in my day-to-day life. I work in counseling, and my clients value me. But now I'm on a one-year sabbatical, discovering another me — my freedom, my individuality, the Catalonia within me."

The smile that spreads across her face is not planned, but rather a reaction to her own words, her newfound freedom. "As a traveler, I'm a less inhibited version of myself. This comes with the freedom from responsibility and a realization that life is unpredictable, and valuable. At home I was caught up in my daily patterns, forgetting that my life was passing by.

"Roy from Vancouver wants to know where I'm from in the U.S. Well, I'm not going to tell you, because I want to remain anonymous. And through that anonymity, I hope to be as real as I can with you all. This is Alexi, signing off from Barcelona. Until next time!"

Chapter 4
Sarah

Two teenage German tourists are looking at her. Sarah hoists the man's backpack with the weird Fucky-van-der-something name onto her shoulders and starts to leave her seat, but just as quickly changes her mind. She shifts it back to the seat beside her and sits down. The German boys have returned their gazes to their cell phones, their thumbs tapping away.

She only speaks a little bit of Italian and she can hardly ask the conductor to turn the train around because she's taken the wrong backpack. She doesn't like the idea of digging through other people's stuff, but she will have to in order to figure out more about this man—a man who possibly has her bag as well, she realizes.

Delaying the invasion of a stranger's privacy, she thinks back to the reception area of the lodge that morning in Cortina. It was busy and lots of people were checking out. She didn't pay much attention, considering how rushed she was, but she recalls a number of the other guests: three families, all Italian; a chummy group of tall European men decked out in expensive polypropylene suits and hiking boots; an American couple and a handful of other people who seemed to have been traveling alone like her. She tries to remember something more. Yes; there were lots of backpacks, she recalls, which makes sense in a hiking area so close to the Dolomite mountains. And that is why she was thankful for that rainbow strap sticking out, making her black backpack so easy to differentiate from all the others. *Or Fokke van der Veld's backpack*, she corrects. Determined not to miss her connection to Treviso, she had picked it up quickly, thrown it on her shoulders and headed out the door.

Okay Fokke. Let's see what you've got. She zips open the side pocket where she would place her sunglasses. She finds sunscreen, lip guard and an unopened pack of XL Durex condoms. Her cheeks flush. So, she has the exact same model of backpack as a young, well-endowed sexually hopeful male. The idea frazzles her. The bottom right side pouch is packed with energy bars and power gel. The bottom left pouch contains a small emergency kit, a pocket knife and compass. Great, she's nabbed his wilderness supplies. So far, no contact information.

She returns to the well-worn leather-bound notebook and flips it open. It's clearly a journal. She looks through the neatly written pages, but it's in German or Dutch. One name that hardly seems of Germanic origin pops off the pages again and again: Jackie.

Sarah keeps her extra cash and passport in the interior hidden pocket— one of the features that led her to select this high adventure model over the others. Sullenly, she opens the backpack up, pushes aside boxers, socks, long underwear and camera lenses and folds open the hidden panel. She unzips the pocket and bingo: a passport, cell phone and at least 400 euros in cash. This must be the heady sensation a thief feels when they find the "hidden compartment". Payday.

She pulls out the burgundy passport labeled Europese Unie Koninkrijk der Nederlanden. She shakes her head at the irony of having a Dutch man's backpack. The coincidence looms up at her like a billboard-sized metaphor—*you have the goods of a Dutch man*. She flips open the passport to discover she is indeed invading the privacy of Fokke van der Veld. He's no scrappy twenty-year-old, but a distinguished looking forty-two-year-old Dutch man with sandy blond hair, light blue eyes, rugged nose and a clean-shaven face. Based on the number of stamps in his passport, he's well-traveled. *Executive type. Probably works for Shell Oil or some other Dutch multi-national,* she thinks.

She picks up his cell phone. She doesn't have any idea where to start, but then the idea hits her. She'll call her own cell phone, which she keeps in the bottom left outside pouch of her backpack and pray to God that Fokke van der Veld not only has her backpack, but can speak English. She tries practicing his name out loud.

"Fuck eh. Fuck eh Van der Field," she mumbles, before bursting out in laughter. It must be the tension of the situation getting to her, because each time she utters his name, she breaks down. She's laughing so hard she has to wipe her eyes. *Focus Sarah,* she counsels, *before mom comes back for another lecture.*

"Folk eh Fan Deer Feld," she finally says with authority. The German boys are completely unfazed by her terrible Dutch pronunciation, but then she notices the angry looking British woman leaning over her seat, her gray hair up in a bun.

"Ma'am. Can you please stop saying the 'F' word? There are children on this train!"

"I am not swearing, ma'am. It's a Dutch name," she retorts. Now she finally has the two German kids laughing. Oh God. Maybe they're Dutch after all.

"Can I see that for a minute?" one of them asks. She hands him the passport. "Fokke van der Veld. Try it like this. Fo-kuh."

"Fucky," she tries, garnering a piercing stare from the British woman. By the time she dials her own number, she has a little audience. Her heart beat is pounding in her ears. The phone rings four times and then goes to voicemail. She decides to take a few centering breaths and try back in a few minutes.

Chapter 5
Fokke

The drive east to Sappada is curvy, the scenery shockingly beautiful. It is
the quietest they have been the whole trip. It might have something to do
with the rounds of Grappa last night, but Fokke doesn't think so. It's
contemplative scenery; perfect for mid-morning introspection. He, at least,
is having a zen moment as he looks toward the majestic mountains. He can
even hear a faint chiming sound that reminds him of a meditation class he
took once in Jakarta, Indonesia.

"Which one of you idiots has a meditation chime on your cell phone?"
Jan asks, clearly annoyed as the tone increases in volume. He doesn't look
contemplative but hung over.

"Not mine," Fokke responds. The others also nod in the negative and
Jan glances at the rotund, mustachioed Italian driver. They all smile secretly
at one another and the silence is broken. They reminisce about a ski trip in
Austria they did together in their senior year at university. Jan starts in on
another story about getting fined for peeing in an Amsterdam canal, how
ten more fraternity brothers, in an act of solidarity, unzipped their pants

right in front of the officer, pulled out their members and joined in the canal pee fest. They all know how the story goes, but they all listen anyway, laughing at their boldness, their stupidity.

They tip the driver well, considering the stories he's had to endure over the last hour and start out on the snowy trail just as the sun breaks through the blanket of clouds. They will hike for two hours in the Dolomites and catch a shuttle on the other side of the trail to a luxury cabin rental.

Jan and Barry forge ahead, while Fokke and Peter take up the rear. They fall a few paces behind when Peter stops to take a leak. As they continue up the pass, Peter puts on his psychologist's hat. They've been talking in English the whole trip for Barometer's sake, and out of default, they continue.

"You know you'll find another woman. One who won't sleep with the Irish Leprechaun of a neighbor."

"Not talking about it," Fokke responds.

"I know. I know. But I'm just saying. It's been over a year, Fok. Time to let it go."

"I'm working on it. I am," Fokke claims. He's not working on it at all. Besides his own mother and sisters, he hasn't so much as smiled at a woman in the last eight months. For the five months before that, he only glared at them. Fokke inhales the icy air and exhales a cloud of vapory breath. As the cold fills his lungs, images of Jackie filter in: her short-cropped blonde hair, her beautiful green eyes; lively American accent; her stomach one giant basketball of baby about to be born. When she got pregnant Fokke was overjoyed. Because naturally, he knew nothing about the affair.

"I wanted it to be mine." He feels a prickling sensation behind his eyes.

"I know man. But she wasn't worthy to be the mother of your child." Peter hopes his words are sinking in, so he waits, giving the idea time to breathe. Fokke is silent; which is a good thing. Peter continues. "There are plenty of women looking for a solid, caring man just like you, who want to start a family."

Fokke gives him a half smile. He knows Peter has a point, but doesn't know if he can ever go through that experience again. "The bachelor life is treating me just fine," Fokke exhales as they climb higher up the pass.

"Is it?" Peter asks, knowing it is a rhetorical question. Fokke is silent once again, but Peter is patient. While he awaits a response, he considers the pros and cons of a pirate-themed birthday party for his seven-year-old, wondering if pirates are still cool. Johnny Depp single-handedly brought the whole pirate thing back into the spotlight just a few years ago. Or maybe he should do a rapper theme. His seven-year old can rap like the best of them. Or soccer? He switches back to pirates, believing for some yet-to-be-justified reason that they are the more noble of the three options when Fokke finally speaks. It takes Jan a moment to remember the topic. Yes, bachelor life.

"Sometimes I think back to that moment; that trip to Venice that changed everything," Fokke says as he glances forward.

"And given a chance to go back? Choose the other path?" Peter inquires.

"Still wouldn't change a thing. I might have been bred to be a lawyer, but I was born to travel." Fokke feels his frustration lift as he utters these words, but Peter goes for the jugular.

"Except that travel doesn't support a healthy relationship with a woman or starting a family. Except that you're not getting any younger."

"Except for all that," Fokke grimaces. He feels a slight vibration from the right side of his backpack followed by a chiming sound—the same chiming sound they heard earlier on the shuttle bus.

"What the hell?" He stops walking and unzips the side pocket. There in his backpack is an iPhone encased in pink faux-leather next to a tube of calendula organic hand lotion. He pulls the pack from his shoulders with a jolt, staring at it. It looks exactly like his backpack: solid black, same rainbow strap, same North Face brand. He opens another pocket and finds maps of Treviso and Venice next to a box of tampons. He opens the main compartment and it's filled with girly stuff — bras, underwear, pink sweat suits, skinny jeans, cashmere scarves.

"Either you're discovering your feminine side, or you've got the wrong bag," Peter bursts into gut-splitting laughter. The other guys turn around and start walking back to see what's so funny.

Fokke finds a map of Ireland in the main compartment with a little Leprechaun in the corner. He waves it in the air.

"You guys plan this elaborate joke?" he glares at Peter. "Some sort of fucked-up humor about my situation? That's just bullshit." But how? When? He'd left his bag alone for the space of five minutes when they were grabbing espresso. But that's all it would take to switch the bags.

"Hold on there, big guy. I swear Fok. We didn't. At least I didn't. But maybe you'd better answer the phone."

"You guys went to great lengths I see. But I'm not falling for it," Fokke retorts.

Chapter 6
Sarah

Once again, no one answers. Sarah decides it's time to talk to some official about her situation. She decides the U.S. embassy would be a good place to start. She opens the phone again. She can't read the menu because Fokke van der Veld's phone is programmed in Dutch. Crap! But there's an icon she recognizes for the internet. That's easy enough. She taps the icon and a little pinwheel pizza of color swirls for a good five minutes, but there's no internet connection. Makes sense with this rocky pass. She's lucky she was able to reach her own phone. The train is fifteen minutes from Connegliano, which means she's almost half way to Treviso. She can either double back to the hotel lodge in Cortina, or continue to Treviso. She's contemplating her next step when Fokke's phone starts ringing.

"Hello?" she answers in a whisper.

"Ja. Hallo. U spreekt met Teun Winders. Is dit niet de mobiele telefoon van Fokke van der Veld?"

"Sorry. I don't understand. Is this Fucky van der Vieeld? Um, do you speak English?"

"Ja, Ik kan een beetje English speaken. I call for Fokke van der Veld. Dit is his buurman."

"His what?" Sarah asks in consternation.

"His person dat lives in het huis next by," the man fumbles. Sarah puzzles through it.

"His neighbor?"

"Ja. His nay-bore."

"Okay. Hi neighbor," Sarah responds, a bundle of nerves. "And your name is?"

"Teun Winders."

"Hello Mr. Tone Windies. I have his phone by mistake. I don't know where he is."

"Winders. Hem. You have his phone?" It sounds like he has a potato stuck in his throat.

"Yes."

"And is hij beschikbaar. Em, available?" he asks, slightly irritated. "Het is important."

"No. I don't know where he is. We. I accidentally got his pack. I don't know if he has mine." Sarah says meekly, wondering if this man understands her.

"You got on his back? Okay, meid. Listen. I know I have promised not to call on his vakantie, maar dit is important."

"So is this. Mr. Windies. I took the wrong backpack. Do you understand?" Meek Sarah is gone. Pissed off Sarah has taken the helm.

"Meneer Winders," he corrects. "You have his phone and on his back?" he accuses.

"I have his BACKPACK. A sort of TRAVEL BAG. By mistake."

"Waar is hij?"

"What? English. Please speak English."

"Waar is Fokke?" he clarifies.

Is he saying War? Or where, maybe?

22

"I have no idea," Sarah replies in consternation.

"Okay. Ja. We make it simple. Jullie twee gaan even door. When you see him, tell him ik weet hij is, umm, he's on vakantie for de volgende twee weken, maar de boom has fallen."

"A bomb has fallen? What?" she startles.

"Nee. Um. Momeentje," he says. Sarah can hear a muffled conversation before the man speaks again. "A tree is fallen across de fens into his tuin. Nee. garten."

"Okay. The tree has fallen."

"Dank you," the man responds. "Tell him. Het is belangrijk. Er . . . impor-tent."

"Please. Mr. Windies. Don't hang up," Sarah implores. "I don't know Fucky van der Field. I was at a hotel ski lodge in Cortina d'Ampezzo, Italy. I took his bag by mistake. He might or might not have mine. I at least, have his bag. I desperately need to get a hold of him. Can you send him an email and tell him?" There is a long pause.

"Listen meid. If Fokke had relations met you and eind it off, I cannot get between."

"Oh my God, no. I didn't sleep with him! I don't even know him."

"You know his naam."

"Naam. Name? Yes. Because I have his BACKPACK and his PASSPORT." She is speaking too loudly. The surrounding passengers are no longer practicing *European Style Detachment*, but blatantly staring. The English grandmother has a guilty smile on her lips, like she's sneaking a peak at a dirty daytime television program.

"His passport, zegt u? Who are you and how does he get to you?" the man asks, suddenly willing to help.

"Call his own phone like you just did?" she suggests, trying not to be sarcastic.

23

"And you are named? Where can he you reach? Welk hotel?" he asks.

Sarah is suddenly wary. What if this is some sort of elaborate scheme? First, they steal your bag, then they call you and act all innocent, or in this case, rude. Then they get more of your personal details and come finish you off. Or worse; place you in a sex trade route.

"Sarah. Just Sarah. Have him call this number." She hangs up the phone. She's made up her mind to go back to Cortina. Maybe her bag is in the lobby of the hotel just waiting for her. And maybe pigs play dominoes.

Chapter 7
Alexi

Alexi adjusts her long dark hair, clears her voice and pushes record.

"Hi everyone. Alexi here. It's day twenty-three of my tour and I'm in Reims, France. This afternoon, I will light a candle in the Cathedrale Notre Dame which you see here behind me. But before I enter those grand wooden doors, I have to tell you a bit about this gothic cathedral. Clearly, it's old. But how old do you think? Seven to eight hundred years old! This was 'the place' for coronation ceremonies for the Kings of France. Isn't it strange to think my feet will soon cross over the same stone floor that royalty crossed in the middle ages?"

She pauses the camera and walks through the front door, dropping a few euros into the donation box. She waits for a group of tourists to walk by before she turns the camera back on.

"Okay. I'm inside," she says, slowly panning the video camera around the interior. "Isn't this structure amazing? Look at how high the ceilings are. It surely created a sense of awe in its visitors eight hundred years ago, and it's still awe-inspiring today.

"Look at these brilliant, circular stained-glass windows. It's like a kaleidoscope, the way the intricate patterns build upon each other in perfect symmetry." As she begins her commentary, a few visitors gaze up, as if noticing the windows for the first time. Alexi pans the camera in a different direction. "Now I'm focusing on a window in rich blues, the figures floating free, its style completely different from what we just saw. How is that possible?" She pauses a beat, as if waiting for someone to answer. "Because these three windows were designed by painter Marc Chagall. I kid you not. I know Chagall wasn't born in the middle-ages. He was commissioned in 1968 to design these three windows in the axial chapel of this cathedral, and they were installed in 1971."

Alexi continues to describe the cathedral, parsing out facts mixed with her impressions. She pauses the video once again, adjusts her hair and rubs her eyes. The interior is too dark to leave on her sunglasses, so she pushes them carefully into her hair. Today she is lucky. It takes no time at all to enlist the help of a Belgian woman to record the next segment.

"It's time for the lighting of the candles. Hope you can hear me, but I have to whisper now. I'm in a church after all, and Francene from Belgium is gracious enough to film this section. Thank you Francene. So, this first candle is for Ted Phillips in Kansas City, Missouri, who wants to find love in his life. I think we all need love in our life, so this is for Ted and finding love. Yes! This tall red candle. That's 3 euros, but I think it's worth it.

"The second candle is for my mother. As you all know, she is the one who gave me the idea for this whole concept. Here's to you mom, and that travel bug you never explored.

"I think of all the cathedrals I have been visiting; all of their secrets, the way they whisper their messages over the centuries to us — connect past, present and future. How tragic it would be if those messages were lost. With that in mind, this third candle that I will light in this ancient cathedral is for Jolia from Syria and for all the other refugees fleeing the Syrian war; for the antiquities that are being destroyed in the ancient cities of Aleppo, Palmyra and many others during this awful war."

The Belgian woman listens on, tears forming in her eyes.

"And the fourth candle is for my little sister, April. She's having trouble deciding between three men. May the best man win!" She can't help but laugh, knowing that April will personally kill her for announcing this tidbit to her followers. But really, no one knows who she is, so what can it hurt?

"Now that the candles are lit, it's time to explore Reims and the beautiful countryside surrounding it. Travel reminds you of how precious life is. We can enjoy what we do have in life, and this is the perfect place to celebrate that message. Why? I'm in Champagne country! I promise to do thorough research for all of you on the bubbly of this region! Signing off in Reims! Alexi."

Francene turns off the recorder and smiles. "What a wonderful project, Alexi."

"Thank you, Francene. I appreciate your help. It's always handy to have someone else film when I'm lighting the candles."

"No problem at all. Would you like to join me for a café au lait?"

"That would be nice," she admits. "A quick break, as I have an appointment in half an hour," she fibs. Although it is nice to interact with someone, Alexi keeps the conversation brief and answers as few questions as possible about the Alexi project.

After a pleasant chat with Francene in the café on the square, Alexi returns to the exterior of the cathedral and sets back up to answer her fan questions: *Where will she head next? How long is she travelling? Is she single?* She doesn't care to answer that last one just yet.

Afterwards, she shuts down the camera and returns to the interior of the cathedral just in time to see the sun escape the gray clouds and stream through the stained glass windows by Chagall. She stands beneath them with the sensation of life streaming into her. For the first time she dares to consider that this sense of being fully alive all by herself might not be a fleeting thing after all.

Chapter 8
Fokke

The guys have finally stopped teasing him for taking the wrong backpack and he realizes it's too elaborate a hoax for them to pull off. He's nabbed some woman's bag by mistake. Or she's nabbed his. If he wasn't still reeling from baring his soul last night, followed by a round of roasting by the guys and enough fucking Irish Leprechaun jokes to last him a lifetime, he might even see the humor in the situation. Except that the sun has come out and he needs his sunglasses, not the girly rhinestone-laden Ralph Lauren sunglasses in the right-hand pocket. And he could use a snack right about now too. The woman's cell phone is down to two bars. He borrows Jan's cell and calls his own phone. It beeps, indicating that the phone is in use. Shit. Maybe his backpack has been stolen. What a complete mess.

"I'll head back to the lodge in Cortina and get this straightened out. I'll hopefully see you tonight in Sappada." He's disappointed that he'll miss the two hour hike they have planned.

"Yeah. You get it all straightened out," Jan says as he retrieves a black lacy bra from the backpack and rubs it between his fingers. He reaches in again, retrieving a pink silky garment.

"Give me that you idiot," Fokke orders, sucker punching his arm as light snow falls upon them. "It's getting all wet."

"That's what she said," Barometer throws in. "Check this out. Is it a wig?" he asks as he pulls something out of the pack that looks very much like a pile of dark hair in a zip lock bag.

"Put it back now, Barry," Fokke orders.

"There are no coincidences, Fokke. You've got a date with destiny." Peter smiles.

"Yeah. Right. Okay you idiots. I'm out of here."

"Want any company?" Jan asks, arching an eyebrow as he thrusts his hips.

"Nah. I think I can use a little break from all of you perverts. See you tonight."

He still has his wallet, but his passport is in his missing backpack. That could be a major hassle if his bag is indeed stolen. It can take months to get a passport replaced, and he's got an assignment in Argentina a little over a week after his vacation. Armed with Jan's cell phone, Fokke heads back down the mountain pass alone to catch the shuttle bus he's just ordered.

***

Twenty minutes later he's at the deserted trailhead. He paces back and forth in an effort to stay warm. Curiosity gets the better of him and he starts looking through the backpack again, trying not to disturb the order of the items. God. Pink bathroom kit. Pink socks. This woman is a fervent fan of his least favorite color. He knows where the hidden compartment is and pushes aside the woman's shirts, gray sweatpants and silky pink pajamas to get to it.

Inside, he finds her wallet laden with cash and credit cards. He pulls out a credit card and discovers her name: Sarah B. Turner. God. Sarah B. Turner must be freaking out. As he sees the dark blue passport, his hand comes to a standstill. Of all the possible scenarios in the universe, he has nabbed the backpack of an American female. He's already picturing Jackie in his mind as he opens the passport.

Sarah Beth Turner is American like Jackie, but that's where the similarities end. Her eyes are a solid dark blue, not feisty green. Her skin has a slight tint, which contrasts well with her golden curls; her cheeks round and full. According to the passport she's five feet ten inches. It's hard to think in feet, but he knows that's tall for a woman. And she will celebrate her birthday in six days, when she'll turn thirty-seven. Which means she's only five years younger than him, not twelve. Hell. Why does he have to compare every woman to Jackie? Including a complete stranger whom he's never met?

Fokke notices that the passport is newly issued, but there are already stamps from seven different countries: Portugal, Spain, France, Germany, Switzerland, Austria and Italy, all within the last four or five weeks. This woman is making a go of it; probably traveling with her husband or boyfriend he realizes as he thinks about the sexy undergarments in her pack. He tucks the passport back into the safety of the hidden compartment.

He is trying to ignore the fuchsia journal, but he's bored and curious. Maybe he could get some relevant information from it. It could be a travel journal, noting where she's heading next. He quickly peruses the journal and it is abundantly clear that it is a combination of travel log and personal thoughts. He flips to the last week of entries.

Monday, October 19th, San Gimignano

Do you have any idea how much fun it is to travel alone? How revealing of character? I wouldn't have thought it possible. I'm so used to being part of a couple, that I didn't have the space to be me; choose what I want to do. Me, Miss High School Counselor, giving advice to others and yet here I am, encountering me on a whole new level.

Travel can be lonely, but invigorating all at once. Deepening my understanding of life, while developing my freedom of choice. I can take my time looking at paintings by street artists if I want to; take the whole day to explore a town and its museums, or simply put my toes in the sea and wrap my coat around me as I take in the sounds and smells of another culture.

I wish you were here with me, mama. You would appreciate the way this little town is perched on a hillside; its cobblestone streets, the smell of freshly baked bread wafting through the shop windows. I mean. I don't really wish you were here, because we'd already be getting on each other's nerves and you couldn't possibly keep up with my pace, but I'd like to at least send you a newsy letter with Italian postage stamps; show you my photos. Have a tea and a chat when I'm back home. Why did you have to go and leave me? Just when things got hard.

He flips a few pages backwards and reads another entry.

Friday, October 16th, Lucca
Matthew is a total ASSWIPE. Ah. That feels good to see in writing. Why did it take me so long to see the light? How could I not notice? And Katie. What a complete freaking bitch. She could win an Oscar for her acting skills — best friend my ass. They're 5,000 miles away and yet right here, seeping into my thoughts and tainting my grand European tour. But if they'd never ruined two marriages, Gregory wouldn't have thought of the perfect revenge! Screw you Matthew and Katie. Ironic choice of words, Sarah. How about this? Rot in your own private hell M and K. Because really, how can you live with yourselves after such betrayal? You deserve each other.
    ***
Okay. I'm back and clear headed again. Just went for a run, did a hundred ab crunches, took a shower and I'm now at Piazza Napoleone eating a rather simple pizza and sipping a very expensive coca cola, but I'm in heaven. It's so beautiful here.
This town! God, it's just as amazing as mom said it was. I doubt much has changed since she and dad were here over 36 years ago. The town of my conception. I tried to find the hotel she wrote about in a letter to grandma Nettie, but I couldn't find it. I climbed some of the church towers in the old walled city center, but most of my afternoon went to a little record shop, flipping through old jazz records. They had CDs as well. There were dozens that I wanted to buy, but I purchased just one. Jim Hall and Joe Lavano playing live in Umbria.
If I ever make love to a man again, I want to have this CD cranked in the background.

Fokke closes the journal. He is definitely invading Sarah Beth Turner's privacy—an act, he admits reluctantly—he is enjoying. He has a strange desire to hear Jim Hall and Joe Lavano's live session in Umbria. Not necessarily under the conditions described, since he doesn't know this woman from Eve, but still. He does love jazz. The chiming starts again, and Fokke pulls the phone from the side pocket.

Chapter 9
A Plan

"Hello. This is Fokke van der Veld," he answers.

"Oh thank God! That means you have my phone and hopefully my backpack?" Sarah pushes away from the hard metal bench where she's been sitting and presses the phone against her ear.

"Yeah. I've got them. And I'm guessing this is Sarah Beth Turner? And you've nabbed my bag by mistake?" Fokke replies, smiling for the second time in the last ten minutes.

"No. I'm pretty sure you took my bag," Sarah counters. "But, whatever, we've swapped them. Can we just figure out how we're going to swap them back?" she huffs into the phone, both flustered and annoyed by his casual tone.

"Yeah. I think that would help us both out. So, Sarah, where are you now?" Fokke asks.

Why does this man sound so calm? She has his backpack, his passport, his expensive looking camera lenses. She's decided the whole bag-nabbing-sex-trade-scam scenario isn't very realistic, so she continues.

"I'm in Conegliano waiting for a train back to Belluno, then the shuttle to Cortina. Are you still at the lodge?"

"I'm at a trailhead near Sappada in the Italian Dolomites. I'm about an hour east of Cortina waiting for a shuttle bus. Should arrive in about 40 minutes. Then it's an hour ride back to the Luciano Lodge. Shall we meet there, or is there a better rendezvous point for you?"

"Well, you could meet me in Belluno? No. Actually, let's just meet at the lodge. I know where that is. But the next train is coming at 13:20. Let me see. That means um . . . "

"1:20p.m." Fokke clarifies.

"Yes. Thank you. So I've got an hour and a half wait, plus an hour train ride to Belluno. Then the three kilometers to the shuttle bus to take me to Cortina. That's another 35 kilometers. That puts me there around 3:30 or 4p.m. Sound good?"

He shakes his head. *Fuck, my whole day is shot.* "Yeah. Sounds good. If you run into any problems, give me a call, okay?" Fokke adds.

"Like what sort of problems?" Sarah responds. She's not nervous. Not yet, anyway.

"Well. This is Italy, after all," Fokke says, as if these words speak for themselves.

"Listen. I've been traveling in Italy for five days without any problems. Until this little situation, that is," she responds. *Oh God. I don't want to jinx myself,* she thinks.

"Yeah. Well, I'm sorry for the inconvenience," Fokke says calmly.

"Yes. Me too. Sorry I have all your hiking gear. Oh. And you might want to charge my phone. I forgot to plug it in last night," she adds.

"Thanks. Mine's fully charged and has a solar back up system. So you should be good. If you need to look something up online, the code is 4119."

"Oh. Thank you. Didn't think of that. My charger is in my bathroom kit," she adds. "If the phone powers off, you'll need my code to log back in. It's 8375." Seems only fair since he gave her his.

"Okay Sarah. I'm sure I'll see you in a few hours and we can work this all out. Safe travels."

"Thank you Mr. van Veld." This is all going rather splendidly, she thinks.

"Call me Fokke," he replies.

"I'd rather not."

"Suit yourself Ms. Turner."

His tone is more formal. *Oh no. Have I pissed him off? Gotta keep the man with my backpack, passport and credit cards on my side.*

"Um. I am not trying to be rude. I just have a hard time saying your name," she blushes.

A grin spreads across his face. He attended university with foreigners; works all over the world. Hell, he survived fraternity. He knows what her problem is.

"Fokke. Not Fucker," he enunciates, trying to teach her the difference.

"Fucky," she responds.

"Close enough. See you in a few hours Sarah."

"Okay. Until then, Fucky."

Chapter 10
Fokke

The shuttle bus is running late and he's cold, thirsty and hungry. He knows he shouldn't, but he can't help himself. He's halfway through her journal. It's all over the place from charming, heart-wrenching and funny to naive, philosophical and sexy. He finds it both interesting and frustrating to learn that men have been pursuing her in just about every country she's visited with varying degrees of intensity, the more amorous pursuits being in Italy. She's from Bend, Oregon, he learns, and has been divorced for less than a year. Her ex sounds like a real asshole, though she occasionally defends him to herself. She's deathly afraid of the dark. She took a leave of absence from her position as a high school student counselor to travel Europe so she could *"get her dignity back and expand her world view"* as she wrote in her journal.

He can't imagine she was making a caboodle as a school counselor, but she definitely has cash flow. He's written about some of the four-star hotels where she's been staying and they aren't cheap. He figures she's burning through a divorce settlement or inheritance from her mother whom he thinks has recently passed away based on the way she writes about her, though he can't be sure. Either way, she's doing her solo trip in style.

The shuttle bus finally arrives and he is thankful for the warmth within the heated vehicle. As he thinks about his friends on the trail, he realizes what a pain in the ass this whole bag mix-up is. But it's also strangely amusing. He's been traveling for years and although he's lost a few suitcases, he's never had a problem like this.

Jan's sarcastic words play around in his head: A date with destiny. He mulls over the idea of Sarah Beth Turner. She's pretty in her passport photo—a feat in itself; funny on the phone and her writing speaks to him. They also have a few unfortunate things in common: they've both been cheated on and lied to by partners they trusted. And a few positives in common: they love their mamas, travel, jazz and writing.

But even as he contemplates her in this way, he knows she's not the type of girl, woman rather, that he wants to get to know any better. One, she's American—*been there, done that.* And two, she's older than the women he dates. He likes young, petite women of child bearing age, not tall American divorcees on the fast road to forty. He sees the hypocrisy in his thoughts. He's forty-two after all. If he started a family today, he'd be fifty-two by the time his son was ten years old and in his sixties by the time the kid started university. *Hell. Why am I even thinking about this?* Fokke frowns.

He reaches the Luciano Lodge just after three o'clock in the afternoon, grumpy and hungry. He chooses a table in the hotel restaurant next to the fireplace in the back and orders a plate of gnocchi and a glass of red wine.

The meditation chime starts again.

"Hello. This is Fokke van der Veld."

"Buongiorno. Sono Giuseppe dell'albergo Palazzo a Treviso. Cerco il Signor Turner."

"Signora Turner non è disponibile. Posso prendere un messaggio?" Fokke replies.

"Dobbiamo chiudere l'albergo questa sera a causa d'un incendio in cucina. Ci scusiamo per l'inconvenienza."

"Incendio nella cucina?" Fokke repeats.

"Si. Si Signore. Non è possibile rimanere con noi. Di solito si potrebbe cerceare di trovare un altro albergo per voi, ma sono tutti al completo per via di un festival locale."

It takes another three minutes and one more bar of Sarah's cell phone battery for Fokke to get the details of the message. The hotel in Treviso where Sarah is booked for the next two evenings is closed due to a fire in the kitchen and although they would like to send her to another hotel, most of the hotels in the area are booked due to a local festival.

Fokke hesitates. He could use Jan's cell to call his own phone to reach Sarah and tell her, or he could tell her in person. Neither option sounds good. Hell. It's not his problem to solve. But based on her diary, she's experienced a slew of problems over the past few weeks: a number of missed trains, one hotel that was closed on arrival, being hassled by men and dealing with her general fear of traveling alone, though she claims to be getting stronger on this last point—and even though it's not yet in the journal, he knows this backpack screw up will be added to the list. He makes a decision. After he finishes eating he'll see if the Luciano Lodge has any rooms this evening. He can at least offer her that. But in the meantime, there's still another thirty pages of flowing handwriting that are calling to him like Sirens from the Odyssey. He knows the Sirens are up to no good, that there are sharp rocks beneath the tranquil waters, but he can't help himself. He turns the page.

Chapter 11
The Handshake

He's just cracking open a John Le Carré novel when he hears the chime go off.

"Hello. This is Fokke van der Veld."

"Hi Mr. Van der Field. It's me. Sarah Turner. Where are you?" She's speaking in stereo. He turns to see her standing in the hotel lobby, his backpack on her shoulders. Her hair is longer than he could have guessed from the passport photo and the curls are messy and damp from the snow.

"In the café behind you," he waves. He experiences an odd, prickling sensation as she spots him and waves back, as if a compelling character in a novel has just stepped out of the pages and morphed into a living, breathing person. Fokke stands as she approaches, extending his hand. "Nice to meet you Sarah Beth Turner."

"Fucky Van der Field," she replies, taking his hand as she looks up into his face, all confidence.

"Please, call me Fokke." He gestures toward the empty seat. She hesitates for a moment, as if assessing him before taking the seat across from him. In place of words, she gives him a simple shrug of the shoulders.

"So, Fucky, do we want to try to figure out who's at fault?" she asks.

"We were running late this morning. So it was probably me. My bag wasn't on the floor in the pile where we'd left them when we went to the café."

"Ah. Then it was me. My backpack wasn't on the luggage rack anymore, and I found it in a pile on the floor. I assumed the rack got knocked over or something, and I was running late too."

Of course she was running late. He knows this about her, or the character in the journal who has made a game of pushing the boundaries of time. If she's too late for a train, there's always another one. Why does she push it? Because her ex-husband Matthew was so damned punctual and controlling of every minute. This lateness is her luxurious revenge.

"So you're the thief," the corners of his lips curve into a subtly gorgeous smile. She smiles back, unfazed by his charm.

"In all fairness, our bags do look exactly alike, down to that great rainbow strap."

"Water under the bridge. Can I get you a tea?"

"A tea would be lovely," she replies. "And then I've got to get going."

"If you're heading to Treviso, I have some news for you. I answered a call on your phone from Hotel Palazzo in Treviso. They had a fire in their kitchen and the hotel is closed until further notice. They apologize for the inconvenience."

Sarah looks at him and nods, taking it in. "Okay. These things happen." She shrugs her shoulders. "Hopefully it won't be too hard to find a hotel on a Friday night." She is acting calm, but the little creases forming on her forehead imply something else. He feels a twinge of excitement about being able to stop those little furrows of worry from growing any further.

"Well, I have some good news on that front. Because it's a busy weekend and things sell out quickly, I booked you a room here in the lodge as back-up," Fokke explains.

The slightly-amused, slightly-pissed-off look on her face confuses him, which causes him to further justify his actions. "You are in no way obligated to use it, but considering how this backpack mix-up made you lose a day of your vacation, and you backtracked all the way here, I wanted to at least have something to offer you before I head east."

She stares at him in disbelief.

Was this a good idea? he wonders.

"That's very kind of you Mr. van der Field, um Fucky. I appreciate the thoughtfulness."

He thought he was getting a sense of what her smile looks like, but he realizes those were half smiles compared to the genuine warmth he now sees lighting up her face. He doesn't care that she keeps messing up his first and last name. He has read her most intimate thoughts in the last few hours and he feels an obligation—no, that's not it—a desire to know her in person. Is he atoning for his sin of invading her privacy? He signals the waiter and orders their drinks in perfect Italian.

"Thanks again for the room reservation. You've saved me a lot of hassle. Well, at least for this latest part of my journey. I was already thinking of spending another night in Cortina. First, it's going to be dark in an hour, and second, there's something really strange going on with the shuttle buses," she explains, her cheeks flushing again.

"There is?" Fokke asks. "I checked this afternoon and they were running on schedule."

"Well, something's going on. It has to do with some poor wounded skier who needs an operation."

"What are you talking about?" His brow is now the one crinkling.

"Sorry," she giggles in response. "I know that makes no sense; that's just me trying to remember the words they put on the buses after they dropped me off. I suppose I'm trying to apply English to Italian, which isn't getting me far. Ski operato was everywhere. My Italian dictionary and travel guide were both in my backpack. That's why I took a few pictures with your phone—I hope you don't mind—so I could look it up in my guidebook later. You speak Italian. Here, just look at the photos," Sarah rambles as she reaches toward his backpack.

There's something strangely intimate at seeing this woman open the side pocket of his bag and remove his phone without the slightest reservation. As she hands him the phone he catches the subtle female scent of her. It reminds him of fresh hay and lavender. Fokke shifts his gaze to the phone in his hands and slides through the photos. He bursts out laughing before he starts cursing in Dutch.

"Sciopero means strike, not a ski operation," Fokke explains. "The shuttle bus drivers are striking."

"No, no. That can't be right. The shuttles were just running an hour ago," she replies with confidence, as if she can logic the strike away. "And who would strike on a Friday evening?"

"The French. The Italians. This is terrible. I'm supposed to meet up with my buddies in Sappada this evening. I was planning on catching the next shuttle east."

"Maybe it's just a one-way strike?" Sarah tries. Fokke opens his phone and starts clicking around to different local news sites. The internet connection is slow. When it finally loads, he shakes his head in consternation.

"Nope. They're dubbing it a 'Flash Strike', playing on the whole flash mob phenomenon. Shuttle and railroad strike from Friday at 4:00p.m. through Saturday at 10:00a.m." Fokke reports.

"It's like they allowed enough time for the locals to get back home for their afternoon siestas and then shut the system down to trap all the tourists for the evening," Sarah adds.

"Yes, something like that," he smirks. "Between this weather and the strike, I don't even know how you managed to get back up here." Fokke realizes the irony of the situation. There will be hundreds of stranded tourists vying for hotel rooms and he has just given the last room at Luciano Lodge to the woman who nabbed his backpack this morning.

"Wow. What are you going to do?" Sarah asks with genuine concern.

"I suppose I'm going to rent a car."

"Ah. Smart," she says, her nose crinkling. "That should be easy enough," she smiles again. He can't tell if she's being sarcastic or not. He rises to go.

"I'd feel a lot better if I knew you made it to your destination," she adds.

Is that disappointment he sees on her face? "Don't worry. I'm a world traveler. I always make it to my destination, eventually." He is fighting a strange, internal battle. He wants to stay and take this woman to dinner and then take her to bed in the room he's purchased for her, and give her about a dozen new memories to counter the sadness he's read in her journal.

"Well, Fucky, this here, is your backpack. Look in the pocket just to make sure." There's that smile again. Is she flirting with him? He offers his hand and they shake. Something catches inside him and he holds her hand a moment longer before letting go.

"Definitely my backpack. Have a great rest of your Grand European Tour, Sarah."

She smiles at him quizzically, caught by his word choice. Those are the same words she's been using to describe her once-in-a-lifetime trip.

"It was nice meeting you Fucky. Good luck getting out of here," she waves.

"Thanks. I'll need it," he smiles inwardly at the double entendre of his words. "Oh. And you'll need this," he remembers, retrieving the reservation number and receipt of payment from his pocket.

"You already paid for the room in full?" Sarah looks at him in disbelief.

"Had to. It was the last room available," he admits.

"I'll pay you back," she states, opening up her backpack to take out her wallet. Fokke can think of several ways in which she could pay him back.

"No. You've already done enough by getting my things safely back to me. Thank you again, Sarah. Nice meeting you," he responds with his best manners.

He looks at his watch and shakes his head, trying to clear the heady experience of talking with Sarah Beth Turner. He needs to get a move on if he's going to catch up with the guys. He's on a reunion trip with his buddies after all, not out to save a damsel in distress. Who is he kidding? This damsel is hardly distressed.

As Fokke heads out the door he is thankful for the snowflakes that soon dust his coat and hair. They are bringing him back to his forty-two-year-old self, cooling down that unfamiliar sexual desire spiraling through him like a tornado.

Chapter 12
Sarah

Sarah Beth Turner. You're attracted to that tall married Dutch man with the banged up nose! I'd say you were even flirting. What has gotten into you?

Sarah stretches out on the queen-sized bed wrapped only in a soft towel, ignoring her mother—even though her mother's got a point, and not just about that prizefighter nose. She will analyze her own actions soon enough, but right now she is marveling at her luck. Not only did Fokke pay for the last room in the ski lodge, but he paid for the Suite Reale that has its own fireplace, kitchen and living room and is three times larger than the room she stayed in last night in this same lodge. Although she has been staying in some upscale hotels due to the insane revenge-budget Gregory provided for her "Grand European Tour", she has never opted for a suite. The bell boy who brought her backpack upstairs lit the fireplace before he left and she's already planning to cuddle up in front of it with a book in the evening.

Her thoughts wander back to her lunch with Fokke van der Veld. She was expecting the same, clean shaven man in the passport photo with those light blue aristocratic eyes. But the man who sat across from her a few hours ago seemed more salt of the earth: disheveled blond hair streaked with gray framing his broad forehead, that fighter's nose, the beginnings of a beard softening the angles of his face and a few more wrinkles around his vibrant blue eyes than in the passport photo from four years ago. And oh boy was he tall.

Besides a few calls home to family and friends and her afternoon call to Nettie, their conversation was the longest one she's had since she entered Italy—heck, one of the longest conversations she's had since she landed in Europe. And although it wasn't particularly deep or insightful, it felt good. The shared experience of being in possession of each other's items for a day seems to have connected them on a subtle level. And the way he looked at her—respectfully, laced with an undertone of attraction—was just what she needed after the past five days.

The *Go it Alone Italy* guidebook had given a word of caution to solo female travelers: Italian men can be very charming and more forward than American women are accustomed. But she wrote it off as fair warning to young university girls, not a woman who'd been married for the last eleven years. She figured that the married vibe might still exist like a residue on her skin, warding off advances.

She was dead wrong. She made the mistake of smiling at one Italian man and he followed her for six blocks trying to woo her with his outrageous flattery and Italian charm. Another young man—he must have been in his early twenties!—asked her to go to the disco, and it took her quite a bit to convince him that she really didn't want to go.

That's why it was so nice to flirt subtly with the well-mannered, married Dutch man with a baby on the way—there wasn't a lascivious bone in his body. And he didn't even ask her marital status; didn't put her in a box; just talked to her as a person.

Something settles in her chest—a warm, relaxed feeling that she recognizes as contentment in the moment. Harmless flirting with a man she will never see again.

She changes into her blue cable-knit sweater and skinny jeans, fixes her hair, slips on her sunglasses and sets up her video recorder to film her daily vlog. She's on tonight. No need for a retake. She uploads it before heading out for a walk on the short section of street lit by gracefully arched lamps. Their amber light casts a soft haze onto the snow-covered ground and illuminates the snowflakes spiraling down from the sky. She is careful to stay within the circles of light, not willing to explore that hazy area where light gives way to darkness. Her boots sink into the growing layer of snow at every step. She is aware of both calm and excitement. She is outside at night, playing with the extended boundaries between light and darkness. She struggles forward, but it's snowing too hard.

Reluctantly, she heads back to the suite. She stretches out on the throw rug in front of the fireplace to do her Pilates exercises and ab crunches, noting the small crack in the thick wooden beam of the mantelpiece. She studies the landscape painting above the couch of olive trees following the curve of a hill in neat rows as she does her crunches.

Sarah smiles at her good fortune as she draws herself a bath in the claw-foot tub. She strips off all of her layers, creating a little pile by the tub. She is anticipating the moment that the hot, lavender-scented water will envelop her naked body; is just about to step in when she remembers the "important" phone call from Fokke van der Veld's neighbor. The neighbor guy was pretty adamant. But if it's so important, he'll certainly call back. But what if he doesn't and there's some major problem at Fokke's house? Maybe she should call him and tell him. Or at least leave a message. Or maybe not. She'll ruin the whole thing by making contact again. Then she remembers the crucial phone call he answered on her behalf; how he not only told her right away about the hotel cancellation, but how he actually purchased the room she's now in. It's been hours since she received the call about Fokke's garden.

She throws her hands in the air, tired of the internal debate. She retrieves her phone from her jean pocket and scrolls through the incoming calls. That last one must be his number. She presses dial.

"Ja Hallo. Met Fokke van der Veld." His voice is gruff, tired.

"Um. Hi. It's Sarah Turner." Heat rises in her cheeks. She shouldn't have called.

His tone softens. "Sarah. Oh. Hi. What can I do for you?"

"Um. I just remembered that your neighbor Mr. Windies called while I had your phone. He said it was important."

"This better not be about that damned tree," Fokke growls. "I can't believe he called me during my vacation. I was very clear about that," Fokke relays, as if she herself were the culprit.

"Hey, don't shoot the messenger! And yes. It was about the tree. The bomb has fallen. That's what he said. And bomb means tree, so the tree has fallen," Sarah relays, rather proud of herself for remembering these details. Her skin prickles from the cold as she stands naked, cell phone pressed to her ear.

"Oh that's just great," he sighs heavily into the phone, ignoring her terrible Dutch pronunciation.

"Are you okay? Is this really bad news?" she asks as she reaches for a towel, trying to wrap it around her body with one hand.

"Yes and no. Not in the scope of things. But right now, I'm, well . . ."

"Where are you?" Sarah asks.

"I'm still in Cortina," he admits.

"You are? You couldn't rent a car?" she asks, stating the obvious.

"No. All sold out."

"Where are you staying?" she questions, her hand stilling.

"Well, I'm not having much luck there either. The hotels are all sold out too. And it's snowing like crazy. I mean, I get that it's October in Northern Italy, but this is unprecedented."

"Well. Um," Sarah hesitates.

"Don't worry, I'm not going to come knocking on your door," he says.

"But, well. You can. Because this suite is huge and there's a living room with a couch. You are welcome to it." Heat rises to her cheeks.

"No," Fokke says quickly. "It's not your problem."

Sarah deliberates, but it is clear what she must do. "Not my problem? Listen, if you hadn't purchased this suite for me, I would've been wandering around in your place, trying to find a hotel room." The very thought of it makes her shiver again. There is a long pause, followed by a few more disapproving grunts.

"Well. I don't think I have many options. So if you really don't mind, I'll take you up on that couch."

She minds. She can tell by the way her body is reacting uncomfortably to the idea. "Okay. No problem. Um, how long until you're here?" she asks, crossing her left arm over her breasts.

"With this snow, I'm thinking about an hour."

"Okay. Be careful. I'll see if I can get some extra bedding," she replies.

"Thank you. That would be great," he humphs.

"I'll see you in about an hour Mr. van der Veld."

Sarah steps into the tub and soaks into the heat and lavender bath salts, thankful for the water pressing against her. She had planned to soak for about an hour, because where she comes from, this is a lot of water to waste. But the idea of a man coming to her suite makes her cut the bath short. What do you wear when you've just invited a shockingly handsome stranger to share your hotel room?

Chapter 13
Fokke

He is a resourceful world traveler who is used to creatively solving the situations in which he finds himself. But the backpack mix-up, the sciopero of the shuttle workers and the snowfall have rendered him dependent upon a relative stranger for shelter this evening. He is fully aware of the keen pleasure he felt when he heard her voice again, and this annoys him. He's not a horny university student; he's a middle-aged man who just went through a serious break-up. Well, just, as in over a year ago.

As he walks, he is caught up in his surroundings. Fokke loves snow for the way it softens and slows down the world. Sounds are muffled. Common footsteps are transformed into a squeaky reminder of how temporary life is. After three and a half kilometers of walking through the building snow, he is filled with a sense of adventure that is hard for a travel writer with his experience to come by.

A few blocks away from Luciano Lodge Fokke runs into a group of teenagers just heading out into the crazy weather and somehow he becomes enmeshed in a snowball fight. He nails a boy on the back of the head, but they team up against him and he is laughing harder than he can remember as he engages in full-blown snowball warfare.

He arrives cheerful but chilled to the bone. The receptionist recognizes him from his reservation that afternoon and hands him a key to the Suite

Reale, accompanied by a quick flicker of the eyebrows. Fokke heads up to the suite and knocks gently on the door.

Sarah opens the door and flashes a low-watt smile.

"Hi Fokke. Come in."

She pronounces his name impeccably, which surprises him. She is dressed as a wife might dress when absolutely confident that her husband loves her: baggy gray sweatpants and an oversized pink-with-hearts sweatshirt that does nothing to accentuate the curves he witnessed earlier today. Fuzzy pink socks peak out of a battered pair of faux-sheepskin boots. Her hair is pulled back in a ponytail and the delicate make-up she had on earlier is scrubbed away, making her look younger, though the natural beauty of her full features is not diminished.

"Thank you Sarah," he says quietly as he enters the private domain of her suite.

"No problem," she responds.

He sets his pack down, and removes his thick, snow-spattered coat.

"Wow. It must be really dumping out there. Here. Let me take that coat. I can put it in the bathroom so it doesn't get the carpet all wet," she suggests. She sounds like a wife too; practical yet considerate.

"Okay. Thanks again. Good idea." He unlaces his hiking boots and tucks them next to the door on the tiled entry. It's a nice suite with plush furniture, old stucco walls and a thick carpet over the wooden floor. He would have never splurged on a place like this for himself. There's a fire going, and he is suddenly aware of how cold he is. "Um. Mind if I change in the bathroom?"

"Of course not," she replies. Sarah is polite in a cautious way; her light humor and bubbly personality from this afternoon gone. Her frumpy clothes and distant attitude suddenly add up in his mind: she is downplaying her femininity while sending him a clear signal that she is unavailable. Although he knows he is not a threat to her, she has nonetheless taken a risk by letting a man share her suite.

Fokke vows then and there to keep whatever strange, romantic thoughts he's been having in check. She is a recently divorced, heart-broken woman traveling alone, not a woman looking for a fling. Is he looking for a fling? Something to take his mind off of Jackie? And why the hell is his mind even recalling that name?

"You look pretty cold. Maybe you should shower," she suggests, crossing her arms over her chest. He has gone a week without a shower on his travels through India and Sri Lanka and he's dealt with harsher climates than this. But she's right. He's cold. Come to think of it, he probably stinks a bit too much to be in the presence of a lady; even if he's sleeping on the couch.

"That would be great. Thank you."

***

As the hot water washes over him, he wonders what it is about Sarah Beth Turner that is turning him on, despite her frumpy clothes she's chosen to wear and the almost business-like way she is speaking to him. But then he thinks back to their lunch together. By the end of the shower, he has a surprisingly long list of things that turn him on about this woman he has just met. Considering how his train of thought is affecting his anatomy, he opts for loose jeans and pulls on a long-sleeved shirt and a wool cardigan.

He finds her sitting on the couch by the fire flipping through a Venice travel guide.

"Thanks again for letting a stranger into your life," Fokke says. She gives him a half-hearted smile as if to say *I'm not letting you into my life.* But she doesn't realize that he's read every page of her travel journal and he's very curious about what the Amsterdam appointment could possibly be. What is it she is going to do in Amsterdam and why does she write about it in code in her own journal?

When I have The Amsterdam appointment, there will be no turning back.
God. I hope I'm ready for The Amsterdam appointment. Now or never!

"So Fokke. You're traveling with your friends?" she asks, pulling him out of his thoughts.

"Yeah. I'm on a reunion trip with some old university friends. Luckily, they made it to our next destination before the strike. But what I want to know is this. How is it that you can suddenly pronounce my name?"

"I practiced." She smiles in a way that makes her eyes go soft, as if she has momentarily forgotten the barrier she is trying to maintain.

"How? When?" he asks, genuinely curious.

"I called my grandma earlier today," she acknowledges. She had called her right after her tea with Fokke to discuss her upcoming visit. Her grandmother laughed along with her at the story of the switched backpacks and hadn't let her off the phone until she could pronounce his name correctly. Who knew it would come in so handy?

"Your grandma? Is she a linguist or something?" he asks. This elicits a cascading laugh from Sarah.

"No. She's Dutch."

"Which means you're at least part Dutch too," Fokke grins. His earlier observation was right. But if she's Dutch, how come she couldn't pronounce his name before? And why would she take the time to practice?

"I'm a quarter Dutch," she clarifies. "I don't speak the language myself. In fact, languages aren't my strong point." She takes the time to explain a rather complicated story of how her grandmother came to America on a study program and met her grandfather on the north rim of the Grand Canyon, how they fell in love and after a long-distance courtship, got married. They lived in America where they had three children, including her mother. "My grandma moved back to The Netherlands two years ago after my grandpa passed away," Sarah adds. "He was the one and only love of her life."

"Sorry to hear about your grandpa. It's nice how they met. Beautiful story," Fokke admits. He is taken by her sincerity and openness, which compels him to share a story about how his parents met during the 1963 Elfstedentocht.

"What's that?" Sarah asks.

"It's this extreme ice skating competition that crosses over 200 kilometers of natural ice—rivers, lakes and so forth—through eleven different Dutch cities," Fokke explains. "My mom was fifteen, my father eighteen. Long story short, due to freezing temperatures, it was one of the worst years ever for the race. Over 9,000 people entered but only 69 finished."

"Wow. Were your parents among them?" Sarah questions as she tucks her feet underneath her on the couch.

"No. They were spectators. Because she was only fifteen, my mom wasn't eligible to enter. My father was an incredible ice skater, but he had law exams the following week. His parents had forbidden him to enter." This detail reminds Fokke of the three-month long silent treatment he received from his own father when he chose travel writing over entering the family law firm. This uncomfortable memory just as quickly fades as Sarah's eyebrows arch upwards, something she seems to do just before she asks a question.

"What happened next?"

Fokke tells the tale he's heard so many times before. "Well, at the beginning of the race, spectators and skaters alike stepped onto the frozen river. Because of the massive weight, the ice began to crack, and the crowd scrambled backward toward the shore while the skaters sprinted forward." Fokke goes on to tell in detail how his mother was thrown against his father during the mayhem of people fleeing the ice and how he held onto her until they were both safely back on shore.

"The van der Veld's like to say that my mother was pushed into my father's arms by fate, and has happily stayed there ever since." Fokke stretches his legs, glancing at Sarah.

"That's such a romantic story! It belongs in a film," she remarks as a rich, cascading laugh escapes her. This pleasant sound enters into him like a fine scotch—heady to the senses while warming him from the inside. She also looks much more like the confident woman he met this afternoon rather than the Sarah that was keeping him at arm's length not an hour ago.

He goes on to tell her about his four siblings, sharing more than he usually would with a stranger. But that's just it; she doesn't feel like a stranger. Through her writing he can almost feel the cadence of her thoughts. They are quite enjoying themselves, talking, laughing and he recognizes without a doubt, the chemistry building between them.

Fully aware of the answer already, he asks her if she's seen any other countries in Europe and she launches into her adventures in Austria. Once again, Fokke is aware of what he's read, and how she tailors it to share with mixed company. He thinks of her diary entry about a man she saw in Austria that looked like her ex-husband Matthew; how she had hidden in a doorway to watch him and his lover pass. But it wasn't her ex-husband after all. The whole experience had humiliated her; made her realize how vulnerable she still was. But that's not the story she shares. She is talking about a dress she saw in the Hofburg Imperial Palace in Vienna worn by the ladies of the court. In her diary she had described the dress as *"both a stunning and tragic representation of fashion and women"* his photographic memory recalls. As he listens to her speak, her written words are playing along in his head like a parallel universe finally breaking off course and intersecting with the now.

"The dresses were beautiful. The fabric so intricately designed," she hesitates for a moment, as if planning to stop there but she goes on. "But at the same time, it's just shocking to think women took those dresses out of their closets and put them on. Cutting off their own ability to breathe, bruising their ribs, for what? To look slender?"

So that's what she meant by tragic, Fokke realizes. "Still happens," he responds. "Women wear high-heeled shoes that throw their backs out just so they can have sexy legs."

"They should work out if they want sexy legs," she returns. Fokke thinks of Sarah's long, voluptuous legs hidden somewhere beneath her baggy sweatpants and can't help but glance downward. It's getting late and Fokke doesn't know what to do with the energy he feels in her presence. Is he wrong in sensing she is attracted to him as well?

He then recalls her more recent diary entries about traveling alone in Italy. Men have been flirting with her left and right. Best not to add to her trials.

"You know. You're a brave woman to travel alone. Especially in Italy."

"Well, thanks. But, I'm only alone for a few days, my hus . . . my friends are meeting me in Rome," she states as she sits up.

He knows what she was going to say; imagines the subtle pain she must be feeling, realizing once again that she's alone after so many years of marriage.

"Sarah, I want you to know that you're safe with me. I'm not going to make any moves on you," he claims. His words are a wakeup call, helping him dispel that strange energy she brings out in him.

"You better not, considering you're married with a baby on the way," she states. "That's the only reason I agreed to let you stay here tonight." As if to emphasize the point, she crosses her legs. Fokke's shoulders involuntarily tense.

"Umm. Well. I hope you're not going to kick me out, but I'm not married. My girlfriend and I separated over a year ago." He clears his throat.

"Are you trying to tell me that beautiful pregnant woman you had your arms around in multiple photos on your phone is not your wife?" Sarah questions. She involuntarily lifts her eyebrows, a trace of panic crossing her face.

For the first time since this whole backpack switch, Fokke feels the discomfort of having his privacy invaded. "You went through my photos?"

"I was trying to figure out who you were," Sarah defends.

"My passport didn't tell you enough?" He sets his cup down on the small wooden table next to the couch and crosses his arms.

"That was before I found your passport," she hesitates.

Her features are changing before his eyes. The lightness that had slowly worked its way back into their dialogue gives way to tension. But he can't help himself. He's angry.

"You had to scroll through quite a few pictures to see those," Fokke stands, tense.

"I'm sorry. I, well. You're right," Sarah admits.

"We broke up," Fokke says, pacing the room.

"And what about the baby?" Sarah can't help but asking.

"What about it?" He doesn't mean to raise his voice.

"Okay. None of my business. Listen. I'm going to call it a night." Her voice is clipped as she stands up as well. "There's extra blankets in that armoire there that the staff brought up earlier," she adds. He can tell she's hoping for an explanation, can see sadness in her eyes. After all, what kind of asshole loser would break up with his pregnant girlfriend and not care about the baby? But he doesn't want Sarah touching this topic.

Even the memory of Jackie can ruin innocent flirtation with a stranger in this romantic setting. Damn Jackie. He wants to stop Sarah's retreat; talk with her more. But how?

"Listen Sarah. I'm sorry. I didn't mean to get defensive." She's an arm's length away, her curls shimmering gold in the firelight. "It's just a very difficult, complicated topic." He can't say anymore. If he does, he'll be opening himself up to a stranger. For what?

"Well, if you want to talk to someone *very familiar* with complicated, difficult topics related to the heart, I'm your girl. I've been through hell in the last nine months."

Fokke nods, hoping it is not too knowingly. Why not tell Sarah everything? What better place to unload your heart than to a sympathetic and honest stranger who will be gone tomorrow? She might need to talk through her heart ache as well. He feels the stranglehold on his tongue loosen as he stands across from Sarah with the golden hair. He can feel his story on the verge of tumbling out of him.

"I'm not good at sharing personal things," he says instead. She is looking into his eyes, as if she knows all about him, as if she is the one who has read his entire journal cover to cover. Hell, he does have an old journal in his bag; one he brought for a very specific reason. But she couldn't have read it. *She doesn't speak Dutch*, he reminds himself.

Her gaze pulls him outward while his emotions form a churning tide within: anger and resentment pounding against desire and hope. She is standing before him in her ridiculous, fluffy sweats, but all he can see is her eyes reading him, stripping him of his armor. His hand is in his hair, pulling.

"That's okay. You don't have to." She waits a beat longer, giving him the chance to suggest otherwise. She sees him struggling on the piercing hook of emotion, and like a good fly fisherwoman, she releases him.

"Good night, Fokke."

She has already turned away by the time he takes a deep breath, breaking out of the trance-like state he was just in. "Good night Sarah. Sleep well," he calls after her.

Chapter 14
Dreaming

Sarah is awoken by the tantalizing smell of coffee. She shifts in bed, slightly confused. Then she remembers the man in the next room—the Dutch man with the funny travel stories and slightly crooked nose who almost opened up to her last night— the same man who had the lead role in the X-rated dream from which she has just awoken. Images of Fokke naked and sweaty making love to her on the floor in front of the fireplace play on the edge of her memory, and her body physically responds.

She sits up in bed, shaking her head. *What the hell is wrong with me?* she thinks as she changes into her sweat suit and heads to the bathroom. The mirror reflects back to her the heat in her cheeks. *Good to know I can still have this kind of reaction*, she thinks. *But still. All those beautiful, charming Italian men hitting on me and I dream about him. Why him?*

It's warmer in the living room. Fokke's by the hearth, loading a fresh log on the fire, which casts its soothing light into the otherwise darkened room. She looks at him through blurry eyes, realizing he's got to be one of those annoyingly chipper morning people. He turns toward her. He's asking her something about how she slept.

"Slept all right. Thanks. And you?" she mumbles.

"Yeah, fine." He runs a hand through his messy hair. "Hope I didn't wake you?"

"Smell of coffee might have woken me. What time is it, anyway?" she asks as she stretches her arms, accompanied by an uninhibited yawn before she thinks to cover her mouth.

"A little after six," he says. She notices the light blue of his eyes, a strangely amused expression on his face as if pondering some sort of decision.

"As in six a.m? Wow," she responds.

"Wow as in early or late?" he asks with mild curiosity. His sweats hang a bit low on his hips where she can see exposed, smooth skin over taut abdominal muscles, their angles defined in the firelight.

"Early," she says. "Too early." She doesn't know if she's talking about the time or the ridiculously lustful nature of her thoughts.

"Would you like some coffee or are you going back to bed?" he asks. "Still five hours before check out time, so you have time to sleep."

If she goes back to bed, those dreams might start all over again.

"Coffee, please. Do I smell fresh bread?" she asks, looking around the living room.

"Yep. Room service," he smiles at her as he retrieves a mug and pours her a steaming cup of coffee, adding a teaspoon of sugar. "Basket's on the table."

Coffee in hand, she heads toward the basket, and ponders the brioche, a fluffy sweet bread, a flaky cornetto and a half-round of bread. She opts for the bread. She sits in the chair across from him by the open fire. The bread melts in her mouth.

"Italian bread is amazing. I'm going to have to add a few miles to my running schedule if I keep eating breakfast Italian style" she says as she takes another bite.

"Yeah. I know what you mean." He taps lightly on his stomach and her eyes follow. Sarah takes a healthy slug of coffee as her eyes linger, studying the musculature of his abdominal region. She shakes her head.

"What?" he asks, looking down at his shirt to see if he spilled something.

"Nothing," she mumbles in frustration. *Am I attracted to him? Or is this some trick of ambiance and firelight?* She assures herself that this attraction is a fleeting thing; the warmth of connection with another after weeks of traveling alone. He will be no more than an entry in my diary or a reference in my Alexi vlog. She tries to let the conviction of this thought placate her as they eat in silence. She notices for the first time how short the couch is in comparison to his height.

"How did you fit on that thing?" she asks, nodding toward the couch.

"I didn't," he laughs. "I ended up sleeping on the floor."

"That's awful," she sighs, thinking about the oversized bed she'd slept in.

"I can handle almost anything for a night." But then he thinks about something that he can't handle any longer; something he needs to clear up. "There's something I want to tell you." His brow creases. "I know I'll probably never see you again after today, but it bothered me last night, to leave you thinking about me as a man who would leave his own child."

Sarah wants to tell him that it's none of her business, but if she's honest with herself, she wants to know. "If you want to explain it to me; if that would somehow help," she offers carefully.

"It would." He seems to be concentrating, as if at a business meeting; keeping his emotions locked away. "It ends up my girlfriend cheated on me and the baby wasn't mine."

She is holding her breath, giving him space to speak.

"I would never leave my own child, Sarah. And the idea that you thought that of me . . . that anyone would think that of me; I had to clear that up."

Instinctively she reaches for his hand. "I'm sorry. That must have been so hard."

"Yeah. It was. Not exactly the type of thing a man wants to admit. Now," he clears his throat, pulling his hand away from hers, "Want to see some travel photos from this area?"

And just like that the subject is closed. She recognizes this technique, senses from her years of counseling others that Fokke needs to talk more about this topic, but now is not the time.

"I'd love to see some photos," she answers.

He gets up and retrieves his iPad from his backpack.

"Let's sit on the couch. Easier to see," he tells her.

She settles in next to him as Fokke turns on the iPad. The screen lights up and she leans toward him to get a better look. He selects the slideshow setting and she watches incredible image after image of Italy pass before her eyes: a roadside shrine hewn out of ancient sandstone with a statue of the Virgin Mary in a bright blue gown, daisies at her feet; sunrise over the Arno river in Florence, the gilt-edged water beneath an ancient stone bridge; a dusty road lined with Cypress trees cutting through a vineyard; the Italian Dolomites crested in snow.

"These are stunning shots. You're a talented photographer, Fokke. Can I see more?"

"Choose a country or city," he suggests. Sarah looks at the folder names on the iPad. There are many places she's never heard of, so she opts for a city she at least recognizes.

"Beijing."

"Beijing it is." Fokke clicks on the map and a whole world opens. As she watches the images go by, she is taken by the emotion the photographs evoke. The city is massive, alive. As the images continue, she sees a pattern evolving.

"This picture is stunning, but eerie. Is it foggy, or is that serious pollution?" she asks.

"Pollution."

"Wow. I can't imagine it's easy to breathe there," she remarks, taking a sip of her coffee.

"It's not. Did you know that over one and a half million people in China die each year because of polluted air? Heart and lung problems, strokes."

"Seriously? How can the government allow that? That's crazy! And that water, it looks like it's filled with, I don't know. What are those gray clouds surrounding that iridescent blue pattern in the middle?" Sarah asks.

"Waste that factories dumped right into a river in the Tianjin province of China. Used to be a water source for the villages surrounding it," Fokke explains, his features animated.

"It always shocks me what industry can get away with," she shakes her head, thinking of clear cutting of old growth forests taking place in her home state. "But there's a strange beauty in this photo. Are you a professional photographer? Do you work for National Geographic covering the environment or something like that?"

"No. I wish." Fokke's lips curve into a smile. It's refreshing that she doesn't know who he is. "I'm a travel writer. Photography's a serious hobby, though. The more I travel, the more I see how much we're screwing up the planet. I like to document it through photography. Gives me the sense that I'm doing something about it." He notices the furrow on her brow and wants to reach out and wipe it away. Is he upsetting her with his doom and gloom photos? "Perhaps a bit heavy handed for your first cup of coffee. Let's go to Costa Rica," he says, clicking on another folder.

Sarah is about to interrupt him, the career counselor in her wanting to discuss the topic of professional photography as a career with him further, but the brilliant images on the screen pull her attention: a rainbow caught in the mist of a waterfall, fluorescent green parrots, monkeys climbing downward from the forest canopy.

"These are amazing Fokke! Did you take these with your iPad?" she asks as she leans in closer to get a better view.

"No. I took these with my Nikon, but everything's uploaded on the cloud for back-up," he explains. "You never know when someone's going to make off with your bag." He glances at her and she can see the teasing kindness in his light blue eyes.

"You're never going to let me live that down, are you?" she playfully creases her brow.

"Nope. I've got to have something on you, especially after I gave you my sob story," he returns. The look in his eyes is friendly, but guarded. She chooses her words carefully.

"Well, I went through a pretty rough break-up myself at the beginning of the year; I was also betrayed. By my husband of eleven years and one of my close female friends." She makes eye contact briefly before dropping her eyes toward her coffee cup.

I know sweetheart, Fokke thinks. "I'm sorry to hear that we have such a crappy thing in common. How you holding up?" he says instead.

Sarah pulls her knees upward and wraps her left arm around them, all the while balancing her coffee cup. Her braid has come loose and her long golden curls surround her face.

"I'm doing better than I thought I would." She weighs her words carefully. "But you know what I find the hardest? Not taking the betrayal personally, you know? Make it all about you or all about the other." She sees the recognition in his eyes as he nods ever so slightly. "But I'm slowly healing," she admits. "How about you?"

"I'm in the numb stage," Fokke responds, a terse smile on his lips.

"Ah. The old numb stage. I like to think of that as the Pleistocene tar pit stage—no forward or backward movement," she replies casually as if discussing soccer, rather than the state of their hearts.

"Is that an official term?" he laughs, realizing he's talking to a trained counselor.

"Nah. But I like visual images."

"And how does one get out of the Pleistocene tar pit?" he asks, sipping his coffee.

"You reach out for a stick, or, in human terms, a helping hand." Her smile is light, friendly, which tricks him into saying more.

"That's logical. But as you saw last night, I'm not very good at that. I'm used to working solo when it comes to the inside terrain." His words combined with his half smile and the fact that they are sitting side by side gives her the sensation of closeness she hasn't felt since this trip began. Hell, since she left Matthew.

"It's comfortable in the tar pit," she remarks, wiggling her eyebrows.

"Very," he replies. "But I'll consider reaching for the stick, counselor. And what stage are you in?"

"Well, I'm not a firm believer in stages, to be honest, but I'd say I'm in the pissed off stage. There's a whole list of stages for break ups." She looks at him, seeing that he's still engaged. "Goes like this: needing answers, desperation, denial, bargaining, relapse, anger, acceptance, hope. They don't line up in a neat little row. These stages can pounce upon you all at once, or arrive out of order."

"You like the pissed off stage?" he muses.

"Yeah. Being pissed off is good. I'm pissed off at Matthew, that's my ex, for betraying me. But also pissed off at myself for not noticing that our relationship was in trouble. The clues were there, but I felt blind-sided at the time. This trip, the distance from it all is helping put things in perspective."

"Pissed off and traveling sounds like a good mix," Fokke shakes his head.

"Are you pissed off?" she asks, shifting on the couch next to him.

"Sometimes. But not at the moment," he replies. His voice warm, friendly.

"As long as you don't get too destructive, anger can be good. It wakes you up, brings you back to yourself. Brings new meaning to your life."

"Here's to anger," Fokke raises his cup. They clink their coffee mugs together and Sarah sees the shift in him; topic closed once again, though there is a tiny chink in the armor.

She points to his iPad. "I'd love to see more. Ooh, Argentina!" she says with enthusiasm.

"One of my favorite places," Fokke admits. "I'm heading there in a few weeks, as a matter of fact." Argentina is close to his heart and the photos feel somehow more personal to him. And for this very reason he wants to share them with Sarah.

This time the pictures that come to her attention are a mix of nature and people; not just any people but cowboys on horses in open country stretching into the distance. These aren't the U.S. cowboys she's used to, with their Stetson hats and wrangler jeans, but exotic cowboys in ponchos and drawstring pants, strength and reserve in their wild eyes.

"Argentinian cowboys?" she asks.

"Yes. They're called gauchos," Fokke explains. "The pride of the nation. They live out in the open plains and mountains with their herds, leading a solitary, nomadic life. Some of them are less transitory; work on large ranches. But they're an amazing, resilient group of people." His voice has dropped a bit, as if discussing something sacred.

Sarah is aware of his hushed tones. She looks up at him for a moment, confirming the look of admiration in his eyes. A photo of three gauchos standing in a small cabin next to their tack comes onto the screen. Sepia tones bring out the intensity of their wild, animal-like eyes.

"It looks like they lead a simple, but hard life. But they look content; as if that solitary life is exactly what they want. Just a gaucho and his horse in the wild," she muses.

"Exactly," Fokke says. She is caught off guard by the look of bewilderment in his eyes. But whatever is passing over him is just as quickly shaken off as he closes the folder. He sees the frustration on her face.

"One more?" she half begs.

"Okay. How about The Netherlands?" he suggests, clicking on a map of photos.

"I didn't see that folder. Yes, please. Take me to The Netherlands." She can't help but notice how different their rapport is compared to their parting words last night. She wishes they had talked last night about the baby, the betrayal; that he had shared this detail of his life with her then. Things might have turned out differently; quite differently.

Chapter 15
Goodbyes

After a quick shower, she changes in her room and packs her things for departure. When she returns to the living room, he is also packed up and ready to go.

"Can I buy you breakfast before we check out?" Fokke asks as he reaches for the door. She's full from the bread she consumed, but she is tempted, which worries her.

"Umm. No. I think this is a good place to say goodbye," she responds.

That's right. Play it safe Sarah. That's your nature.

Sarah shakes her head, wondering why the ghost of her mother dressed in a purple nightgown is choosing this moment to taunt her.

As they step into the hall, an impulse streaks through her and before she can rein it in, she leans into him, arching her long neck upward and kisses him on his sensual lips, and just as quickly pulls away. Fokke stares at her, clearly taken by surprise.

"Wow. To what do I owe the pleasure?" he asks.

"I just wanted to kiss you once before saying have a good life. You're a good man, Fokke, and I'm already jealous of the woman who will end up winning your heart," she smiles, ignoring the rush of energy pulsing through her body.

"You surprise me Sarah," he says, pushing a strand of hair behind her ear. She is touched by this personal gesture, which feels somehow more intimate than the quick kiss she so daringly bestowed upon him.

"I surprise myself. Have a good life Fokke," she winks at him, one final flirtation.

"Sure I can't buy you breakfast?" he asks. He can see her hesitation, and is about to try to talk her into it when he hears someone in the hall behind them.

"Ah. Bongiorno Signore en Signora van der Veld." They turn to see a hotel worker with a letter in his hands standing in the hall.

"Oh, we're not married," Sarah explains, feeling slightly ridiculous.

"Ah. Yes. Well, we are telling all of our guests of the situation and our policies."

"Is it illegal to share a room in Italy if you're not married?" Sarah whispers to Fokke, catching the earthen scent of his cologne.

"No. I don't think that's the situation he's talking about," Fokke whispers back, trying to suppress a smile. "And what is the situation?" he asks the hotel worker.

"Too much snow and a large snow storm moving in. There's government warning issued for people to stay inside. Freezing temperatures, snow drifts, no vehicles moving," the employee informs them. "Don't to worry. We have plenty food in our kitchens and so far, the electricity and gas are still proficiente."

"Are you telling me we have to stay here?" Sarah responds. *With this Dutch man whom I just kissed on a wild whim?!*

"Yes signora. The rooms will be 50 percent sale," he explains. "You come to breakfast in the restaurante. Later we have games and dance night too."

"I have to go to Venice," Sarah explains.

"Non possible, Signora."

"I'm supposed to go to Sappada today," Fokke adds.

"East. No, no! Non è possibile. Ci sono nevicate record. Tutta la città è coperta di neve." He sweeps his hands in wild motions as he walks them to the hall window and draws open the blinds.

"Oh my God. Don't they have snow plows in this country?" Sarah exclaims as she takes in the snow piled half way up the doors and the heavy spirals of snow falling from the sky. "What did he just say?"

"Record snowfall. The whole damned region is snowed in," Fokke informs her.

"Okay Signore. Signora. You stay then?"

"Considering we have no choice?" Fokke responds. "Yes. I think we'll be staying. Any idea of when this storm is supposed to be over?"

"Ah," he shrugs his shoulders casually. "A few days." He hands them the envelope.

That could be a week in Italian time, Fokke muses. As the hotel worker recedes down the hall, Fokke turns toward Sarah.

"Looks like it's not quite time to say goodbye after all," he teases.

Sarah feels the heat in her cheeks. "I'm so sorry about that kiss!"

"You are?" Fokke's smile drops a notch.

"Well, not entirely sorry. I guess I've been traveling alone for too long," she lets out.

Fokke looks down into her eyes. "Yeah. Traveling can be a lonely business."

Sarah's cheeks burn as fear creeps into her eyes.

"You okay? Us sharing a suite for some unknown period of time?" he asks pointedly.

"Honestly? Not really," Sarah tenses. "Listen. Not that I don't trust you." She is looking at his lips, thinking of how he tasted like almonds and coffee. "I just, I don't think it's a good idea."

Fokke sees the flush on her cheeks, the way she's looking at him. He wants to take her back into the suite and show her just how good an idea it is. "Okay. Um. Let me talk to the receptionist and see if there were any last minute no-shows," he says instead, squeezing her hand.

Sarah feels their connection like a current of electricity flowing through her body to his and back again. She's staring at him, confusion on her face. "Yes please," she says hastily.

PART TWO: GRAND SNAFU

Chapter 16
Roommates

Fokke tries to get his head around the situation: that kiss, her flirtatious words, the energy reverberating between them. Yet she looked scared out of her wits at the prospect of continuing to share a hotel room with him. And to tell the truth, the idea scares him too. This is the first time in fourteen months he has felt anything for a woman, and oh bloody hell would he like to explore those feelings. But he can't screw around with her; not after reading her diary page-for-page, knowing, that despite her strong appearance, how emotionally fragile she is. He has also read her musings about what it would be like to eventually experience the *"taste and feel of another man besides Matthew,"* is keenly aware of how he's been picturing himself as the one to provide the comparison. *There sure as hell needs to be a room available for me,* he thinks, *or we're going to do something very stupid.*

She has come with him to reception, determined to be the one to move to another room, despite his insistence to just the opposite. But the lodge is still sold out. Not only sold out, but a handful of people in the game and reading area of the lobby are sitting next to folded blankets. Considering most of them are having a collective bad hair day, he's guessing they slept there. Sarah's also looking at them, concern on her face.

"Those poor people! Do you think they slept in the lobby?"

"Looks like it," Fokke confirms.

Sarah contemplates them as if choosing a dog to take home from the animal shelter. "We should offer to share our suite. It's big enough for at least two more if there are extra mattresses," she suggests.

Fokke looks at her skeptically. Is she just going to invite strangers into their room? But of course; she's already done so. "Listen, Sarah. How are you picturing this working? I mean, I'm impressed by your kindness—that you let me stay last night. But these are total strangers. They could steal our things in the middle of the night. Happened to me in a youth hostel in Sri Lanka."

"This isn't Sri Lanka," Sarah points out, crossing her arms. "This is a high-end ski resort. And plus, if they stole from us, where would they escape to?"

"I've also been robbed in Italy. In a four-star hotel," he adds.

"How about that woman in the green sweater?" She motions her head toward the lobby, ignoring Fokke's list of travel-related robberies. Fokke takes in the bulging curves of a sturdy woman in a woolen skirt, her silvered hair cascading down her back like a cloak, a cross dangling between her sagging breasts.

"That old Irish woman?" Fokke asks.

"A green sweater and a cross and you assume she's Irish?" Sarah is looking around the lobby. "Or those two younger women; they look like sisters."

Fokke rubs a hand across his face and glances in the direction she has just indicated. Two twenty-something girls in jogging suits, brightly painted nails and matching suitcases are sitting close to one another, deep in discussion.

"I don't know," he sighs.

"Or that middle-aged couple," Sarah nods toward an athletic Italian man and woman in jeans and hiking boots. "They look nice enough."

"Everyone looks nice on the surface, but let's be strategic about this. We've got to choose someone we can tolerate for an unknown period of time," Fokke reminds her. The irony of his comment is not lost on him as he thinks of the primary reason they might want extra company in the suite tonight.

"Let's go check out the titles in the bookcase," Sarah suggests.

"You short on reading material?" he asks, surprised by the sudden change of topic. She winks at him, walks toward the bookcase in the middle of the lobby and begins to silently peruse. Fokke joins her and is amazed at what they overhear; it's almost as if they are invisible instead of standing within earshot of multiple, uncensored conversations. Though the Italian couple glances over at her a number of times speaking rapid Italian, they largely go unnoticed. Within five minutes they have all the information they need.

"Shall we have breakfast then?" Sarah asks quietly.

"Sure darling," he raises his voice, making it clearly audible to the others as he drapes his arm around her shoulders. She shoots him a look as they walk from the lobby toward the queue for the small café.

"What was that about, *darling?*" she emphasizes when they're out of ear shot of the roomless travelers. "You can take your arm off my shoulders any time now," she raises her eyebrows at him.

"In a minute. You have no idea what that Italian hiker man was saying about you; even though you were within ear shot. Damn," Fokke is almost bristling with anger. "Just wanted to be clear you aren't some 'tasty morsel on the menu', in need of 'devouring,'" he translates, using air quotes. Though the asshole has a point; Sarah does look delicious in her slim-fit jeans and tunic sweater, something that could be devoured. Fokke shakes his head again, reluctantly taking his arm away from her shoulders.

"Ah. So you're protecting me. That's very kind of you." She liked the feel of his arm around her, but she needs to keep herself in check. "I could sense he was talking about me, but without understanding Italian, I missed the content," Sarah lowers her voice, leaning closer to Fokke conspiratorially as they wait in line.

"Best to leave it that way. He was crude." He wonders how many other men have been gawking at Sarah during her travels.

"And the sisters? I've got to see this hotel worker!" She laughs out loud, her head leaning toward his. "I thought guys were bad, but those girls, Australian, don't you think? I'm seriously hoping they're not sisters . . ."

"Yeah. That made me feel cheap just overhearing it!" Fokke concurs. "Looks like they'll be getting a bed tonight, one way or another."

"There's still the older lady, who based on how nice and friendly and Irish she looks, must be an Italian mafiosa," she concludes.

"Now you're catching on," Fokke winks at her.

Sarah looks up into his face, sees the playful creases around his eyes, pleasantly surprised how they get one another's humor.

A table opens up and they settle in.

"So Fokke. Good call on getting a bit more information," she admits as she picks up the menu. "Looks like we won't be sharing the suite with anyone else after all." She imparts this information without any of the reservation she had earlier, and Fokke feels relief followed by a pang of angst.

"Thanks. And that was clever, looking at the bookcase. I'm always amazed how people forget they can be overheard; as if focusing on their own conversation blocks them off from the rest of the world."

He realizes that at some point between coming down this morning to look for another room and the last twenty minutes waiting in line, that he and Sarah have become a sort of team, the rapport between them easy.

"So you're the chivalrous type," Sarah concludes.

Her assessment catches him off guard. "Haven't figured that out by now?" he responds, the playfulness leaving his voice.

Sarah is aware of the shift. "Did I say something wrong?" she asks, as she pulls on the ties of her sweater.

"No," Fokke shakes his head. He studies the delicate mosaics on the salt and pepper shakers, silently counting the colors. How can he explain that she just said something that Jackie once said to him, verbatim? *So you're the chivalrous type.* Okay. Not exactly original words. But just like Jackie, Sarah pronounced "chivalrous" as if it's an antiquated concept. Do American women think chivalry is passé?

"You just reminded me of someone else right now."

"Of Jackie?" she ventures.

"How do you know her name? I didn't tell you that." Fokke stares at her.

Sarah freezes. "You said her name in your sleep last night," she improvises. "I heard you, when I got up to use the bathroom." Does he see her flushed cheeks? Can he tell she's lying?

"Are you serious? I said her name in my sleep? So much for moving forward. Damn I'm pathetic," Fokke's face contorts.

Sarah inhales and exhales deeply. She knows better than to play with someone like this.

"Okay. Fokke. You're not pathetic. I am. You didn't say her name in your sleep. I saw her name in your journal. And before you get upset, no. I would never read your journal. I couldn't if I wanted to, considering it's in Dutch. But that was before I found your passport. I was trying desperately to figure out who you were. Her name was one of the few words I could read." Sarah's shoulders tense and relax. Better to be honest.

"Um. Okay. This is awkward." Fokke looks at her, his eyes glinting. She stares back at him with her big blue eyes, clearly upset. Now would be a great time to tell her he read *just a wee bit* of her journal too, in a language he fully understands. "It's okay Sarah," he starts, "I . . ."

"Signore, Signora. Bongiorno," the waiter interrupts them. Sarah orders fresh fruit, tea and toast with jam and Fokke chooses the ciabatta with thick slices of Parmigiano-Reggiano and sundried tomatoes. Another server is making the rounds with coffee and tea, and their conversation is derailed.

After breakfast, Fokke is trying to figure out the best manner in which to broach the topic of her journal that he *accidentally read in its entirety*, but before he can get around to it, she heads off to a bread and pastry baking class, which Fokke assumes is the hotel's clever way of enlisting guests to help with the cooking. Fokke joins an impromptu chess tournament in the bar.

He's spent many an hour playing in the chess clubs of Amsterdam and Bombay, Melbourne and Hong Kong and it is clear that he is one of the better players in this tournament. That is until he encounters Celeste, a sixty-eight-year-old French woman who puts him in check mate in twenty-six moves. Celeste treats him to an espresso. He soon learns that she owns a bookstore in the Quartier Latin of Paris, which she opened after retiring from a life as a French correspondent in the United States.

"So where did your wife get off to?" she asks him.

"Not my wife," Fokke clarifies.

"Ah. Yes. I know," she chides. "I can tell that you two are quite new, based on the charming flirtation." Fokke wonders when Celeste could have possibly observed them together.

"So you're a detective as well as a bookstore owner. Ah. And former journalist," Fokke retorts. "Snooping out a story?"

"It comes second nature to me, I'm afraid." She adjusts her silver-rimmed glasses.

"And you'd like to know our story," he concludes. *Perhaps she recognizes me,* he thinks.

"Oui, Oui Monsieur." She is bold, but he likes that about Celeste. Her approach is like her clothing; elegant, yet concise. He would like to visit her book store in Paris, see her in action helping customers, intuiting which section they will seek out. He does nothing, however, to satiate her need for a story.

"We'll have to have a re-match before this snowstorm is over," Fokke says, bidding her adieu. He heads back to the room. He wants to try his cell phone one more time to try to reach the guys.

Chapter 17
Doors

Sarah and the other guests who have signed up for the baking workshop are surprised to discover a professional kitchen behind the ancient wooden doors of the entry. In fact, the only thing that seems out of place among all the shiny stainless steel appliances is the sooty brick pizza oven.

The first two hours they work on sourdough bread, thin pizza crusts, raviolis and brioche. While the dough is resting, the cook asks them if he could enlist their help with this evening's dinner. Everyone is in good spirits, happy to be doing something useful. Sarah is teamed up with Espen, a fit Norwegian man in his mid-to-late forties who is quite handy with a knife. Like Sarah, he has also admitted to having a lot of cooking experience. They make short work of a large mound of kale, then move onto a 20 kilo bag of gnarled carrots that come in a variety of exotic colors: purple, white, blood orange.

"You're amazing with that knife. Are you a chef?" Espen asks her.

"Grew up in the kitchen. My mother was a chef. I'm more of a hobby chef. I love trying out new recipes or inventing my own. And you? You look like a pro."

"I own a restaurant in Stavanger. I cooked the first few years, but now I spend most of my time in the front of the house."

As she gets into the rhythm of chopping, she is struck by the pleasant feeling of six strangers working together, which helps take her mind off the snowstorm. She knows why the setting is so comforting. She is picturing her mother, her sister April and their younger twin brothers Eric and Aaron all around a kitchen island, helping with one of her mother's many grand recipe experiments. For the first time since she landed in Europe, Sarah misses her siblings, and she misses her mama so much it makes her chest hurt.

Espen hums to himself as he chops, a comforting melody in contrast to the staccato clicks of their knives. The kitchen is warm and well lit, but the wind comes in harsh gusts against the high windows. Instead of blue or even snow white, the glass displays a menacing patchwork of the storm outside: ominous, dark clouds, hail, snow flurries.

"Good thing they're prepared for this sort of thing in this region," Candy, a woman from New York, comments as she follows Sarah's gaze. "Imagine if you were snowed in in one of those cheap hotels without a full kitchen—just those cereal boxes and a few bruised bananas at the breakfast bar."

"They have a larder here," Espen points with his chin toward a door at the far end of the kitchen. "Fully stocked. I don't think we're at any risk of going hungry."

"I don't suppose they have any vegan ricotta or parmesan stored in there," Sarah says.

"I highly doubt it, but I'll ask for you," Espen volunteers. Before Sarah has a chance to say she can do it herself, he is conversing in Italian with one of the cooks on staff.

Sarah doesn't need to speak Italian to follow their conversation. The hand gestures and raised voices make it all clear: a ravioli without cheese is a ridiculous request. Espen keeps talking, gesturing toward Sarah. Both men smile appreciatively and the conversation seems more amicable as the cook pulls in his upper lip and rubs his chin. He is now nodding and laughing as he leads Espen away to the pantry.

Sarah continues chopping carrots as Beatrice strikes up a conversation.

"This little bit of work is a blessing," says Beatrice. "Helping prepare the food. The staff clearly has their work cut out for them."

"Yes. It's fun as well," Sarah responds. She couldn't be more pleased to have Beatrice in the group—the same woman that she had jokingly called an Italian Mafiosa earlier in the morning.

"So is this your first time to Sappada?" Sarah asks her.

"No. No. My husband and I had our honeymoon here when this lodge first opened. That was many years ago. We always talked about coming back here for an anniversary, but he passed away last year." Beatrice pushes her large spectacles up on her nose. Magnified by the thick lenses, her eyes appear owl-like and Sarah sees the tears forming in the corners of her eyes.

"I'm so sorry," Sarah responds as she reaches for Beatrice's hand.

"Thank you. We had many lovely years together. I decided it was time to come back to the lodge and honor the memory of our love," Beatrice finishes.

"What a good idea, Beatrice. That love between you carries on, will always be with you," Sarah adds, hoping she's not being too assertive.

"Yes. I can almost feel him with me," Beatrice says. "I'm glad to be here. Though we weren't snowed in during our honeymoon."

Beatrice is a fountain of knowledge when it comes to the lodge. Sarah learns that the lodge usually holds forty guests, but they are far over capacity, especially since the employees cannot leave. Their crew of ten slept in the basement level, which although lacking the luxury of the guest rooms, is equipped with beds as well as bathrooms and showering facilities.

Ten minutes later, Espen and the cook return from the pantry with a handful of ingredients and commiserate near the six burner industrial stove where Espen is placing a cup of raw cashews in a pan to cook. She sees the bag of flour labeled tapioca and she has a good idea what is going on.

She heads to where he's standing and sees the tell-tale ingredients. In addition to the cashews and tapioca flour, there's garlic and something called lievito nutrizionale, which must be nutritional yeast, she guesses.

"Are you making vegan cheese from scratch?" Sarah inquires.

"Yes. Vegan mozzarella. My ex-wife was a vegan, so I became quite proficient in vegan cooking," he explains. "I thought you might appreciate some mozzarella in your raviolis."

"This is amazing. And very thoughtful," Sarah acknowledges. "Thank you, Espen."

"You're more than welcome Sarah. I like the idea of making something special for you," he smiles, revealing a set of nearly-perfect teeth.

"Oh. Well," she sighs, drawing in a breath to calm her nerves. "I'm going to get back to that mountain of carrots."

When Espen returns to the group again, Candy is talking about her three girlfriends who are on the trip with her. Espen joins the conversation and they soon learn that he is traveling with his mother. By the sound of it, she is the type of woman who is accustomed to the fineries in life. Although Candy, who is a fairly attractive woman in her mid-forties, is doing her best to gain Espen's attention, he keeps steering the conversation back toward Sarah.

"And you Sarah, are you traveling alone?" Espen asks.

"No. I'm traveling with my husband," she answers automatically. She recoils from her own words just as soon as they leave her lips. But of course, for most of her adult life, this is how she would have finished that sentence. As images of Matthew enter her mind, she quickly revises her statement. "My husband is Dutch. We're on our honeymoon."

"Oh. Excuse me. I didn't notice a ring," Espen says, a trace of disappointment on his face.

"The ring was too flashy to wear while traveling," she explains. "We thought it best to leave them at home." The lies roll off her tongue seamlessly.

"You're on your honeymoon!" Beatrice repeats. "Oh dear. My meeting you during your honeymoon here in the lodge. It's *a sign* from him," Beatrice states, a beatific smile on her face. "Love does conquer all."

Sarah nods politely as guilt pierces her conscience. She will certainly go to hell for such trickery. The ladies in the group naturally want to hear all about her wedding and her groom and Sarah can't help but continue weaving her tale. That's the thing about lying; once you start, it can be a slippery slope, and she is sliding head first as she answers their long list of questions. Her story sounds so plausible that the initial guilt begins to lift. After all, what's the harm in sharing a happy love story, even if it's not true? It's not like she'll ever see these people again after the storm ends—and it will end, eventually.

They are given leave and Sarah bids adieu to Candy, Espen, Beatrice and the others and heads to the café for a cup of tea. Alone once again, it is only a matter of time before a middle-aged man from Austria approaches her table and asks if he can join her. His predictable banter and questions ruin her peaceful moment.

She politely excuses herself and heads back to the suite, suddenly realizing how tired she feels. She enters the suite and is relieved to find it empty. She strips down and hops in the clawfoot tub and turns on the shower to rinse the smells of the kitchen from her body.

As the water washes over her, she feels her eyes prick; the emotion rising higher and higher. Her body is shaking, willing the tears to come. Her shaking gives way to uncontrollable laughter. She laughs so hard that her sides hurt. She does not analyze it, does not try to suppress it.

By the time she is all laughed out, she is emotionally spent, but calm. She dries herself off and combs out her wet curls before they get too tangled and then blow dries her hair into loose curls. She wraps the fluffy hotel robe around her and heads to the small kitchen to make a cup of tea, enjoying the warmth of the hot liquid. She draws the curtains open and peers outside. The snow is falling in tight strands, layer after layer blocking all visibility.

She thinks of Matthew, and this time she comes up blank: no anger, no pain, no sadness. Just a thought that she watches, like seeing a stranger cross the street. It helps, she realizes, to have a handsome, single man in her midst. But now that she knows they are both single and attracted to one another, it complicates things. Or perhaps just the opposite.

***

When she awakes, she knows there is someone in the living room. It takes her brain a panicked moment to sort out the sounds and remember that she has a suite mate. She stretches and slowly gets out of bed, feeling refreshed. She has dreamed of Fokke again, but this time they weren't engaging in wild, orgasmic sex by the fireplace, but sitting in a café, holding hands like long time lovers, laughing. She realizes her mind has pulled the setting from one of the photos of The Netherlands Fokke showed her this morning.

There's a soft knock on the door.

"Sarah, you awake?" he asks.

She props open the door a crack, looking out. "Hi Fokke. I just got up," she says through the door. "Is it late?"

"It's getting late. The kitchen closes in an hour. I'm heading down pretty soon. Would you like to go with me?" He's dressed in black jeans, a deep blue cashmere sweater and stylish leather shoes with blue stripes that only a European man could pull off with style.

"Yeah. That would be nice. I just need to get dressed." She is aware of how considerate Fokke is, making sure she doesn't miss dinner—the very dinner she helped prep.

When she comes into the living room, he is staring at his iPad, deep in concentration.

"Hi. Is there wifi again?" she asks as she crosses over the living room.

"No. Still no connection. I'm reading an eBook," he answers, glancing up at her.

"Ah. Which book?" But her question is lost on him. His eyes wander slowly over the stockings that cover her long, sensual legs, over her short gray skirt to the light pink V-neck sweater that accentuates the curve of her breasts, and finally to her face.

"You look amazing, Sarah," he lets out.

"Thanks. Once in a while I wear more than sweats. Shall we head downstairs?" she says, brushing off his compliment.

"Sure." He slips on his suit jacket. "Do you have something you're going to wear over that . . . to keep warm?" he suggests.

"Oh. Good idea. I'll grab my cardigan and a shawl."

They are standing by the door, about to head out when Fokke turns toward her. He steps closer, leans into her, his hand on her cheek. She takes in the details of his touch, the heat coming off his fingers, the thickness of his forearm, the hooded look in his eyes. Her heart rate increases rapidly as a pleasant shiver passes over her skin. She doesn't know whether to run or lean into him and close her mouth over his.

"You're a good woman, Sarah," he states before breaking away from her.

"Thank you," she replies. She looks up into his eyes and the heat she saw a moment ago has given way to something else; frustration, consternation. "You wanted to kiss me, but now you don't," she states.

"Oh. I still want to kiss you. But I'm not going to," he winks.

"Good. That would definitely be a bad idea," she says firmly.

"Yep," he nods as he takes her hand and leads her deliberately out of the room. "My thoughts exactly."

Despite the way Fokke is pushing his lips into a straight line, his facial muscles work hard to suppress the right corner of his mouth from curving upward into a smile.

Chapter 18
Lights

"Special vegan dish for the signora," the waiter announces as he sets a plate in front of Sarah. Fokke has already received his plate and he raises his glass to hers for a toast before they begin to eat.

"To making the best of being trapped in Sappada."

"I'll drink to that," she responds. She bites into the carrot vegan mozzarella raviolis with sage, and can't help but let out a sigh. It's delicious.

"You made these?" he asks with a look of admiration on his face. She nods, pleased to know that all of that work this afternoon resulted in something so tasty.

"They're amazing, Sarah."

"Thanks. I didn't do it alone. There was a team of us." As she sets her napkin on her lap, Fokke refills her wine glass and continues with the conversation they had begun before the food arrived.

"As a school counselor, do you also get into personal issues? Not just career guidance?"

His question pulls her out of the moment, back to Bend, Oregon to her office, conversing with a young adult across her desk.

"Yeah. More and more in the last five years. Kids are growing up quickly these days," she begins. "One minute I'm in a guidance role for academic progress and the next we're discussing bullying, safe sex or school shootings."

"That sounds tough. If you can handle those sort of issues with teens, you've got to be able to handle just about anything," Fokke comments.

"You would think," she replies. "But I needed a break after everything went down with the betrayal, the divorce." She loved her job, believed it fulfilled her completely. Until it didn't. Until her new best friend did the unimaginable. She went from sought-after counselor to a broken woman who didn't feel qualified to counsel others while she was falling apart inside. She feels the tug at the corner of her mouth, negativity pulling at her happiness.

Fokke seems to be able to read her like a book, because his right hand scoops up hers and he's staring into her eyes. His touch is like a shot of whiskey that warms her to the core.

"Whatever's troubling you, let it go, woman. We're snowed in in the middle of nowhere, we're eating amazing raviolis you helped make and I'm going to dance the evening away with you."

She is staring at him as the warmth builds within her, taken aback by his confidence, by how his words encompass her with a buoyancy that pushes away her sadness.

"Sarah!"

She turns to see Espen with an elegant older woman by his side.

"You look gorgeous this evening. And this must be your Dutch husband," he states. Sarah nods discreetly, introducing Fokke to Espen.

"Nice to meet you," Espen responds. He introduces the woman at his side as his mother Sissel, who nods with an elegant smile.

"Your son is quite a talented cook. Once again, thank you for your thoughtfulness, Espen," she says.

"You're most welcome," he answers. They chat for a bit before Espen leads his mother to another table.

"Nice title I've acquired," Fokke raises his eyebrows at her quizzically.

"Sorry about that," she starts. "A certain man was giving me a fair amount of attention."

"Espen," Fokke clarifies.

"Yeah. He even made me vegan mozzarella from scratch! I thought it was just friendliness until he asked if I was single," she explains. She can feel the heat on her cheeks as she continues. "I said I was married. It just slipped off my tongue before I even had a chance to think about it. And then, that brought up thoughts of Matthew, the bastard, and before I knew it—"

"You had claimed me as your husband," he finishes.

"Yes," she admits. "I'm sorry. Lying was much easier than explaining the whole divorce, bag mix up, strike, sharing a grand suite with a man I just met thing."

Although he is frustrated by the potential repercussions her fib could have on them both should anyone recognize him, he quite likes the idea of being her husband for a few days; one who wouldn't cheat on her with one of her best friends—a best friend who happens to be the now ex-wife of Gregory Golder, Sarah's ex-husband's boss. Damn he knows too much.

"I get it. I come in handy to fight off your legions of suitors. Use me all you want," Fokke returns. His words are playful, but there's something dark in his eyes.

She thinks of the way he touched her cheek before they came downstairs; how important it was that he broke it off before it went any further. And yet outside of the spontaneity, their absurd situation, there's a natural spark between them she felt from the moment she shook his hand.

The music starts. To her relief, it's the tried-and-true tunes one might expect at a party in America. Sarah starts tapping her feet as the dance floor fills with guests of all ages.

"Shall we?" Fokke asks. It's a simple invitation to dance, but it feels like crossing a threshold, granting this relative stranger permission—but for what she's not quite sure.

"Yes. Let's." Sarah takes his hand and they head to the dance floor. Cold air radiates from the glass windows. She looks toward them, realizing the dark shadow on the second window pane is piled up snow. Are they now completely snowed in? The thought makes her shiver. She pushes the idea out of her head as she dances with Fokke, the rhythm of a familiar number washing over her. She is just getting warm when a slow song starts. Fokke gazes at her as if once again asking permission and she steps closer to him, resting her hand on his shoulder.

"I'm enjoying dancing with you," Fokke admits. "Better than a movie, or chess."

"Was that supposed to be a compliment?" she teases.

"Yeah. It was." Fokke gazes at her intensely, as if he might kiss her. She closes her eyes in anticipation, but the kiss never comes. Instead, he pulls her close and she leans her head against his chest, taking in the cinnamon and musk of his cologne. The scent tantalizes her, sending her thoughts back to that quick kiss. He's clearly a man to take things slowly. Considering she's only been with one man in the last eleven years, taking things slowly is probably just what she needs. Sort of.

One song merges into another and Sarah luxuriates in the strange sensation of being nestled in Fokke's arms. What would it be like to have a fling? Could she be like her sister April and experience a man physically without any strings attached? The idea has never appealed to her, and yet, as she touches his chest, leans into him, she feels the first inklings of the idea working their way into her. She is actually disappointed when the music changes and Fokke pulls away.

"Bathroom break," he says. "To be continued."

As Fokke heads toward the lobby, Espen approaches her.

"Can I have this dance?" he asks.

"Sure," she says. The funky James Brown song is clearly popular in this crowd as adults and children flock to the dance floor around them. Espen keeps a polite distance as they groove in time to the throbbing baseline. He's a pretty good dancer, and she is admittedly having fun until a loud thud followed by a crackling sound fills the room. She whirls around toward the noise and sees it—a dark mass pressing against the windows, the frozen glass cracking in an eerie pattern.

"It's going to burst!" Espen yells. Others see it too, and start running backward when the window explodes, shards of glass flying, snow and wind billowing inside as a large tree branch falls upon the dance floor. The lights flicker twice before going out. It takes only a few seconds for the votive candles on the dining tables to succumb to the howling wind and they are enveloped in complete darkness. Sarah considers herself a brave woman, but one thing she cannot take is the pitch black.

Apparently, she's not alone. Screams fill the room. People are shouting in different languages, trying to find their partners or children. She has lost contact with Espen. Though she hears him calling for her, she can't make out the direction of his voice. Someone bumps into her with such force she almost loses her balance. She hears the cries of children close by.

The panic is rippling through the crowd, rippling through her. She mentally reconstructs the space in her mind, trying to get to a wall, out of the way of the chaotic scene. But she's not quick enough. A large bulk of a person is coming toward her. As she tries to get out of the way, she trips over something right in front of her and lands painfully on her hands and knees.

"Maman!" cries a small voice. She scrambles to her feet, pulling the small form with her.

"Scusami," the man calls gruffly as he lumbers forward.

"Maman!" the child's voice is high, presumably a girl. "Où est ma mère?"

"What is your name?" Sarah asks, but the child doesn't understand. Sarah wraps a protective arm around the little child as she guides them blindly through the darkness.

"My name is Sarah," she says, doing her best to comfort the child. "Sarah."

"Je m'appelle Adeline," the child responds between gasps. "J'ai si peur."

Peur . . . that means frightened, Sarah remembers. She finally reaches the wall and can feel the little girl shaking, her breaths coming in quick gasps.

"Please. Breathe slowly, or you're going to hyperventilate," Sarah says with a calm she doesn't feel. "We'll find your mother. Maman," she tries.

Cell phone lights appear like ghostly boxes floating in the darkness. In the midst of the shouting, she hears a clear and steady voice calling her name.

"Sarah Beth Turner!"

"Fokke! Over here! Against the wall." The little girl is shaking in her arms.

"Keep talking Sarah, I'll find you." One of the cell phone lights starts to come in her direction and she finally sees him.

"Fokke! I'm to your right!"

He navigates toward her and is finally close enough to make out her features by the light of his cell phone. He reaches for her hand.

"I leave for a few minutes and all hell breaks loose! What happened? You all right?"

"The window exploded. I think from a fallen tree. Must have uprooted a power line with the fall. I've got a little girl with me," she says into the darkness. "Adeline. She's French. Do you speak French?"

"Yes. Of course," he responds. Still holding onto Sarah in the darkness, he finds the child's hand, then wraps her in a simple embrace as he speaks calmly. Whatever he says seems to work, as the little girl holds onto them both as Fokke leads them through the crowd like a bodyguard protecting the royal family. As more cell phones flash on, the darkness is punctuated by light, easing the hysteria.

"I think she's hyperventilating. Tell her to breathe into her hands to slow her breaths," Sarah instructs.

Fokke nods, and speaks calmly yet efficiently to the little girl in fluent French. Adeline follows his instructions and her breathing calms within minutes.

"Adeline!" a panicked voice yells through the crowd.

"Adeline est ici!" Fokke calls back into the darkness. He turns on the flashlight function of his cell phone and waves it in time with his words, successfully drawing the panicked mother toward them.

"Merci! Merci!" the mother cries as she takes Adeline into her arms.

Now that she's no longer concentrating on keeping the little girl safe, the panic Sarah was so successfully keeping at bay slams down on her and her own breaths begin to speed up. Fokke turns his attention toward her.

"How are you doing, Sarah? Your skin is ice cold! Where's your sweater?"

"I left it on the table. In the café somewhere."

"Si prega di mantenere la calma. Adesso vi portiamo delle candele," an authoritative voice says through the darkness. Sarah thinks she recognizes the voice of the head waiter.

"What did he say?" she asks Fokke, leaning into him as she tries to gain control of her breathing.

"He's telling us to stay calm. They're working on getting us candles." He leads her by the light of his cell phone toward the inner lobby by the bookcases, which is slightly warmer.

"Can you stay put right here? I'm going to see if I can find your sweater and then help somehow."

"Stay with me, would you? Just until I catch my breath, until the candles arrive." She doesn't like to ask, but the idea of being alone in the dark constricts her chest and pushes down on her shoulders like an invisible force.

"Of course." He rubs her arms again and she barely feels his touch. "You're freezing Sarah. I'll take you up to the room. You can get under the covers. Warm yourself up," he states, rather than suggests. "I'll build a fire so it won't be dark. Then I'll come back down to help out."

"No. I'm fine. I just need a minute," she whispers. "Then I can help too."

"Listen Sarah. I know you're used to helping others. But I think you're in a bit of shock right now. And your teeth are chattering."

"I'm fine," she states, but the shaking won't stop. "Maybe you could warm me up a bit?"

Fokke pulls her into his arms, opening up his suit jacket so she can slip her arms under it. He cradles her against his chest, planning to keep her there until her breathing slows and the warmth returns to her arms.

As she presses against his chest, feels his arms on either side of her, she has the sensation of settling into a warm, safe place. Minutes pass. Her breath calms, her skin begins to warm. There is only this moment, this warmth. She wants to stay there indefinitely, to open her heart to him, let him inside. Her thoughts cut into her and she pushes herself away.

"Better?" he asks.

"Yes, thank you," she responds, biting her bottom lip. "I'm going to be fine once I get a candle," she comments.

"Ah. Well, here they are." He steps away from her and walks over to a hotel worker, talking with him for a few minutes before returning with a stack of candles.

"You want to help? You can pass out these candles to the people here in the lobby," he says as he takes her scarf and wraps it around her shoulders. "And use this one to light the others." The candlelight breaks the darkness, pushing her fear a little further away.

"Okay. I can do that," she replies.

"They could use my help getting a tarp up over the window. I'll be back soon. Otherwise I'll see you in the room."

"I'll wait for you here," she responds.

He kisses her quickly on her forehead before leaving. She watches him disappear into the darkness, surprised how that simple kiss suggests an intimacy between them that shouldn't be possible in such a short time; is even more surprised by how much she holds onto it. *This must be what happens when people are in threatening circumstances,* she reasons. *Time speeds up; barriers break down.*

She slowly distributes the candles among the other guests huddled in the lobby—mainly women, children and older men. She is frustratingly aware of how quickly traditional roles can fall into place in threatening situations. Each person thanks her for the candle. As she transfers her flame to theirs, the light grows and the lingering tentacles of fear slip away into the shadows.

She hears the steady chanting of the Hail Mary prayer coming from her left, and discovers the woman sliding her fingers along the beads of her rosary is Beatrice, whom she met in the kitchen earlier today. As the candlelight grows, the atmosphere lightens. A handful of children in the lobby are clearly excited by the candlelight and Sarah is swept up in the moment.

"Papa!" a child calls out, and Sarah turns to see a group of men heading toward them. Fokke is among them and sits down next to her, damp with snow.

"We got the window covered with a tarp, but the power lines are snapped. We're in for a cold, dark evening. The heat is out as well."

"At least we've got the fireplace," she remarks.

"Good point. Shall we head up to the room?"

"Yeah. I really need to get warm," she admits. They break away from the growing crowd and head toward the stairs when Sarah realizes something.

"Fokke, we have to go back. We have to see if Beatrice needs a place to stay."

"Who's Beatrice?" he asks.

"You remember Grandma mafiosa from this morning? She was cooking in the kitchen with me. Ends up she's Irish, just like you guessed, and she's lovely. She slept in the lobby last night. I just saw her there. With the broken window and all, it's way too cold to sleep there again tonight."

"Of course. You're right. Let's go get her."

"And just remember, you're my husband," Sarah adds.

"Was she hitting on you too?"

"Yeah. I'm irresistible to old Irish ladies," she smiles. "She was in the group with Espen and me. So naturally, when I mentioned my Dutch husband ..."

They find her sitting on a chair in her winter coat by a votive candle, halfway through the rosary.

"Hi Beatrice, it's Sarah. From the kitchen?" Beatrice looks up at them, the candlelight reflecting eerily in her large bifocals.

"Ah Sarah. Some adventure we've got ourselves into," she says conspiratorially, her hair a fuzzy halo around her face.

"It is a big adventure," Sarah replies gently. "Did they ever find you a room Beatrice?"

"Well, they said I can stay in the basement with the workers, but I'm not sleeping in a room with a bunch of people. I'll be fine here."

"Or you can stay with us. We have a suite and there's a cozy couch just your size."

"I don't want to impose on you two on your honeymoon," Beatrice sighs.

"Oh, um, it's okay." Sarah blushes. Fokke squeezes her hand, laughing out loud.

"You okay there young man?" Beatrice asks.

"Fine, thanks. You can have the couch, which is much better than a cold lobby. You won't disturb us in the least. Shall I help you with your bag?"

"Well, aren't you a gentleman." And just like that it is settled.

Fokke notices that Sarah is trembling.

"Just one more thing. Be right back," Fokke says as he uses the light of his cell phone to head to the dining room. He returns in a few minutes with Sarah's cardigan and wraps it around her. She thanks him as the three of them head up the stairs together, guided by the candles. As they open the door to the suite, ice cold air greets them.

"Make yourself at home, Beatrice, while we change into warmer clothes," she says. She and Fokke both head for their packs, putting on extra layers. Dressed in her warmest layers, she makes up the couch for Beatrice. As she tucks in the bedding that Fokke used last night, it dawns on her what her generosity combined with her "we're on our honeymoon" lie means: Fokke will be staying in her room tonight. The idea both intrigues and frightens her.

He works on the fire as she makes tea for the three of them. She and Beatrice chat on the couch, both wrapped in blankets.

"He really is a handsome lad, despite that nose of his," Beatrice whispers very loudly to Sarah. "And such a romantic proposal. Top of the rock of Gibraltar."

"Yes, it was." At least the embarrassment is warming her up. A strange coughing sound comes from Fokke's throat.

"How many children do you plan on having?" Beatrice asks in a polite tone.

"Oh. We're thinking five or six," Sarah says loudly. She is pleased by the corresponding coughing fit this elicits in Fokke. The fire finally catches and he comes closer, a mirthful look on his face.

"Since we're planning on so many children, we better—" Fokke cuts himself off mid-sentence as he sees Sarah's sweat pants. "Is that blood on your knee?"

She looks down toward her white sweats, seeing the red stain over her left knee. "I must have gotten cut from the broken window," she realizes.

"Okay. We've got to clean this up and see if there's any glass in there. Does it hurt?"

"No. I didn't even realize I got cut," she responds, looking downward.

"Can you take off those sweats and stockings? I've got a first-aid kit in my bag."

At the mere mention of Sarah's stockings, Beatrice clears her throat loudly.

"You two just head into the other room now," she orders.

"Well, if you need anything, just let us know," Sarah responds.

"Good night Beatrice," Fokke says politely as he takes Sarah's hand.

"Good night you too. I'm taking out my hearing aids now. You'll have to tap me on the shoulder if there's anything. *I can't hear a thing* without these," she emphasizes.

Chapter 19
Tar pit

"Five or six children?" Fokke says once he shuts the door. "Are you a sadist?"

"Thought you'd like that," she winks.

"And we got engaged on the Rock of Gibraltar? That is so cliché. I'm a travel writer for God's sake. I'd do you much better than that," he laughs.

"Okay, then. You try coming up with a spontaneous, romantic engagement story when confronted by a table of women wanting to hear all about how you proposed."

"Should have thought about that before you started spinning lies," Fokke laughs again.

Sarah is laughing as well, despite the tension filling her body. In the last forty-eight hours she has both dreamed and fantasized about Fokke. Fantasies are one thing. This situation is downright uncomfortable.

"Um. Fokke. I'm sorry about this whole mess I got us into," she says.

"You mean the whole newlywed, sappy romantic, honeymoon thing? And that queen-sized bed staring at us?" Fokke does his best to control the smirk on his face.

"Yeah. That," she replies, aware of a tightening sensation low in her belly.

"It's pretty awkward, but I'm more worried about your knee right now. You don't want slivers of glass working their way in any deeper. Now, can you get out of those sweats and stockings?"

She shrugs her shoulders, as if it is no big deal that she is about to partially disrobe before this man who will be sharing her bed this evening. She slips off her sweats, shivering in the ice cold room before slipping off her stockings. She pulls her sweatshirt down over her butt, and lifts up her knee, trying to examine it herself, but not only is there too little light, the angle is all wrong.

Fokke retrieves a small flashlight from his backpack. "Here. Let me take a look. Sit down on the bed Sarah. I've got to see what I'm doing." He takes tweezers, gauze and iodine out of his first-aid kit and kneels in front of her.

As Fokke moves closer, she is thinking more about how he is perfectly positioned to see her red lace underwear, than the potential slivers of glass in her knee.

His hand touches her thigh and she jumps involuntarily.

"Stay still please." He forces his eyes to focus on the tweezers, not on her firm legs, or the view he has of her sexy underwear. But as he sees a piece of glass sticking out of her skin, his thoughts are entirely focused on getting it out. He extracts the small sliver on the second try.

"Got it," he says.

"Thank you," she responds, looking at the top of his head beneath her.

"I think there's something in my right hand too," she admits, placing her hand in her lap within the beam of light. Fokke takes it in his, running his fingers over her palm. She shivers at his touch, as much from the cold as the strange pulse of energy his touch generates in her.

"Ouch! There."

He finds the tiny shard of glass and manages to get it out, then squeezes the wound until it bleeds. He hands her a cotton ball doused with antiseptic to dab at the blood as he begins to examine her other knee, rubbing his fingers over her smooth skin until she squirms.

"Where does it hurt?" he asks.

"Actually, it kind of tickles," she laughs. He looks up at her and the expression on his face is the same, brooding look he gave her earlier in the evening.

After more disinfectant and bandages, he stands again, looking down at her. "You're all set," he says, his voice hoarse.

"Thanks for that. Thanks for everything tonight," Sarah responds earnestly.

"You're welcome." Fokke's smile is tight, as if he is trying to suppress something. She has an idea what that might be as she turns away from him and slips off her clothing, and as quickly as possible, pulls on her pajamas before climbing under the covers.

Fokke changes into his long underwear and is standing before the bed.

"Mind if I get in? It's pretty damned cold out here."

"Of course. This bed is definitely big enough for the two of us."

Fokke crawls in next to her and they both lie beneath the cold covers, shivering.

"We can warm each other up by combining our body heat," she suggests.

"Good idea," he mumbles. *Terrible idea*, he thinks. Fokke wants to do more than warm her. He spoons her against him, wraps his left arm around her waist, feels the small of her back, her buttocks and the backs of her legs pressing against him. Damn she's cold. He rubs her arms, the side of her hip. He wants to kiss her so badly. He fights it for a good ten minutes, just focusing on getting warm. But as her body heat slowly begins to come in little waves against him, he can't take it anymore.

He turns his head ever so slightly and grazes his lips against her neck, causing her to tense. The sigh that escapes her lips encourages him to kiss his way up to her ear. She responds to his touch, turning toward him so she is on her back. He tilts her chin upward until her lips are against his and he probes gently with his tongue. As her body presses against him, her breathing becomes ragged, uneven. She gazes into his eyes, wanting, needing.

I could have this woman, he realizes. But she's not just any woman; not someone to bury his desires in for one evening. All that he knows about her floods his senses. Christ.

"What do you want, Sarah?" he asks, but doesn't give her a chance to answer as he bruises her mouth with a passionate kiss. She is falling into the kiss, her pulse rising, desire pooling within her.

"This. You kissing me," she whispers.

He pulls away from her and leans over toward the night stand, lighting the last candle and placing it next to the remains of the other. His features come into focus in the soft light of the flames, and she is amazed at what she sees in his eyes: desire, yes, but also kindness.

"Sarah. You are like a renaissance painting in the candlelight," he whispers in her ear. She is melting into his words, into his touch. The longer they kiss, the further she shifts beneath him until he is lying on top of her, his arms on either side of her face. She is pinned beneath him, his chest against hers. She can feel his heartbeat as she strokes his chest; can feel how thoroughly aroused he is; can imagine how good it would feel for him to shift himself inside of her.

As the thought plays through her mind, she is suddenly conscious of what this would mean; Fokke would be her entry into the post-Matthew world. Is this how she wants it to be? Fast and intense with a sexy stranger who will leave her tomorrow? Will she ever be with a man again after the Amsterdam appointment? Who will want her then? Is Fokke her only chance? Is it fair, knowing what she does about him, to even start anything?

"Fokke," she whispers into his kiss.

He pushes himself up on his elbows, looking down into her eyes. "Yeah?"

"I'm not sure if I can do this," she says haltingly.

"That's okay," Fokke replies. "You don't have to explain." Because he knows. She hasn't been with another man except for her jack-ass of an ex-husband for eleven years. Just this afternoon, when he came into the room to check his cell phone, he'd heard her in the shower laughing in a way that didn't sound natural. She's in a process. He can't screw around with her; that much he knows.

"I want this, Fokke. But I have no idea how to be with someone casually. A one-night stand, or two nights if this storm has its way." Her body is tingling, wound up in anticipation, but her mind is sending an entirely different set of signals.

"That makes sense. I'm not an affair type either. But my body is doing its best to convince me otherwise," he adds, fully aware of his erection pressing against her.

She takes in his rugged features in the candlelight: full forehead subtly creased with lines that suggest mischief, broad prizefighter's nose, untamed eyebrows above sensual eyes, stubble accentuating his square jaw. And those lips. She brings her lips to his for a moment and then pulls away.

"Have you ever had a one-night stand?" she asks.

"Yeah," he admits, "but not since my university days. Back then I would have tried to convince you to let me make love to you right now." His words fall over her like devil's candy. She squirms involuntarily, her lips full and lustful in the candlelight.

"And now?" she asks.

"And now?" he lowers his face to hers, kissing her slowly, tauntingly. "I have a feeling we'd be incredible together." Her breasts are pressed against his chest, her body formed to his. It would be so easy. His lips linger at her ear, breathing heat into her. But her words in that damned diary float up to him. He shifts his weight, looks at her more gingerly, as if she might break.

"But I know you're recently divorced, and the last thing I want to do is hurt you."

His words temporarily sober her. "You're right. The last thing I need is more pain, or to be dependent upon a man."

He rolls off of her, but pulls her into his arms. "You just want to depend on yourself from now on, is that it?" he asks, playing with one of her curls.

"Yeah. That's the plan," she replies, staring at him with a look that burns through him.

"No reaching out for that stick? Stuck in the Pleistocene tar pit, just like me?"

"I'm willing to reach out for support," she counters. "But just not to a man."

"Does that include pleasure?" he counters, a grin spreading across his face.

His eyes seem to be flickering in the candlelight, taunting her. And even though the luxurious weight of his body is no longer upon her, she sees the desire in his eyes, knows it matches her own.

"When I'm ready, I definitely want a man to bring me pleasure again." Her voice is thick, suggestive.

"When will you be ready?" he asks.

"Believe me. My body is ready right now," she stares at him. "But my heart. It's still on the mend. I don't need it broken any time soon."

These last words still his libido. "I can respect that," he says as he chastely kisses her forehead. "You deserve love."

As the words leave his lips, he knows in his core that he envies the man that will be in a position to give her what she needs.

"We both deserve love," she returns.

"True." He strokes a finger over her cheek. Her eyes are shining and bright. "This is one hell of a honeymoon: snowed in, lying in bed by candlelight with my beautiful, fictitious bride, both totally aroused and we can't even consummate the marriage."

"Life's tough," Sarah counters as she grins.

"Yeah. And I don't think this man is going to get much sleep tonight."

"Or this woman," she responds as she nestles into his arms. "But I'd love to spend some time right here."

"You got it," Fokke replies. They shift around, finding a comfortable position. She is surprisingly relaxed in his embrace, feels natural and safe there. She is tired; more so than she realized. Her eyelids grow heavy and she drifts off within a few minutes to the sound of Fokke's heartbeat. He, on the other hand, is far from sleep. He is concentrating on doing long-division in his head; thinking about the shade of blue he wants to paint his den wall; anything to keep his mind and body clear on what he can and cannot do with this amazing woman asleep in his arms.

Chapter 20
Kindling

It is late at night in central Kyrgyzstan and it's cold inside the yurt. He is dizzy from the altitude and aware of his aching muscles from the hike up Kyzart Pass. Fokke huddles by the ashes of a campfire still trying to feel its warmth, even though it has burned out long ago.

He is alone in the yurt, though it could easily sleep eight. He pokes at the ash and is startled as he unearths a small ember. Its deep red glow streaked with powdery gray ash promises heat if he will only feed it— provide it with the kindling it needs to grow. He discovers in his hand a few tiny, matchstick-sized shards of wood. He places them gently against the ember and blows. It takes a little effort, but they catch, causing bright, delicate flames to lick up the wood. He needs more kindling, he realizes, or he will never get the fire going. He looks around the darkened yurt and sees kindling stacked neatly in the corner, but his fingers are suddenly bound, and he cannot move forward. The cold is gnawing at him, but he feels warmth at his back and he presses into it.

Fokke comes out of his recurring dream to discover Sarah lying beside him wrapped up in the thick comforter. He is only partially covered, yet his back is warm where it is in contact with her. He is vaguely aware that the dream has shifted, but the details fade as he sees how Sarah's curls are a tangled mane of gold framing her face, her hands delicately tucked under her head. She is like an apparition from a dream—not some dream of perfection, but of a vision of a potential future life where he awakes to find his partner sleeping beside him, lost in her own dreams or dreamless sleep.

Despite the fact that she has stolen most of the covers and left him exposed to the chilly morning air, her exposed limbs are cold. He gets out of bed and searches through the dark wood armoire, discovering a woolen blanket they hadn't noticed last night. *This will warm you,* he thinks as he straightens the comforter and throws the second blanket over her.

Faint morning light enters the room as he pulls open the curtain and looks out the window. The snow continues to fall, piling up against the side of the building. They could be here a while, he realizes. He is cold and revels in the idea of crawling back under the covers and pressing against her. But first, he needs to address his full bladder. He opens the door to the living room and walks toward the bathroom.

"Shit!" he yells as he sees an apparition across the room, its silver streaks backlit by the firelight, its beady eyes four times the size of human eyes. "Ah. Sorry Beatrice," he calls. "I forgot you were here."

Soft laughter comes from behind him as he runs to the bathroom and quickly shuts the door. While he's in there, he brushes his teeth and decides to take a shower only to discover there's no hot water. He shaves instead. By the time he exits the bathroom wrapped in a robe over his long underwear, there is no sign of Beatrice. Sarah, on the other hand, is standing in the living room, blinking her eyes sleepily.

"What did you do to scare Beatrice away?" Sarah laughs as she yawns.

"You know I didn't do it on purpose," he muses, catching her smirk. He is happy to see no signs of discomfort on her face as she meets his gaze.

"I spoke with her briefly," Sarah says. "She said she was thankful for our hospitality, but that 'God wouldn't want her to stay with the newlyweds any longer, especially when we are trying to conceive our first of six children.' Those were her exact words."

As she shares Beatrice's comments, her smile doesn't quite reach her eyes.

"Well, that's too bad. Another casualty of your lies," he winks at her. "And she can make a good fire for an old Irish lady."

"Yes she can. And don't be a sexist pig, or you can sleep in the lobby with those university sisters," Sarah returns before ducking into the bathroom.

It's 7:48a.m. and the bedroom is freezing. Fokke pulls the comforters off the bed and makes up a nest in front of the fireplace just as Sarah re-enters the living room.

"Wow. What's this?"

"It's going to be another snow day," Fokke tells her as he crawls under the covers. "Come here. Get warm."

Sarah casts him a dubious glance, trying to fight the warmth spreading through her.

"You're just after my body heat," she says sternly. She's not fooling anyone, including herself as she keeps her distance.

"That's all I'm after," is his casual comeback. The light smile on his face is all it takes to break down her imaginary resistance and she finds herself walking toward him and slipping under the comforters.

He has made a sort of lounge chair with the cushions propped against the base of the sofa. They are reclining next to each other, the comforter pulled up to their chests.

As she settles in next to him, she is aware of their arms touching, the pressure of his legs against hers. And even though she shared her bed with him last night, fell asleep in his arms, this new round of contact next to the firelight feels like a further opening between them.

It suddenly hits her that she wants to share something with him; something both personal and daring. "Want to see a project I've been working on?" she asks.

"Sure," Fokke responds. She pulls away from him and heads into the icy cold bedroom to retrieve her iPad and headphones and runs back to the nest of blankets, curling up beside him.

"Okay. So. This is my alter ego you are about to see," she begins, taking a deep breath. She clicks on a folder called The Project. As it opens, Fokke notices that there are at least thirty videos in the folder.

She puts on her headphones and taps on one video, listening carefully before she pulls out the headphone jack so Fokke can hear. On the screen Sarah begins a monologue, her gaze confident in front of the camera. It is early morning, the light soft inside her hotel room, but she has her sunglasses on—those pink rhinestone ones that seem to have been a mismatch of her personality, and her hair is dark brown instead of blonde. Her words are eloquent, yet upbeat and playful. It is as if he is indeed watching a bigger-than-life version of Sarah; one that can certainly handle rhinestone sunglasses. She is sharing her impressions of La Sagrada Familia in Barcelona while tying in her personal thoughts, extolling her wisdom. It is Sarah the counselor, he imagines, but amped up on the intoxicating freedom that comes with solo travel. Her dialogue is creative yet genuine and she sparkles on film.

"You posing as a school counselor? Because based on this vlog, I'd say you're more like a talk show host—a mix of Dr. Phil and the Dog Whisperer."

"I'm definitely a school counselor. The sunglasses, wig and bright pink lipstick are my attempt at concealing my identity. I don't want this coming back to haunt me when I return to work, or when I try to find another job."

"I think you should call yourself the travel whisperer," Fokke smiles.

"Are you making fun of me?" She wrinkles her nose at him, arching her eyebrows.

"No. No. I'm giving you a compliment. You have a really unique angle, Sarah. You're discussing the place you're visiting, explaining its history, its charms, but also making it personal; what it conjures up in you, and in doing so, imparting wisdom. It's great. I like the candle lighting as well. It's something that thousands of tourists do every year, but you make it unique by turning it into a gift to others."

Fokke sees how his compliment works its way in: her shoulders relax, the corners of her mouth turn upward.

"Thank you. It seems to be helping me move forward," she explains.

"Can I see another one?" he asks.

By way of answer, she scrolls through the videos and selects one. As it loads, she gives a brief introduction.

"This is one of my favorites, but also one I'm still struggling with." She sits up straight as she taps on the video. She puts on her headphones, listening to the text and once again skips the introduction.

"Why don't you play it from the beginning?" he asks.

"Protecting my pseudonym," she answers just before she unplugs her headset and presses play.

" . . . live from Bern, Switzerland on my solo trip through Europe. There are many women who have traveled alone before, and it takes bravery, constant assessment and the ability to roll with the situation around you. It also takes trust—both in yourself and occasionally in others."

Fokke watches the screen, perplexed once again by this other version of Sarah. Three worlds are melding: the raw and vulnerable voice of Sarah's journal; the gently confident, self-composed woman who is sitting next to him, whom he has kissed, slept next to for an entire night and who has managed to get inside his head faster than any woman before, with no apparent agenda; and now Sarah on screen—a glossy, bolder version ready to take on the world, yet true to her own nature.

"Trust is one of the hardest things to do. Especially if you've been burned," dark-haired Sarah is saying. "Who hasn't been burned by love? Or rather, the failure of love? If you've been through a break up, you not only fall out of love with that other person, but you also break up with yourself—with that part of you that dared to believe this man or woman would love you forever."

The camera pans to a statue of two lovers above a dry fountain half-filled with leaves, discarded cigarette butts and random trash. Fokke listens to Sarah's wise words, her impression of this lover's kiss caught forever in bronze in a public square—how love isn't frozen in time, but in constant development. "If we try to capture it, still it, mold it, it flees from us." As the words sink in, he has the unreasonable feeling that Sarah has made this vlog just for him; laying a path for him to move forward, to step out of the "frozen moment" he is still holding onto, even though life has continued forward on its unpredictable path.

When the video stops, Fokke turns toward her, leaning in for a kiss. She does not rebuke him, but rather than the heated exchange they had last night—before they both forced themselves to stop—their kiss is chaste. He doesn't realize it, but he has closed his eyes. When he opens them again, he sees a confused expression on her face that is hard to read.

"What's going on in there?" he asks her, tapping his pointer finger gently on her forehead.

"I'm just thinking about how much I enjoy being with you," she acknowledges. "How I already feel like I understand you. How crazy that is, considering I've known you for about three seconds."

Fokke traces his fingers along her face, across her forehead, massaging at the worry lines he sees forming there.

"I feel the same way. Strange, isn't it?"

"Yeah," she responds. "But I'm ready for the next three seconds of getting to know you."

Chapter 21
Newlyweds

Hunger is the reason they finally leave the cocoon of blankets. They bundle up in layers and head downstairs to the lobby. Just like Sarah and Fokke, most people are wearing their winter coats as they wander around or sit at the tables. They discover that the window has been covered by plywood. Just as they are crossing the lobby, they hear an enthusiastic cry from the crew who has just managed to get the generators going. They welcome the news that the ghastly chill in the air will slowly be replaced by the warmth of radiator heating.

As they enter the restaurant, they see a few familiar faces including Espen. He is at a large table and invites them to join him. He introduces them as the newlyweds, which causes a round of congratulations from total strangers. Fokke's bemused smile and the color on Sarah's cheeks are incorrectly interpreted as that awkward mix of bewilderment and excitement of newlyweds, adjusting, for better or for worse, to the concept of forever.

People are talkative, seemingly in need of interaction, and they are pulled into conversation as they break bread with this group of familiar strangers. Sarah is enjoying a debate about the future of education in France with Celeste, an acquaintance of Fokke's from the chess tournament yesterday, and Uva, a German mother of three.

Espen proclaims this freak snow storm to be a side effect of global warming, which launches a passionate discussion around the table.

"The superpowers need to switch to renewable energies if we want to reduce global warming," a middle-aged man with a surprising amount of ear-hair states.

"They don't have the infrastructure in place, and by the time they do, it'll be too late," Uva responds.

"Actually, there's a much quicker way to address it," Sarah interjects. "Become vegan."

"Explain," Celeste responds, waving her fingers in a polite yet commanding manner.

"It's complicated. But like fifty-one percent of all greenhouse gas emissions come from the livestock industry—more emissions than from cars or from factories. It sounds crazy, but it's true, if you do the math."

"Fifty-one percent of greenhouse gases? Where did that statistic come from?" Espen asks inquisitively.

"World Watch," Sarah returns. "If we all stopped eating meat and dairy products, we could change the world."

"Good luck with that one. I think we'd rather go extinct than give up our meat products," ear-hair man comments.

"Go extinct as a species just to satisfy your taste buds?" Sarah counters. She launches into the logic behind the statistic as everyone listens on intently. She mentions Cowspiracy, the documentary where she first discovered this information and smiles hopefully as half the people take the time to write down the name.

"I've visited many cultures that thrive on a vegetarian diet," Fokke throws in.

"I'm vegetarian, and I live in France. If I can do it, anyone can," Celeste states evenly.

"Yes. But vegan is much more rigid. Could you give up your dairy products and eggs?" Espen asks. The reactions range from "that would be hard" to belligerent "no ways" and "not in this lifetime." The conversation shifts to cheeses from different regions of Europe, and the entire concept of veganism is quickly forgotten.

After lunch, Fokke challenges Celeste to a game of chess and Sarah decides to do a 2,500-piece jigsaw puzzle of an island paradise.

As she scatters the pieces on a large table, she is thankful for the simple distraction—anything to take her thoughts off of Fokke for a few moments. Because that is about all she has been doing in her spare time: thinking, wondering, imagining.

Considering their current snowed-in situation, the turquoise waters and the tropical light of the jigsaw puzzle seem to mock her. She forms the edge of the cerulean blue lagoon and imagines its wet warmth caressing her body. The lush vegetation and sturdy stalks growing along the edge of the lagoon penetrate her mind. Her fingers fumble with a piece of sky. As she finds its place, presses it into the skyscape she is now creating, she imagines the heat of that tropical sun warming her skin. A pulse of pleasure radiates through her body. She is slightly embarrassed, mildly amused that a simple jigsaw puzzle can set her off like this. But of course it has nothing to do with the puzzle and everything to do with him. Although she would lecture any woman who would dare to compare a man to the heat source of the entire solar system, she finds herself secretly likening Fokke's bright personality to that tropical sun. She has never met anyone like him and she wants to get to know him better; get close enough to get warm, a sunburn even. She already spent the entire morning in his company talking, laughing, and all she wants is more. As it finally dawns on her in what way she wants to get to know him better, she hears a beep coming from her phone.

"The internet connection is back!" Candy says, who is sitting in a chair nearby. Numerous people react to the news with relief, pulling their phones and tablets from their bags. Conversations are abandoned as faces turn toward their devices.

"Storm is letting up," someone reports. "We could be out of here by tomorrow."

Sarah should be happy with this news, but she feels what is akin to a twist in her gut as she realizes what this means—her time with Fokke is coming to an end, and more than anything, she wants his heat to melt away the storm brewing inside her. And if their connection last night was any indicator, he would melt her to the core.

She casts what is supposed to be a casual glance in Fokke's direction. Their eyes lock, and she feels the warmth radiating through her. She tenses her stomach muscles in response to the twisting sensation expanding in her belly and working its way south. His gaze is electrifying, penetrating. She brushes her hand self-consciously across the top reaches of her sweater just to make sure she isn't as naked as she feels. She doesn't realize she has been licking her lips until she slips the tip of her tongue back into her mouth where it belongs. *Oh-my-God*, she thinks as she turns away trying to get her bearings.

She takes a healthy chug of her chamomile tea, wishing it was something stronger. Candy and her travel partner are sharing tips on Venice with her when Fokke breaks into the conversation.

"Sorry to interrupt, but I need to get my bride back upstairs." His statement is met by laughter and coy looks.

"Maybe they need my help in the kitchen again for this evening's meal," she protests, not appreciating being read like a book.

"We've got that covered," Candy intones. "Go. Enjoy your honeymoon."

Fokke stretches out his hand and she slips hers into his.

"That was classy," she reprimands as they gain distance from the group. "You do realize they all think we're going back to our suite to have passionate sex?" She had gone for brazen humor, wanting to keep it light, but her words backfire on her as her pulse quickens, the sensation of his hand around hers sending a shock of electricity through her body.

"I just want some more time with you, before all this serendipity comes to an end."

His words are like oil on the hinges of her heart, which spring abruptly open just for him.

"I want that too," she responds, not daring to look into his eyes. They are out of sight of the group but their hands stay firmly clasped as they reach the suite.

It is pleasantly warm inside from the radiators along the walls that have been running since the heat went back on. They notice the rumpled pile of blankets in front of the fireplace at the same time. She turns to face him, her hand still in his. It is unclear who moves toward whom, but they are pulled into each other as if by magnetic force. Somewhere in the back of her mind, she still believes she can keep their connection light, flirtatious. But then Fokke places his large hands on either side of her face and kisses her so deeply that she is lost in want and need. He grazes her neck, bites her earlobe and she is on fire. The mewling sound that escapes her lips only encourages him further. His hands make their way from her face to her shoulders and slowly downward to the small of her back as they continue to kiss.

Their jackets have already found their way to the floor. Her sweater is being lifted over her head, half by her, half by him. He traces his fingers gently over her clavicles, as if fascinated by her bone structure. His mouth finds its way to the taut skin now visible where her shirt scoops around her neck. His teeth graze her, the prickle of his stubble taunting her, sending another shiver down her spine.

She is following him—or is he following her?—to the pile of blankets. He takes a moment to stir the fire and place a fresh log on top of the hot coals before joining her on the floor. She tugs at his sweater and he helps her slide it over his shoulders before she starts working on the buttons of his shirt with precision. She rubs her hands over the fine cotton of his undershirt; reaches beneath to explore the contours of his pectorals and his smooth stomach as he shivers in pleasure at her touch.

117

He pulls her shirt off, pausing to take in her form in her black bra before his mouth is on hers again, ravishing her. He expertly unclasps her bra and pushes it aside, exposing her full breasts. He flicks his tongue over her nipples and she arches in response. Her jeans are stripped off her, then her panties and she is completely naked. He drinks her in, his eyes roving from her face all the way to her toes before he reaches for the buttons of his jeans.

He nuzzles into her neck all over again, breathing into her ear gently before spreading his searing kisses slowly downward, skin on skin, heat building heat. Each press of his lips is like a healing balm, erasing every ounce of sadness she has stored in her body. He looks upward, checking in with her, reading her continued surrender and opening.

He explores her with his fingertips, his tongue, his lips until her entire body is thrumming with excitement. The weight of his body upon hers, the sensation of his manhood on the verge of entering her feels primal, right. He finally shifts into her and she gasps, overwhelmed by the sensations flooding her body and mind. He fills her perfectly. And as he builds a thrusting rhythm, she wraps her legs around him, securing him to her.

They are locked together, consummating the undeniable connection between them. Although they do not exchange words, their love making is far from silent. The pleasure escaping their lips, the way they look into each other's eyes communicates more than she would ever dare to say.

He brings her higher and higher until she is pulsing around him, her vision blurring as she lets out a scream of pleasure. His mouth ravages her neck as he continues to thrust, groaning as he finally releases into her.

It isn't until afterwards, as they lie panting beside each other, completely spent by their passionate lovemaking that the other part of her mind returns. Her critical mind, with its harsh list of judgments, biting at her euphoria.

This man will be gone tomorrow! You don't even know him. This is just for the time being. Your future is already set.

This must have been how Eve felt, she thinks. Something as beautiful as being naked and intimate together in the garden is suddenly seen as shameful. Sarah doesn't want this snake in her head. It is trespassing.

He traces a finger over her forehead, rubbing at the creases on her brow. He grazes his fingers along her cheek until she looks into his eyes. As they make eye contact, the trespasser is evicted and she is back in the moment, feeling blissful, ignorant, ready to believe in the power of now; Eve before the fall.

"You okay?" he asks, concern in his hooded eyes.

"Yes," she sighs. "That was incredible," she strokes her hand across his cheek, holding nothing back. "You just undid me, threw me off a cliff of pleasure. I haven't experienced that kind of pleasure . . ." Has she ever been loved like this? "for a very long time," she says instead.

He kisses her forehead gently, a blend of lust and pride in his eyes.

"Glad to be of service. But I'm not finished with you yet."

Chapter 22
Camera

Fokke awakes to the sensation of someone touching his chest. He opens his eyes and sees Sarah cuddled up beside him, her hair bathed in a stream of sunlight coming through the window; her dark blue eyes speckled with a flinty green he hadn't noticed before.

"I had the most interesting dream," she says.

"Tell me about it." Fokke reaches lazily toward her, pushing her hair away from her eyes.

"You and I owned a restaurant along a canal in Amsterdam. I was this amazing Italian cook, and people came from miles away just for my homemade cornettis."

"Three nights in the same hotel room and we're already in business together?" Fokke traces his finger across her cheek to her lips. "What color were the chairs?" he asks as his hands begin to move lazily over her body.

"I don't remember the chairs. Why?" She doesn't stop his hand from wandering to her butt, which he massages gently.

"I collect chairs. I have a warehouse full of them."

"A warehouse full of chairs?" She's trying to stay calm as he traces a circle on her stomach.

"Yes. From all over the world," he admits. He doesn't tell people about his chairs. She is so firm, so responsive to his touch. He climbs on top of her, pulling the covers over their heads, and starts kissing her belly. She squirms beneath him, but he suddenly stops.

"Be right back," he announces, pulling himself off of her. She watches him walk to the bathroom, stark naked. She takes in his strong legs, his firm butt.

He's back by her side within minutes with minty breath. He pulls the curtains further open, letting in beams of sunshine.

"I've been looking forward to making love to you in the sunlight," he whispers into her ear. Fokke doesn't want to think what the sunshine and the constant sounds of dripping outside mean, but it presses on his mind. He could use a week of being snowed in with this woman, just getting to know the richness of her body. And another week to talk with her, learn her quirks and kindnesses. And then another to travel with her, show her some of his favorite spots in Southern Europe. But he's got a few hours if he's lucky. He unrolls the condom, slides it on. She's watching him the whole time, her eyes big and full of longing.

"You're beautiful, Fokke," she whispers, her eyes locked on his as he enters her.

"If you say so," he smiles wickedly as he lowers himself onto her, moving in rhythm. She doesn't want this to be the last time. He is certain that is what she's thinking. He doesn't want that either. Something from her diary comes to him, causing him to slow his pace.

"Please Fokke, don't stop," she pleads.

"Any chance The Netherlands is on your itinerary?" he asks, looking down into her eyes.

She startles.

"Your grandma and all?" he adds.

"Oh. Yeah," she replies, relaxing again, though not completely. He feels a shift, her carefree openness closing off.

121

"Maybe I could do this to you on my homeland soil," he says as he increases his pace, working her into a frenzy.

"Oh my God," she cries. She arches up to him, pulls on his hips, guides him. He's about to release in her but he wills himself to hold off.

"I want you on top of me," he commands. They manage to roll over and he watches her as she takes control, intoxicatingly aware of the pleasure this angle brings her. He catches her left breast in his mouth, suckling until she is gasping in pleasure, then switches to her right breast.

"I love . . . being with you," she whispers as a shudder pulses through her. She collapses on top of him. He cherishes the weight of her, the warmth of her skin. He wants to shower with her; to make love by the fire again; cook her dinner and chat for hours; be in comfortable silence with her; know her in a way that only time can offer. Christ, is he just torturing himself?

"The snow is melting," he observes.

"Yeah," she sighs. "The snow plows have been at it all morning."

"Guess we're free to go."

"Most likely," she responds.

"Shall we just get it over with and get married for real?" Fokke asks.

"Might as well. Oh, except that I don't believe in marriage anymore," her eyes are soft yet vulnerable behind her smile.

"Okay. Good point. Marriage is kind of a big step, often filled with disillusionment. How about we start with breakfast and exchanging emails?"

"Now there's a commitment I can keep," she smiles at him sadly. This is going to be hard, Fokke realizes. A lot harder than he ever imagined.

"And if I'm pregnant?" she asks, before she thinks how sensitive this topic might be. He's apologized more than once for their reckless second round last night.

"You know what I'll do if you're pregnant," Fokke replies, all seriousness. Sarah's heart swells as she nods.

"But if you wanted me to get you pregnant, we should have kept him unsheathed the whole time," he smiles wickedly.

She is staring at him in disbelief, her eyes moist. *That's right*, he remembers; *this woman wants a baby. God, if the stars were only aligned differently.* He suddenly licks her cheek.

"What are you doing?" she asks, swatting at him.

"Licking your cheekbone. It will bring me luck and change your mood instantly."

He's right. She's laughing, smiling, despite the sadness screaming at her: *Hang onto this man; find a way to extend this moment.*

***

They shower together in subdued silence, gently washing each other's bodies as if trying to memorize the forms and contours. They dry each other off in what could easily be a tribal matrimonial ritual—slowly, soundlessly, laced with reverence.

She changes into her travel clothes and comfortable walking shoes—her uniform that represents adventure and freedom. But it doesn't match her mood. They pack their bags with some difficulty, considering how many times they stop to kiss. Finally, they are at the door, double checking the room for any missed items. They head downstairs to discover the café is closed due to repairs underway on the shattered window.

They turn in their room key and Fokke pulls out his card to settle the account.

"Signore en Signora van der Veld. We hope you had a pleasant stay, considering all the problems," the female receptionist says.

"We did," Fokke responds, squeezing Sarah's hand.

"The next shuttle to town is due in twenty minutes. I'm afraid the restaurant is closed, but we have pastries and coffee in the lounge."

Fokke holds her hand as they walk toward the lounge. Other guests gaze at them longingly, as if they are love incarnate.

"Good morning Fokke, Sarah," Celeste greets them. She is dressed in elegant wool slacks and a tailored wool coat, the subtle earth tones set a backdrop for her rich blue scarf.

"Hello Celeste. You must be glad the snow storm is over so you can get back to your bookstore," Sarah comments.

"Yes. I have an author signing two days from now and I'll be quite lucky to pull it off at this rate. If you two are ever in Paris, for your anniversary or otherwise, please do look me up," Celeste says, placing her business card in Sarah's hand and then one in Fokke's. "I'd love for you to do a book signing, Fokke," she adds, but continues on before Fokke can respond. "I wish you a long and happy marriage."

"Thank you," Fokke replies cordially, but his eyes give Celeste a warning look that Sarah doesn't quite understand.

"Book signing?" Sarah asks as Celeste moves away.

"The travel writing. I've been published a number of times," he responds casually, waving his hand in dismissal.

"Oh? That's great," she smiles.

After coffee and pastry, they head outside to meet the shuttle that will take her to town. He will be catching a later shuttle, heading East.

"I guess this is it," she says, burying her head in his chest. "I don't want to say goodbye to you." Despite weeks of willing the tears to come, she is now doing everything she can to keep them back.

"I don't either. How long will you be in Europe?" he asks, wrapping his arms around her.

"That depends," she answers cryptically. Fokke turns her head upward, removes her dark gray "Sarah" sunglasses so he can see her eyes.

"Depends on what?"

"On some business I have in Amsterdam," she answers vaguely. Sarah doesn't want to tell him what she has signed up for with the PNC Institute; not after what she has learned about him; and especially not after how intimate they have been.

"I live in The Hague. That's a 50-minute train ride from Amsterdam."

"Maybe I can visit you there," Sarah suggests, aware of the immediate tingling sensation in her stomach.

"That would be great, if the timing works. I have that assignment in Argentina in a few weeks. But before or after that . . ."

The bus arrives, and Fokke is pulling at his hair.

"Can I call you?" he asks, after he kisses her again.

"In America?"

"Well, eventually, if, well. I mean during the rest of your vacation."

"That would be nice. I'd like that." *Very very much* she thinks.

He loads her backpack under the bus and takes out his camera. Sarah is getting out her voucher ticket, talking to the driver when she hears a clicking sound. She spins around to see Fokke taking pictures of her, one after another. She stares at him, thinking about his touch, his kindnesses as he clicks away.

"Stop that," she says. Other passengers are getting on board and she steps aside.

"No. You belong among all the other photos of natural wonders; all the beauty I've seen on this trip."

She rolls her eyes. "You're a romantic Fokke. The Dolomites will look relatively the same in a hundred years, but I'll be dead and gone long before then." She doesn't know why she's doing it; maybe to create some space. She can't take the kindness, the positivity for a moment longer, or she'll break like that window the night before last, shatter in a thousand pieces and let all the bitter cold seep in.

125

"I'll be dead in less than that, too" he returns. "Doesn't mean I can't enjoy the essence of life when presented to me."

These are the words that stay with her after she kissed and hugged Fokke one last time and waved to him from the window until she couldn't see him anymore. Is she now in the category of essence of life to Fokke? If that were the case, she would be a thing to keep, to cherish. Not to be loved and thrown away. He's leaving her too.

She knows it's not fair; that she's mixing up her pain from the affair and the divorce; the death of her mother and the hopelessness she feels. These things have nothing to do with Fokke. He is more like a bright flame of goodness, of love. This last admission unsettles her.

She leans against the window and closes her eyes; replaying memories of her time with Fokke van der Veld, wondering if she will ever have the pleasure of seeing him again.

Chapter 23
Definitions

The cabin is warm from the blazing fire that Peter has kept going. They are passing around a bottle of Speyside single malt Scotch and talking soccer, despite the lack of a television or any other modern technology. Fokke is half listening, half somewhere else when Barometer's voice breaks into his thoughts.

"Something happened with backpack woman, because we've lost you, man," Barometer intones, kicking the sole of Fokke's left hiking boot.

"Nothing happened besides that freak snow storm," Fokke lies. "Just didn't get a lot of sleep." At least that part is true.

"So if nothing happened, why do you have a picture of her on your cell phone in her pink silk pajamas?" Jan asks.

Fokke sits up straight, suddenly aware that he has left his cell phone on the counter. He never took a picture of Sarah in her pajamas. But how could Jan know the color of those delicate silks Fokke stripped off of her on more than one occasion? Did Sarah take a selfie on his phone? A surprise for him?

"What the hell were you doing looking at my phone?" he returns.

The smile on Jan's face is growing as Fokke sets down his whiskey on the oak coffee table, stands and walks to the counter to retrieve his phone. He swipes it open and taps on the photos, discovering zero pictures of Sarah in her pajamas.

"Asshole," Fokke grumbles.

"Liar," Jan launches back.

"I concur on the liar status," Barometer laughs. "You definitely got intimate with backpack woman."

"Her name is Sarah Beth Turner. And all right. Guilty as charged. But how did you know about the pink silk pajamas?" Fokke asks Jan as he heads back toward the leather chair.

"We looked in her backpack, remember? On the trail?" Peter adds, a friendly smile on his face.

"Shit. That's right. I forgot about that," Fokke grazes his hand over his hair, a grin on his face.

"Yeah. If you're going to straight-out lie to your buddies, at least be strategic about it," Jan suggests.

"There's a difference between lying and protecting a woman's dignity." Fokke is still holding his cell phone, glancing at the screen as if willing a photo of her to appear.

"I think you've fallen for this little sex kitten," Barometer chides.

Fokke is on the verge of lying again, but he can't muster a clear answer. Instead, he retrieves his scotch and takes another sip.

"Your silence is full admission!" Jan persists. "You've fallen hard for Sarah Beth in the course of, what? Three days?"

Fokke shakes his head in consternation. He could desperately use someone else's perspective on this one, but he is not having this conversation as a foursome, and not with this crew; that's for damned sure.

"You're on kitchen duty, Fok," Peter interjects. "We've been without your cooking for long enough."

Fokke gives him a warm smile of thanks. "Sorry guys. I guess I get a pass on the inquisition. Have to show you lousy cooks what a real meal tastes like."

"Consider it a moment of reprieve," Barry replies just before Fokke leaves the room.

Cooking is one of Fokke's favorite pastimes and he's the one who usually cooks when the four of them get together. He's happy to see the fridge stocked with fresh fruits, vegetables, ground beef and steak, just as he ordered from the luxury vacation rental company. Onions, shallots, peppers and garlic fill a wooden box on the counter top. Hell; there's even ripe avocados, roma tomatoes and lemons. Where do you get avocados this time of year? Among all the beer filling the middle shelf are two cartons of eggs, milk, butter and cheese. He checks the cupboards to find a proper herb and spice collection in a sealed plastic box, as well as a large tin can of Italian olive oil. Glass jars with suction-seal lids line the top shelf, each labeled with standard baking fare: flour, sugar, salt, baking powder, bread crumbs.

He can definitely work with this. He pictures the meal he wants to make and starts gathering ingredients. Before he starts, he checks his phone again out of default. Not a single bar of reception. It cut out halfway up the mountain pass, just as he was trying to send her a text message with two concise sentences: *Already miss you. Can I meet you in a few days?*

He's used to being cut off from technology in the far reaches of the earth. And although it's inconvenient at times, he usually takes it in stride. But right now he wishes there was a cell phone tower poking its ugly head through the pristine tree line, connecting him to the world; to Sarah.

It takes Peter ten minutes to amble into the kitchen. Fokke is expecting him.

"Need some help in here?" Peter asks.

"Sure, you can give me counsel," Fokke replies as he finishes off a red sauce and places it on the stove to simmer. He deftly cubes vegetables, then heats oil in a larger pan before throwing in first the onions, then carrots, and eventually the zucchini. While the vegetables are sautéing, he adds spices and breadcrumbs to the meat.

"You really like this woman," Peter states, rather than asks.

"More than I care to admit," Fokke replies as he stirs the vegetables.

"And what does that mean to you? You want to start a relationship with her?" Peter asks.

"Well, hell. I don't know. It's complicated, seeing as she's here temporarily and lives on another continent," Fokke admits. "But if there was a way . . ." he trails off.

"You would go for it," Peter suggests.

"Yeah," Fokke responds. "I think I would."

"What if this was just a fling? I mean, last time we talked about the subject of women—a mere four days ago—you weren't even over Jackie," he probes. Fokke points to the vegetables and hands him a wooden spoon.

"I'm over Jackie. I'm just not over the betrayal. This woman. Sarah. She's so different from Jackie. She's honest; almost naively so. Yet wise at the same time. She's a communicator; no head games, you know? And she knows what she wants."

Fokke turns off the fire and folds the vegetables into the meat and breadcrumbs and kneads it into a loaf. As he ladles the red garlic tomato sauce over the top, he wonders what Sarah is doing at this very moment.

"She wants to see you again?"

"It sure seemed like it," Fokke says. "Though she was cautious."

He makes a kick-ass meatloaf. But this is one of many dishes he could never cook for vegan-minded Sarah. He covers it with foil and pops it in the pre-heated oven.

"So how did you leave it?" Peter continues, his easy-going nature loosening Fokke's tongue.

"I told her I wanted to be with her again."

"And what did she say?" Peter encourages.

"She said that would be nice."

"Nice?"

"Hell. You haven't heard Sarah Beth Turner say the word nice. That four-letter word is transformed into poetry when it passes over her lips."

"You've got it bad," Peter chuckles.

"Yeah. I do. Here," Fokke tosses the avocados toward him. "Help me make some guacamole."

***

They enter the living room to find Jan and Barometer playing cards. As Fokke sets the chips and guacamole on the table, they stop their game and dig in. Peter grabs the bottle opener and pries the caps off the beers, passing them around.

"So you're in love," Barometer states.

Fokke glares at him.

"Walls are paper thin," he explains.

"I didn't say anything about love," Fokke counters, acutely aware of the fear this four-letter word invokes in him.

"Maybe not, but you're on your way," Barometer explains. "You want this woman in your life."

"Lust? Yes. Passion? Yes. But no. He can't fall in love that quickly," Jan states matter-of-factly as he plows a tortilla chip through the guacamole.

Peter shakes his head in disagreement. "I think it's possible. I mean, love at first sight. We've read about it in literature. Remember that poem by Jan Willem Berg? 'In één avond heeft zij mijn hart veroverd. Zij heeft mijn ziel omgetoverd. Zij heeft betekenis aan mijn leven gegeven. Ik ben benieuwd wat de dag na morgen zal brengen.'"

"Translation please," Barometer demands.

"She conquered my heart in just one evening," Fokke begins. "She has transformed my soul with her magic. She has given meaning to my life. I am curious what the day after tomorrow shall bring." Fokke says the words with a sorrow that takes all teasing off the table. The four friends sit in silence, each man lost in his own web of thought.

Jan finally breaks the silence. "You are so fucked."

Laughter, including Fokke's own, fills the room. The fire pops loudly as it melts a mound of sap on the aged pine logs, and the earthy scent filters into their senses.

"What are you going to do?" Peter questions.

"I suppose I could go after her," Fokke answers. "See if she feels the same way I do."

Peter observes him closely, as does Jan.

"You do mean after we finish our vacation, don't you? And after the reunion in Amsterdam?" Jan asks accusingly. "You *are* giving the keynote speech, and plugging your charity," he adds.

"Yeah. Of course. I—" Fokke starts.

"You'll be useless to us in this state," Barry cuts him off, shaking his head in disagreement. "Except as ridicule material. And although that's very tempting, I agree; I think you should go after this Sarah Beth Turner and meet back up with us at the reunion," Barometer concludes. "But if it backfires, you need to go to a shrink so you're not scarred for life." He's got his steely blue eyes fixed on Fokke.

"I think you should go into therapy regardless of what happens, but, no. I don't encourage this. We need to keep you here for at least forty-eight hours," Peter counters. "Make sure this isn't some sort of temporary infatuation. That, and we need your cooking skills."

How the hell did my personal life become a group discussion yet again? Fokke wonders. "Infatuation, huh?" he rubs his hands together, looking at his friends. "I don't think so." It feels a bit like infatuation, seeing as he can't get Sarah out of his mind. But he doesn't want to either. Certainly, each and every one of them has experienced this.

"Tell me about the first time you met Hilde," he says to Peter, aiming his beer bottle in his direction. Barometer and Jan regard Peter with bemused interest. They all know he met his wife Hilde at the architecture firm where he worked right after finishing university, but they don't know how it all began.

"Ah. You sure you want to get me started talking about Hilde?" he chides. Peter's not exactly succinct when it comes to storytelling, but they're not exactly in a hurry. They shift in their seats to get comfortable as he recalls the first day he met his wife.

"She was at a project site in Dubai my first week at the firm. I'd met everyone else, but noticed the empty chair to my left. When I asked about it, my colleagues had said, 'Oh, that's Hilde's desk. The smartest designer in the firm.'" He lights up when he talks about her. Fokke has always admired this about him; especially seeing as they've been married for 16 years.

"So I was picturing this gaunt, nose-to-the-grindstone woman. You know, the defensive type that's had to deal with all the hierarchical, sexist bullshit and fight her way upward in a male-dominated industry," Peter is explaining.

"And then you saw Hilde walk into the room," Barometer interjects.

"Yeah, and she took my breath away," Peter says with reverence. "She was so hot."

"She's still hot," Barometer acknowledges. "Even after four kids."

"Watch it," Peter arches an eyebrow at him.

"And funny as hell. Not a reserved bone in her body," Fokke adds.

"It took me weeks to get the nerve up to ask her out and then one Friday evening as I'm shutting down the computer, she asked me out."

"So was it love at first sight?" Jan questions dubiously.

"Lust, love, awe, mixed with a sense that this could be the woman I would want to bear my children, spend the rest of my life with."

All four of the men are nodding now, Barry and Peter thinking of their wives, Fokke of Sarah Beth Turner, and Jan of a woman named Piper who works at the herring stand close to his work.

"We're just a bunch of pussy-whipped bastards," Barometer says.

"Speak for yourself," Jan returns; but Fokke and Peter are slower on the uptake.

Although they will still tease each other mercilessly, they have crossed a new bridge and are now standing on the other side—an unfamiliar place where men can talk about their feelings for their children and wives, their hopes and dreams of true love. And Fokke feels like a fish out of water.

"Can we get off this whole topic and get back to our regular routine of poker, beer and general rudeness?" Fokke suggests. Everyone is game. Barry deals out the cards.

When the timer for the meatloaf finally goes off, Fokke is down fifty euros. Barry gets up with him and retrieves plates and cutlery while Fokke takes the meatloaf out of the oven. The four friends settle into the high-backed chairs surrounding the dining table and dig in. As his old university buddies taste the meatloaf, they nod appreciatively in Fokke's direction. Before the meal is over, Jan is talking about a woman named Piper; how he can't get her out of his mind.

"She might be my Sarah Beth Turner," he confides.

Chapter 24
Gondola

Venice, the City of Love, her guidebook says. Everywhere she looks, she sees it: couples walking down the streets, holding hands in the café; in the two Italian teenagers leaning into each other, kissing at the edge of an elegant sea-nymph fountain the entire time it takes her to eat her gnocchi, drink a glass of wine and read an entire chapter of her guidebook. *Their lips must be getting chapped*, she thinks irritably.

Even the architecture of the city oozes romance. She gazes upward, taking in the geometric patterns of arches over windows and doorways, the stone balconies worn smooth over the centuries by the elements and by hands caressing the ledges to gaze upon the age-old square.

She thinks of the layers upon layers of cultures that have formed this city: The Moors of North Africa, the Greek Byzantines; ancient Roman, Christian and Islamic design styles intermingling over the centuries to become the Venetian architecture that makes this city so romantic and mysterious.

And then there are the waterways that run through Venice. The Grand Canal carves an S shape through the whole city, defining the mariner lifestyle. Whereas the Grand Canal is a heady display of Palaces and villas such as Ca' Foscari and Ca' Rezzonico along the water, the side canals branch out like liquid roots, winding their way through the neighborhoods.

She is certain that the stone footbridges crossing these smaller waterways have been witness to many an intimate exchange between lovers: lips on lips, whispered passions, planned and spontaneous proposals. She knows she's in trouble when she sees erotic shapes in the paintings of Vasily Kandinsky and Paul Klee in the Peggy Guggenheim museum—paintings she would usually not describe as even remotely erotic.

Her Grand European Tour up until this point has been about self-discovery; expanding her boundaries, rediscovering her passions. Now it's all about a tall Dutch man who hasn't even bothered to call or send a text or email in two days.

She is tired of thinking of Fokke's crooked smile, his humor, his intelligent way of describing things, his kiss. Has she ever been kissed so thoroughly? Loved so thoroughly?

Stop stop stop! she tells her mind. But it doesn't listen today, and didn't listen yesterday either. She blames the City of Love for the state of her heart, but she is quite worried that when she moves on to another city less steeped in romance, that her thoughts will be the same.

She is contemplating a gondola ride on the canal even though the air is chilly, the sun low in the sky. She wants to see the city from this perspective in a smaller vessel; has wanted to ride in a gondola her entire life. But she hesitates. Isn't that about the most romantic thing a person can do? Won't this just create further torment? She presses forward, completely aghast with herself. *This is not about him! This is about me!*

The gondolas were full most of the day, but the crowds are thinning and she is able to catch the eye of a gondolier who smiles at her as he guides the sleek black boat in her direction. She is not the only one interested in the gondola. A striking dark-haired Italian in a meticulous pin-striped suit is also approaching.

"Hello beautiful lady! You going for a ride?" he asks as he reaches the water's edge. His smile is friendly and inviting.

"Um, yes," she responds. He is drop-dead gorgeous and his attention flusters her.

"Let me treat you to a gondola ride. I get the company of a beautiful woman with golden curls, and I show you my beautiful Venezia!" he proclaims, sweeping his arm toward the canal.

"Very kind, but no thank you, sir," she states. "I'm meeting my boyfriend shortly."

"Ah. Of course," he teases. "But perhaps you need a second boyfriend?"

"No, no." Sarah waves him away as she steps into the gondola and sits on the plush, but well-worn leather seat before wrapping the provided blanket around her.

"With such beauty, you cannot fault me for trying. A fine journey to you signorina." He raises his eyebrows and sends an imaginary kiss in her direction. She feels the flush on her cheeks, as if this handsome Italian man has actually kissed her. His grin is slightly devilish, pleased with himself for affecting her.

She waves awkwardly as he continues to watch her, wishing the gondola would start moving. Finally, the gondolier pushes off from the shore.

"I show you my city without hassling you signorina," the gondolier says. She nods in appreciation, though she does not miss the way his dark chocolate eyes brush over her.

Venice was stunning from the edge of the canal, but now it takes on a new life from the water. Within a few minutes, they are before a stretch of buildings she read about at home, back when a trip to Venice was just a fanciful dream. She knows from her guidebook that the ocher-hued grand building to her right is the Palazzo da Mosto, a beloved Palazzo dating back to the 13th century. Ancient Romanesque-Byzantine arches cap the ground floor entries. Its surface is weathered to a state beyond a pleasant patina. Cracks break through the stucco, exposing sections of ancient brick and mortar. Watermarks are clearly visible along bases of the pillars, demonstrating that the water has crossed the threshold on numerous occasions throughout the centuries. Cross-hatched bars block the entry, giving it an abandoned look. Yet the building still exudes a form of beauty she has not experienced in America. She eyes the series of eight windows on the first floor loggia, delicately capped by arches and she tries to imagine what this building was like in its heyday. Friezes and coats of arms are carved into the stone above the delicate arches, but their meaning is lost on her.

As the Italian man in the striped shirt guides the gondola down the canal with an oar—also known as a "remo" she has learned in her guidebook—her thoughts are back to Fokke. What she would give to have his arms wrapped around her, to be able to lean into his chest as she takes in Venice from the water.

She flips open her phone and powers it on. One new message. She hugs the phone to her chest, saying a silent prayer it's from him. The gondolier is talking loudly in Italian and Sarah glances up to see another boat slipping closely by on her left. She holds the phone out in her hand, glancing at the screen when she is suddenly jostled, the other gondola bumping into theirs. She startles, her hands pulling back and the phone slips from her grasp. She watches in horror as her cell phone hits the edge of the gondola before plunging into the water. She springs up from her seat and reaches after the phone, causing the gondola to tilt to the left. Rapid Italian assaults her ears as the gondolier motions wildly at her, which she correctly interprets as sit down immediately.

"My cell phone!" she cries. "That could have been Fokke that texted."

Mom looks younger this time, how Sarah remembers her from childhood.

Is that your first thought, you love-sick woman? How about the telephone number for your grandma? Your ability to call home? The hotels on your future itinerary who have this number? And all you think about is your Dutch lover. Must run in the family.

Sarah closes her eyes, frustration building. *I'm not in love*, she responds firmly. *I'm in passionate like*. Her mom wiggles her eyebrows, begging to differ.

Sarah's international, pre-paid phone was more than those numbers. It was her safety net; her connection to home and the only place she stored Fokke's number. She is about to really lose it when a beautiful, operatic voice fills the air.

She opens her eyes to see the gondolier, his hand outstretched, singing. She forgets everything else as she listens to the melody, to the Italian language, watching his movements. She wraps the blanket tighter around her as they pass under an arched stone bridge and head down a smaller canal. Grand palazzos give way to more modest palazzos turned into living quarters. Her gaze drifts upward as if following the notes into the deep cobalt sky.

She sees lights on in the ancient upper floor apartments; catches glimpses into peoples' lives: families preparing for dinner; a man polishing his shoes on a balcony; a plump woman wrapped in an orange and green shawl leaning out the window, staring skyward.

She smells onions sautéing in butter; oregano-heavy sauces, cigar smoke. There are tourists still wandering along the canals, but also locals returning from work or shopping. An Italian pop song drifts from an apartment, its heavy beat sparring with the operatic voice of the gondolier before it fades into the distance as they glide forward. She returns her attention to the gondolier and listens raptly. He is no longer looking at her, but at his beloved city as sunset approaches. It is clear he is just as enamored with Venice as she is. His voice is in a full vibrato as he sustains the last note of his song and bows in her direction.

"Grazie Signore," she says, fervently clapping her hands together.

"You're welcome, lady," he winks back at her.

Long after the gondola ride is over, she is still in a heightened state of awareness, completely enthralled with the city and happy to be on her own. She wanders along the sidewalks edging the canals with new eyes, taking in the surroundings with all of her senses.

The peeling paint of an old wooden shutter looks like shavings of jewels in the golden rays of sunset. She has seen so many beautiful marble statues since she's been in Italy that they seem almost common place. But as she comes upon a small statue of a winged lion in a nook of a crumbling wall, red candles at its feet, she stops and stares. She is taken by the intricacy of the carving; the way the fur looks like it could almost be soft to the touch, the marble tail so life like, it is on the verge of twitching. She knows the lion represents Saint Mark, the Patron Saint of Venice. She closes her eyes and whispers a silent prayer to the saint, to God, thanking them for giving her this journey, this new beginning.

She arrives at her hotel well after dark, immensely proud of herself for walking without fear, for finding it again. She got lost yesterday, but today she has been using the compass Fokke gave her along with her map.

It isn't until now that she thinks of her phone problem. But then again, there's always the internet. The hotel has Wi-Fi; she has an iPad. She can look up all of the hotels she has booked through the email confirmations, can use her iPad as a phone if need be. Even her grandma's telephone number is in an email.

She unloads the shopping bag with dried nuts, fresh bread, basil, herbed olives and roma tomatoes she purchased at a small deli and opens a bottle of sparkling water. She sets up her makeshift dinner on the small table in the hotel room and flips on the radio. She recognizes the Italian pop song on the radio as the same tune that drifted down to her while she was in the gondola.

She recognizes something else as well; the now familiar sensation of being happy in her own company. After she finishes dinner, she showers and changes into her freshly laundered pink silk pajamas and settles into the single bed to read.

Being under the crisp white sheets with a comforter over her reminds her of someone. She lets the memories of Fokke embrace her anew, and this time, instead of the longing and the familiar pain in her chest, she is awash with happiness of having known him.

But it doesn't hold. Longing nudges its way back in, nagging, demanding action.

She has to forget him. If she holds onto him, she might undermine the progress she is making on her own. And with that, she opens her book on Andrea Palladio. But before she can finish even one chapter, her mind is dwelling on another topic of interest. She huffs out loud and tries to convince herself that this 16th century architect, described as the most influential person in the history of architecture, warrants her attention far more than a modern day Dutch travel writer with a banged up nose. But who is she trying to fool?

Chapter 25
Fokke

He's had that damned yurt dream again. The ember was there in the ashes, and he fed it kindling one fragile stick at a time until he was out of kindling and the sudden heat was just as quickly fading.

As usual he is the first awake. He climbs down from the top bunk, his weight creaking with each step on the small ladder. He heads into the kitchen and does his morning stretches, push-ups and sit-ups before downing a large glass of water.

He has made a decision. He has to wait. He can't just drop his trip with his buddies and follow after this woman—no matter how he feels about her. To do so would compromise his own integrity. *Fokke van der Veld doesn't chase after women.*

He turns on the espresso machine, waiting for it to warm up as he contemplates what he can prep for this evening. He settles on a lemon basil chicken dish he can marinade and place in the refrigerator, a green salad and roasted potatoes with garlic.

He notices a piece of paper sticking out from underneath the basket of fruit and pulls it out. Instructions for the rental. He is about to set it down when his eyes land on a few key words: *For internet reception, turn on the modem and router in the hall cupboard in the loft.*

He climbs the stairs quickly and it takes him only moments to locate the cupboard and turn on the electronics. Within minutes he hears the familiar pinging sound of his cell phone coming from the living room and quickly runs down the stairs. Fokke watches, trance-like, as his fingers take on a life of their own, ticking away a 200-character message to Sarah and pressing the send button before he can even think. *That was pre-coffee auto pilot*, he reasons. *I can't be responsible for anything that happens pre-coffee.*

He takes the time to clean out the ashes and build a new fire in the fireplace. He has no lack of kindling and he goes a bit overboard building a fire he just can't seem to finish in his subconscious. The cabin is piping hot by the time the others have rolled out of bed.

After a hearty breakfast, he and his buddies head out on snow shoes, exploring the pristine blanket of white. Besides sighting a pair of sparrow hawks, they seem to be alone in the wilderness. But out of the corner of his eye, Fokke sees a shift. Armed with his camera, he points his lens in the direction of the movement, discovering a fox just at the base of the tree line hoping for a rabbit. He clicks away, capturing its pointed ears, its alertness, eyes trained in his direction. The men are silenced, each taking a turn to look through the lens and see the fox staring back at them as if they are the prey he seeks.

The fox scampers out of sight. The silence lasts a beat longer before Barry starts giving Fokke some serious shit about being pussy-whipped. The jokes become more and more ruthless as the day continues. At least they're no longer talking Leprechauns, a callous reference to the red-headed Irish man that stole away his last girlfriend. He's not giving them anything else to add to the list. Instead, he digs into Jan and his herring stand lady and pulls a twenty-year-old event from his memory to harass Barometer. He does not glance at his cell phone until the sunlight is leaving the sky and they're on their way back to the cabin, cold and hungry.

As Barry and Jan head into the kitchen to place the dishes Fokke prepared this morning into the oven, he quickly checks his phone, discovering a number of text messages. Not one is from the sexy Oregonian vegan he's dying to see again. Her absence of reply, along with the serious roasting he's endured from the guys are both working against him.

Was it just a fling? Have I blown this whole thing out of proportion? After all, he and Sarah didn't talk about their love affair, didn't label it at all—didn't make any plans for her visit to The Netherlands besides a generally noncommittal *that would be nice, if the timing works out.* Why, then, is he so stuck on the idea that there is a future for them?

He checks his email and over a hundred messages pour into his inbox. But once again, there's nothing from Sarah Beth Turner. He flicks his finger across the screen, turning the phone off and heads into the kitchen to see if his help is needed.

After dinner, cigars on the front porch and a few rounds of cards, they spill into the hot tub under a full moon. The sky is loaded with stars, not a cloud in sight to block their vision. Peter lights a joint and passes it around. Fokke passes, as he always has, and always will. They know this about him, but as they all begin to mellow, he catches their mood.

"You think our grandchildren will see foxes in the snow?" Barry asks. His question doesn't need any explanation. It hangs in the air, mingling with the transitory mist where hot steam from the jacuzzi meets crisp winter air.

Fokke thinks of the report he heard on satellite radio just a few months ago while driving to Costa del Sol in Andalucia. It had been one of those perfect days impregnated with a promise that all things are right in the world. The sky was an azure blue with sheep-like clouds floating across its canvas, the Mediterranean a shade of cerulean stretching to the horizon, whispering eternity in his ear. After the jazz show came to an end, a talk show commenced. *The number of wild animals on earth has halved in the past 40 years* the host stated to his guests. *What can we do about it?* He felt the two worlds colliding and his heart ached for a moment before he switched off the radio. But its presence endured as did the emasculated feeling of trying to escape from the facts. *Human expansion is deadly to other species.*

His thoughts shift to Sarah and her claim that going vegan would solve so many problems. Overfishing would come to an end; land used for raising food for livestock could be used to raise food for people and create more open space; methane gases and water-polluting excrement from livestock would disappear. Could he live with a vegan? Or become a vegan? Half of his best recipes are based on a savory cut of beef or a succulent fish. The word succulent plays around in his mind and he sees Sarah lying beside him, her hand toying with the fine fuzz of his chest hair.

"Nature has a way of enduring," Peter says. "It understands the path of least resistance, but also how to use everything it has learned to adapt to the current situation and thrive."

A shooting star rips across the sky and they all see it, staring at its majestic arc long after it has disappeared.

"I hope you're right," Jan intones.

"There must come a point when human impact is too much, when nature can no longer self-correct," Fokke adds.

"Kill mother earth, you kill us along with her," Peter says. "But it won't come that far."

"Nope. We'll wake up before then. Do what's right, set things right," Barry says.

Fokke doesn't share their optimism, but he remains silent. His head is getting foggy from the second-hand smoke. He uses a trick he has used in many situations like this; recall a passage of text from his photographic memory and recite it back to himself. Sarah's journal comes unbidden into his mind. He sees the way she curls the bottom of the letter G and puts a full circle above her I's. There it is; *itinerary*, with two little circles above the I's like floating whole notes on a musical score. He scrolls through the text in his mind. Ms. Sarah Beth Turner should now be in Venice, Italy at the Hotel Ai Cavalieri di Venezia for four more nights. She had a day trip to Vicenza planned today to see Palladio's architecture. He has a sudden desire to send her an email, something he has yet to do.

"I'm going to call it a night, guys. I'll see you in the morning."

Fokke is out of the hot tub, dried off and headed inside when he hears their voices, heavy with humor calling after him.

"Phone sex is overrated."

"When you're done masturbating, clean that shit up."

"Tell her we love her too."

Chapter 26
Correspondence

Sarah is met with that strange sense of excitement she gets every time she uploads her Alexi vlog to share with the world. It's one of her better ones, she thinks—beautiful architecture, elevated thoughts, romanticism.

Vicenza hadn't even been on her original itinerary. It was Gregory Golder's idea. Sarah thinks back to that conversation where they ate lunch on the deck overlooking the Deschutes River in Bend. That moment seems a lifetime away, yet transformative.

"If I'm going to send you to Western Europe in style, you have to go to Vicenza to see Palladio's villas," he had insisted.

"Is he a friend of yours?" she had asked.

"Might have been if I lived in the 16th century," Gregory had responded drily, leveling his gaze on her before launching into an explanation of the architect Andrea Palladio and the significance of his work. She soon learned that Palladio's works and writings influenced architectural design throughout Europe and America.

"He used symmetry, harmonic and mathematical proportion to create rich designs while paying homage to antiquity," he went on, taking in a breath to continue before she had cut him off.

"Stop, Gregory. I'm not an architect. Speak in layman's terms."

"Hmmm. I thought I was. Let me try again. Ever seen The White House?" he had asked, causing Sarah to glare at him before she nodded.

"Those great columns? The proportion and symmetry? They are of Palladian influence." He had gone on to mention Thomas Jefferson's famous Monticello estate and a handful of other famous buildings she could easily picture.

"Okay. So palatial, classical buildings with columns out front. How could that be Palladio? Wasn't ancient Rome and Greece full of those types of designs long before the 16th century?" she had countered.

"Yes. Very good Sarah. That's what I meant by paying homage to antiquity. Palladio was greatly influenced by Vitruvius, a Roman architect from the 1st century B.C. Vitruvius would have also been my friend had I lived in the first century. He wrote *De Architectura*, on architectural design. Fifteen centuries later, Palladio wrote his own treatise on architecture called *I Quattro Libri dell' Architettura* or *The Four Books on Architecture*. These books were 'The Bible' of architecture for hundreds of years."

Today, as she walked the gravel path leading to Villa Capra La Rotonda, staring at the massive building with six columns spanning its grand entry, she thought of Gregory.

La Rotonda was massive yet elegant. She stood at the far side of the front lawn, studying its perfect symmetry. As she came closer, she regarded the life-sized statues ornamenting the roof and staircase as if they were sentries, demanding respect for the structure and past occupants. If it weren't for the tourists ambling around in jeans, hiking boots and windbreakers, she could have imagined herself transported back in time; arriving at a regal estate to dine with the gentry of the countryside.

The Basilica Palladiana in the town of Vicenza had affected her the same way. As she ambled along the tiled walkway of the upper level loggia gazing through the massive arched openings to the street below, she felt elevated by the experience. Not only elevated above the street level, but it was as if the very proportion of the architecture was responsible for elevating her mood and thoughts. She captured this idea in her Alexi post. Now, just an hour after upload, she is already getting hits.

And speaking of hits, Alexi seems to be gaining momentum. According to the statistics that YouTube sent her just yesterday, 76 percent of her followers are female with a median age of 34. Her sister April, who works in IT, has also been tagging her posts, and applying her IT voodoo to boost her ratings. April has sent more than one email saying that Alexi is a sensation just waiting to happen. But April tends to be overly optimistic when it comes to her siblings.

Yet, there's something going on. Alexi has 3,600 followers, which seems like a lot to Sarah. But she knows better. Some of the kids she counsels back home have over 60,000 followers for their fan fiction, and have had a few posts that received over 100,000 likes. Relatively speaking, her 3,600 followers make her popularity feel quaint, unexposed. Yet it is enough of a following to suggest her project is making a difference to people.

Tired from a long day of walking and taking in such rich history, Sarah is ready to crawl beneath the covers. She only had to politely stave off one would-be pursuer today, which felt like a cake walk compared to the day before that.

She yawns, about to turn off her iPad when she decides to check her email. Twenty-two unread messages. She scrolls through them, flagging those that need follow-up. Then her eyes land on a name that makes her sit up in bed with a jolt.

October 25, 22:30

Dear Sarah,
Enjoyed every aspect of meeting you. You are a bright and shining light. Hope we can rendezvous in The Netherlands.
Fokke.

She cups her hands over her mouth as she opens the second email.

October 25, 22:34

Dear Sarah,

If my memory serves me correctly, you have a birthday coming up. Any chance I could take you to dinner? And if my memory doesn't serve me correctly, could I take you out to dinner anyway? Your phone is going directly to voicemail by the way. Miss you.

Fokke.

Sarah jumps, cradling the tablet as she re-reads this last message that was written just half an hour ago. Maybe he's still on line. She starts typing.

October 25, 22:57

Dear Fokke,

Nice to hear from you. I'd very much like to celebrate my birthday with you. But it's tomorrow. Do you know any good restaurants in Padua? Maybe we could meet there in a few days.

Miss you too. Sarah.

October 25, 22:59

Dear Sarah,

There's a lovely old restaurant in Padua about four blocks from the Piazza delle Erbe that I'd like to take you to, but I have to be back in Amsterdam in four days. How is Venice?

Fokke

October 25, 23:02

As you probably know, Venice is the City of Love. Strange city to visit on your own.

Alone in Venice in a hotel room, Sarah

October 25 23:04

I could change that scenario for you in a few hours.

Alone in bed and thinking of your beautiful earlobes.
Fokke

October 25, 23:05

Beautiful earlobes?
Sarah

October 25, 23:06

If I start writing about all of the delectable parts of your body that I would like to touch right now, you won't get any sleep tonight. Earlobes are reasonably safe.
Fokke

October 25, 23:07

Try me.
Sarah

October 25, 23:12

When I think of you, I see first your dark blue eyes, framed by golden curls. I see the creases around your eyes that indicate a woman who lives life with a sense of humor, who knows how to be compassionate and loving. I see the flinty green specks in the blue of your eyes that I only noticed in the sunlight, before I made love to you for the last time. Then I see the smooth skin of your neck, the gentle curve of your breasts. Your ample thighs and butt, that taut stomach that I want to kiss right this minute.
Sleepy?
Fokke

October 25, 23:14

Want to meet me in Venice? Just a few more days here. Destined to be awake all night.
Sarah

October 25, 23:15

If you're serious, I could be there tomorrow in time for your birthday. Shall we talk on the phone?
Fokke

October 25, 23:17

Very tempted. But you have to sign the 'I won't break your heart' contract before I say yes. No phone. Dropped it in a canal.
Sarah

October 25, 23:18

A contract to come to Venice? As long as you sign it back. I'm a bit saturated on Venice, but I'd go again for you. Will have to hear that canal story in person. Have a phone in your hotel room?
Sleepless in Sappada
Fokke

October 25, 23:20

Yes. See you tomorrow then. Bring your pj's and toothbrush. And how can anyone get too much of Venice?
Good night.
Sarah.

October 25, 23:22

It's a big city. Where shall we meet?
Will pack my toothbrush among other supplies.
Fokke

As Sarah starts to type in the address of the Hotel Ai Cavalieri di Venezia, she hesitates. Is this what she wants? To extend this fling? She already can't think straight. What will it be like if she has more time with him? Will she get attached? Ultimately, she can't start a relationship, considering her upcoming interview with PNC. Plus, she is enjoying being on her own.

Her mother is smoking a cigarette, the tendrils of smoke hanging in the air. Her unkempt curls are pinned up loosely with two pencils.

Relax baby. If this is meant to be a fling, it will be. If it's meant to be a lifelong love, it will be. There's room for you in all of this. So don't worry. Push send and get some sleep.

Her mother's words—wise or completely misguided—give her courage as she finishes her email and pushes send.

Chapter 27
Reunion

As his watch clicks over to 9:00a.m. the train crosses the Ponte della Libertà bridge over the lagoon into the City of Love. He's questioned his own sanity at least four times on the early morning trip south, but keeps coming back to the same conclusion; life is short.

It can also be long, harrowingly long if you have witnessed atrocities in the world as he has; if you have experienced betrayal, loss. But even longer, he reasons, if you don't take any risks, appreciate the beauty and grace along the way. And Sarah is all grace.

But the internal alarms are going off anyway. Danger! Risk!

Keeping a beautiful woman company in Venice should fall into the pleasure, not risk-category, he argues as he arrives a few blocks from the Hotel Ai Cavalieri di Venezia. And he must keep the cliché though surprisingly wise words of Barometer in mind: Don't approach this with expectations or you're sure to end up disappointed.

He heads out in search of the print shop he looked up last night online. Forty-five minutes later, present in hand, he enters the four-star hotel. As he walks over the polished marble floor of the lobby toward the front desk, he sees her. She is sitting on a gold and ivory toned couch reading a book. She looks like an advertisement for the hotel, her golden curls draped over her shoulders as she casually reads a novel; a vase of pink, red and orange

Gerbera daisies on the marble table next to her, a painting depicting gondolas on the Venetian canals just above her head.

As if sensing him, she turns his way. Once they make eye contact, a now-familiar heat fills his heart area then radiates outward, sending rapid signals to various parts of his anatomy. *Either the beginnings of a heart attack or lust,* he reasons. She sets down her book and stands. Heat rises to her cheeks as she moves toward him. He's not quite sure how she ends up in his arms so quickly, but she is buried in his embrace and emotion washes over him as he takes in the familiar lavender scent of her shampoo.

"Happy birthday, Sarah," he says into her thick curls.

"Thank you, Fokke, I'm so glad you came," she responds as she hugs him, her arms slightly hindered by the backpack on his shoulders.

They would have behaved like the responsible adults they are if it weren't for the kiss; a simple press of lips against lips that might happen between friends. But that slight contact brings it all back—every intimate memory they have been replaying in their minds—and they forget about the public lobby; lose all sense of etiquette. His mouth devours hers and a tiny moan, barely audible, escapes her lips as she presses herself against him. It takes every ounce of reserve he has to break the embrace.

There's no discussion as they head up the marble staircase. They can't get the door to her room open fast enough. Fokke drops his bags on the wooden floor as Sarah hastily shuts the door behind them. He is far from gentle as he pushes her against the wall, one hand pinning her arms above her against the velvety wall paper as the other tilts her face to his. He kisses her hard, parting her lips with his tongue as his body presses against her. The mewling sound coming from her lips undoes him. He can't wait a moment longer.

Their clothing forms a scattered path over the wooden floor as they stumble together toward the large bed. He is on top of her, amazed all over again at her firm, yet feminine shapes, at how she seems to fit his body. But there is no time to revel right now; barely enough time to slip on the condom.

He nips at her breasts, her nipples hardening in his mouth as she opens herself to him. He thrusts inside her, his weight pressing upon her and she thrusts against him, taking him in inch by inch until he fills her completely. Their lovemaking is fierce, full of mutual urgency. She is quivering, arching, calling his name. He tries to slow the pace but she is bucking against him. As he feels her tightening around him, the spasms jolting through her, it pushes him over the edge and he cries out her name as he empties himself into her.

As they slowly come back down to earth, Fokke looks into her eyes, wondering if he's crushing her with his weight.

"Hi darling," he whispers.

"Hi," she exhales.

"Not too rough?" He shifts more of his weight to his forearms.

"No. But we'll have to see if I can still walk," she sighs.

"Damn. I'm sorry, I thought you . . ."

Sarah presses her lips to him, silencing him with kisses. "You thought right."

"You like it rough?" he asks.

"I've been thinking about you non-stop for the last three days and I needed a serious, um, re-alignment. I think we've got that taken care of now." Her eyes are bright, sated.

"Good," Fokke answers. "I think that makes two of us. I promise to take it more slowly next time, but right now, we have a birthday to celebrate and I have some plans for us."

Her eyes shift, another expression forming on her face; gratitude, surprise. This woman who is lying beneath him, his manhood still buried in her, is turning him inside out, opening his heart as if it's there for the taking.

He couldn't get to Venice fast enough to see her again, but now that he's here, his feelings for this woman are scaring the hell out of him. He shakes his head as if to dislodge this thought. He pushes away from her and rises to dispose of the condom in the waste basket before walking toward the entry to retrieve the medium-sized plastic bag.

He observes her from across the room, her mussed up curls, the sheen of sweat on her chest and belly, most likely half his, the sated repose of her body. Satisfaction settles over him, as if he's just won some sort of competition. But before he can fully appreciate the feeling, he has to wipe away that uncertainty he sees forming on her face. Whatever the hell it is the two of them have gotten themselves into, this moment doesn't need to be tarnished by doubt. He strolls languidly back to her, bag in hand, and leans down to kiss her. The wrinkles of concern she doesn't even realize have formed across her brow dissipate as his lips press to her forehead.

"I have a present for you. Didn't have time to wrap it," he admits as he sits beside her. It does the trick. She is clearly excited, but trying to hide it. He knows about Sarah and presents; knows that dickhead Matthew forgot her birthday two times in the last eleven years, their anniversary more often than that.

She reaches into the bag, extending the moment by feeling the present within. She pulls it slowly upward, and her cheeks heat up as she stares into her own, naked eyes in a framed photo. They are wide open, sparkling, dark blue. The expression on her face is candidly raw, full of longing, desire, sadness; a half smile tugging at her cheeks.

"Just before we said goodbye," Fokke informs her. She looks up at him, embarrassed by the emotion he has captured. Is she so transparent to him?

"You're beautiful, Sarah. Your kindness radiates from this picture."

Good. That's what he sees; kindness, not vulnerability, she thinks. "Thank you, Fokke. I really appreciate this." She props the photo up on the nightstand and snuggles into his chest.

"Glad you like it," he responds as he finally notices the room around them. The nightstands with marble tops and delicate gold lacquered legs are French, probably Louis XIV style. Thick white curtains with gold sashes frame the large windows complementing the gold and green striped velvet wallpaper. "Amazing room," he adds.

She just smiles at him and kisses him slowly on the lips. Fokke notices how good it feels to have her pressed against him, naked and relaxed. Since his break-up fourteen months ago, he is used to an uncomplicated, woman-free lifestyle; living out of a suitcase or backpack in the company of strangers, viewing their worlds from a distance, distilling and packaging his personal observations and experiences into appealing copy for best-selling travel guides and luxury lifestyle magazines. He's met plenty of women in that time and disregarded them all.

But this woman? She's doing something to him; casting some Sarah-style voodoo on his anti-woman heart. It excites him as much as it scares the hell out of him. *Don't freak out*, he tells himself. Jan's words come back to him; *you are so fucked*. If he had ended it in Cortina, his heart would mend. But now, here, it feels different. In the act of opening up to her, his heart feels raw with emotion, a vulnerability he has spent the last fourteen months trying to avoid. Inside, his team is on a counter mission, quickly assembling scaffolding, calling all hands on deck to get the wall back in place as soon as freaking possible.

"You know Fokke. I really enjoy your company; how honest you are. How you seem to get me, even though you know so little about me. How I want time to get to know you better." She pulls the sheets over her breasts, either feeling cold or exposed.

"I want that too," he manages.

I'm honest? Fuck. I know a hell of a lot about her because of what I read in her journal. I have to come clean. Talk about taking risks. Will she hate me? Kick me out?

She must also feel uncomfortable with the weight of the situation as she shifts suddenly, her lips pursing in distaste.

"Okay. Enough of all this seriousness. The birthday queen wants a shower. With you," she says lightly. He and his frightened, walled-in heart rejoice at the change of subject, though his conscience makes a note to bridge the topic of the journal at the first reasonable moment; after they are clothed and fed.

"I'd like to bathe with you, but Italian showers tend to be small, especially for a man of my height—that bath tub back in Cortina was an exception to the rule."

"Let's go see," she coyly suggests, pulling him from the bed. What he is observing now as he and Sarah head to the bathroom together, is not for any travel guide. His eyes graze over her ample butt, firm calf-muscles and ham strings, the golden curls cascading down the middle of her long back. "This looks big enough, don't you think?"

Fokke is standing in front of one of the most elegant bathrooms he has seen on Italian soil.

"Do you always rent rooms with an extra-large bed and a shower with two shower heads?" He marvels as he closes the glass door of the shower behind them.

"No. I upgraded when you decided to join me. You wouldn't have fit through the door of the room I had yesterday."

"That was thoughtful," he replies as the water begins to heat up, mist swirling around them. *Seems like divorce settlement money well spent*, he thinks as he pulls her into his arms. He doesn't think it possible, but the sensation of her wet skin against his pulls him to attention. He pours a handful of Sarah's lavender shower gel into his palm and massages it slowly into her shoulders, slowly working his way South. *Definitely won't be clothed, fed or confessing any time soon.*

Chapter 28
History

Fokke's first encounter with Venice was as a seventeen-year-old on a class trip on Italian architecture. Its liquid roadways, ancient architecture and maritime lifestyle had so impressed him over that long weekend that he vowed to come back again. Just after finishing his law degree, he made good on his promise, and spent three months in this grand city writing *van der Veld's Pocket Guide to Venice*. This guidebook was so popular that it led to a contract to write *van der Veld's Guidebook to Italy*, which led to *van der Veld's Guidebook to Austria*, which led to *van der Veld's Guidebook to Indonesia*, which led to *van der Veld's Guidebook to*—so on and so forth.

That initial Venice pocket guide was the catalyst that changed the course of his life from yet another van der Veld in the family law firm, to renowned travel writer of a series of guidebooks that has kept him richly employed and on the move for 20 years.

After he announced he would not be joining the family law firm, his father didn't speak to him for three long months. Fortunately, the silence was broken when Fokke credited his law degree as the key to his success.

To this day, Fokke believes it is his lawyerly approach—detailed research, cross examining the information and going to great lengths to understand the clients, or in this case, locations he is representing—that makes him a successful travel writer. As is the case with most of the books and articles he has written, more than half of the information he researched for *van der Veld's Pocket Guide to Venice* didn't make it into the final draft. But it's there in the background, informing his writing style, framing his confidence to speak definitively about a city and culture that is not his. In short, he has exhaustively explored this city's hidden secrets. Although Venice has not divulged all of her secrets to him, he is tired of extolling her charms to the world.

He selfishly wishes that all of the tourists (himself withstanding) would just go home so he could know the city in a purely Italian light. *One other tourist could stay behind as well*, he muses.

For reasons he doesn't understand, he has never been to Venice in the company of a woman. Until now. As he and Sarah begin their journey through Venice together, he sees it through her eyes: fresh and awe-inspiring and, yes, damn it, romantic.

As they walk the streets, taking in the sights, sounds and smells, she brings him up to date on her adventures thus far. She has tackled a number of top tourist attractions over the past three days: The Doge's Palace, Saint Mark's Basilica. She has crossed the Ponte de Rialto bridge, which he knows was re-built between 1588 and 1591 by architect Antonio da Ponte. He also knows that da Ponte competed with both Michelangelo and Andrea Palladio for the contract to re-design this bridge, and won. He keeps his internal narrative to himself as he listens to the excitement in her voice.

She has traversed the Grand Canal by "vaporetto," the Italian water taxi, to visit the Church of San Giorgio Maggiore, which, like many buildings in Venice and the surrounding regions, was designed by Andrea Palladio. She has even slipped across the liquid roadways of Venice in a gondola at sunset—all of these without him. *Pity*, he thinks. *It would have been something to see these old friends through her Virgin-Venice eyes.*

They see a small café with heat lamps above the outdoor seating and decide to stop for a cappuccino and Brutti e Buoni, an almond biscuit that is a perfect counterpart to Italian espresso. As he places their order, Sarah flips through her Lonely Planet guidebook, completely unaware that there is a living and breathing guidebook sitting at her table.

"I was thinking maybe this place," she says, pointing to a picture of a building with a gothic facade.

"Palazzo Moncenigo," Fokke nods appreciatively.

"Yes. They have a clothing collection from 17th and 18th century Venetian nobility. I could see it another day if that sounds boring to you. Or we could split up and meet back up later?" she suggests.

"No. I'd like to go with you if you don't mind." Fokke is pleasantly surprised by her choice. It will tie in perfectly with something he has planned for them tomorrow, which he alluded to this morning before they left the hotel.

"I'd love for you to go with me. Have you been to Palazzo Manchigeno, um, I mean Moncenigo before?" she asks.

"Several times. It's one of the most prestigious 17th century Gothic style palazzo's here. The Moncenigo family was an important Patrician family of Venice. They had seven Doge's in their lineage. The Palazzo was the residence of the San Stae branch of the Moncenigo family for centuries, right until the mid 1950s when the last family member died. They only opened to the public in 1985."

Sarah tries not to stare as the details flow out of him.

"A Doge is like the town mayor?" she asks.

"The chief magistrate. The leader of Venice elected for life."

"Wow," she responds.

"Yeah. But that's not all. The Moncenigo family was full of procurators, another elected life-long position, which was the equivalent of a manager for the Saint Mark's Basilica. Procurator was considered the second highest appointment after Doge," Fokke goes on. "They had a rich military history as well . . . sorry. Please cut me off at any time," he laughs.

"No! No! I find it fascinating. But let me guess; you've written about this palazzo," she smiles.

He hasn't told her to what extent he knows this city, because if there is one thing he can't stand, it's a show off—thus the reason he cut himself off mid-sentence just a minute ago.

"I've written quite a bit about Venice, but not Moncenigo. Strange, considering it's one of my favorite palazzos. Oh, and there's also a perfume museum housed within," he adds, nonchalantly gauging her reaction.

"That's right! I read about the perfume museum." Despite the fact that Fokke is right here beside her, she is filled with a strange longing as she thinks of the earthy, yet sophisticated scent of Fokke's cologne. She has come to know this scent on his body over their short time together; has seen him spray it sparsely over his chest after his morning shower. That musky forest scent had been her first clue that she had the wrong backpack, way back when Fokke van der Veld was just a name in permanent marker on the inside of a bag—like a whole week ago. She leans toward him as she casually reaches for a sugar cube, trying to get close enough to smell him. And there it is: Happiness, understanding, lust, humor, warmth, protection. It's all there inside that scent of cologne interacting with his skin. She knows her olfactory nerve is sending certain sensations to her brain that she now associates with this smell. But logic doesn't help in quelling the emotions welling up within her.

"Tell me more about the Moncenigos," she encourages, seeking both distraction and the sound of his voice. As she listens to his slightly animated stories of military battles, of love affairs and influence on Venetian society, she realizes she could listen to Fokke for hours. He could have been a historian. He'd also make an excellent teacher, she decides, taking in the unassuming way he imparts information; knowledgeable yet friendly and enthusiastic. She decides something else; she doesn't want to be inside with him just yet, but outdoors, the sky stretching endlessly above them, the architecture and canals of Venice their landscape.

When he finishes talking about the Moncenigos, she shares her thoughts.

"Before we go to see this amazing Palazzo Moncenigo, I'd love to just get lost in the city with you, maybe have lunch at a small sandwich shop where locals hang out. Oh. And I need to get a new phone."

Considering his familiarity with the city and his superior navigation skills, he doesn't think it possible to get lost, but he likes the idea of trying. Especially with Sarah by his side.

"Sounds like a plan. We'll keep our eyes open for a cell phone outlet. Why don't you lead the way," he suggests. He notices her shoulders relax. If there's one thing she can't stand, it's a man leading her around. He knows this from her journal. But he believes if he had not read a single page of her curly handwriting, he would have known this about her intuitively. He's not one to follow either, but for her sake, he's willing to try.

They find a mobile phone shop within minutes, and Fokke proves to be instrumental in helping her select a pre-paid plan with a SIM card that will work in multiple countries, 'including The Netherlands so you can reach your grandma' he emphasizes.

They stop at a record store and he leaves her to explore the jazz section while he checks out the classical music. A half hour passes quickly and he sees her deflect the advances of two men in the short time he is not by her side.

"What a pain in the ass my gender can be," he comments after she has swatted them away like flies.

"Yes. Quite a nuisance. But at other times, they can be extremely useful," she responds as she wiggles her eyebrows at him.

"You're just using me for sex?" he asks.

"Of course."

"Do you have any idea how much trouble I'd be in if this conversation were reversed?" he toys with her.

"I would be slapping you right about now," Sarah says as she leans in for a kiss. Her touch is so gentle and loving that Fokke can't help but pull her into a hug.

They talk easily as they continue to walk. She leads them across bridge after bridge without rhyme or reason but still he is not lost. They have talked about architecture, veganism, nature, farming, city life, bands, politics, cultural differences and even though they differ on their opinions here and there, they have navigated all of these topics without tension.

She doesn't dwell in gift stores, which he appreciates, but seems more drawn to the architecture. She walks quickly and agilely but doesn't mind stopping to discuss the facade of a building or the history of a coat of arms. She is not afraid to state her needs, but she is also capable of compromise. In other words, she is his perfect traveling companion.

He is vaguely aware of something brewing inside of him. Something so subtle that it's just a whisper circulating in his subconscious. It was there in Cortina, and it is here now, slowly coming forward from the shadows. As he tries to give it definition, it blurs like an enticing shape beneath the water's surface. *Deep, still waters like an underground spring*, he muses. He has discovered a secret well within her, has sipped from that well and it is good; pure; essential. And he is thirsty for more.

He breathes in, imagining what this analogy forming in his mind means. Has he ever likened a woman to a well? To water? An element essential to one's existence?

"I'm thirsty," she says.

"What?" he asks. Can she peer inside him? Was he speaking out loud?

"Hungry too. Maybe we should start looking for a restaurant," she remarks.

"Oh yeah, sure," he responds with relief. They have been walking for a few hours and he can feel the rumblings of his own stomach as they enter the Santa Croce neighborhood of Venice.

"Do you have any suggestions?" she asks.

"I do," Fokke says as he kisses the back of her hand. "There's a great little restaurant called Bacareto da Lele in this neighborhood. And if I'm not mistaken, it's close by." He knows, in fact, that it's three blocks away. She asked for casual and local. Bacareto da Lele is about as casual and native as you can go. This unimposing hole-in-the-wall has delicious ciccetti's and a decent wine list. And it's cheap.

As they round the final corner, she spots a green awning with the words Bacareto da Lele stamped on its surface in faded white letters.

"There it is! Wow. You really know this city," she comments.

"Yeah. I guess," he returns, casually deflecting her praise. The line is full of not only locals, but tourists galore. He shakes his head. Looks like it's gained in popularity over the last few years. That's the problem with sharing hidden gems in guidebooks, or online on Yelp or Trip Advisor for that matter. The gems are unearthed and become crowded. And like an idiot, he hadn't thought about Sarah being vegan. Most of the little snacks are meat-based. But she goes with the flow and orders a bottled water and a sandwich with artichokes, tomatoes and basil. It only takes them two times to leave off the meat, the cheese and the butter.

"Delicious," she murmurs as they sit on the steps of a nearby church, sunshine pouring over the white and orange swirled marble. "Though I think I'll need a few more of these."

"Yeah. Me too," he responds as he bites into the thin layers of prosciutto on a freshly baked roll. "These snack bars always have small proportions, but they're cheap and tasty."

Sarah is contemplative yet relaxed as they continue to eat in comfortable silence. He stands in line to get them another round of sandwiches while she tilts her head to the sunlight, closing her eyes. After they finish eating, they linger on the steps, enjoying the cool, bright sunshine.

"It's strange being outside with you," she says.

Based on the open smile on her face it's a good strange. He feels it too.

"Like before we were cocooned in a dream—snowed in. And now we've been released into reality," Fokke replies.

"Sort of like that," she agrees before taking another bite. "But Venice has a dream-like quality to it too."

"Yes. But it's real at the same time," Fokke states.

"Yes. It is," she agrees.

***

After lunch, he begins to guide them toward their destination. He is not fond of public displays of affection. But as they head down a side street five or six blocks from the grand canal, she stops their progression to point out a row of white undershirts interspersed with blue baby onesies airing on a clothes line two floors above them. Her pure joy at this common sight stirs something within him and he pulls her suddenly into an arched doorway, a cherub above their heads and kisses the small constellation of freckles on her neckline.

"What are you doing to me Fokke?" she replies as she leans into the doorway.

"What are you doing to me?" he returns, aware that his navy pants, sturdy cotton that they are, are doing very little to hide his arousal as he tastes her slightly salty, lavender-scented skin. He can't seem to get enough of her. He indulges himself, taking his time kissing her until they are both flustered and out of breath.

He rakes his hand through his hair, adjusting his clothing as he breaks their embrace.

"My God, woman," are his only words as he takes her hand and guides them forward. As they approach their destination, Fokke imagines what it might be like to really be with Sarah. He pictures them as a couple, living in the city of love, or better yet, traveling the world together. They could be happy; very happy. Just before the idea can take hold, something inside of him—a haggard thing with hunched shoulders and a sharp pointer finger—pokes ruthlessly at him, ordering him to cease and desist with these nonsensical thoughts. *No!* He counters vehemently. *If there is any city in the world where a bit of romantic fantasy can be tolerated for a time and then be left behind, it is here. What happens in Venice stays in Venice*, he thinks.

Inside the Palazzo Moncenigo they explore the grand rooms. Sarah closely observes the rich fabrics on the walls and the costumed mannequins in Venetian finery as if attempting to record every detail. Fokke feels a sense of privilege being here with her, as if this palazzo, this city is his to give. He points out a ceiling fresco created for a wedding within the Moncenigo family, explaining the allegorical figures of Fame, Marriage and Glory.

They spend a good deal of time in the rooms dedicated to the Italian contribution to the perfume industry. Sarah dwells on the elegant perfume bottles in brilliant glass and jewel-encrusted vials and listens raptly to the explanation of the connection between scent and emotion. Fokke comes closer and she smells that faint forest musk powdered with cinnamon. Her olfactory nerve sends a series of intimate messages to different areas of her body, brain and soul, and she is tricked for a moment into believing she is falling in love with Fokke van der Veld. As a counselor, she is aware how emotions can lead you astray. But Sarah is too smart and wise to fall for these kinds of tricks.

Chapter 29
Scent

Just like the last four mornings in Venice, she is awoken by the steady clanging of church bells. Fokke is usually an early riser, but is miraculously still asleep. No wonder, considering the amount of energy he expended last night. She stretches contentedly as she recalls the details of last evening.

After the Moncenigo museum visit, he had taken her to dinner at Pinzimonio, a small vegan restaurant on the Viale Garibaldi. *It's not fair*, she had thought. *He's not only infiltrating my sense of touch, sight and smell, but now taste.*

They had headed back to the hotel to discover an urgent message from her sister April. Sarah had called America right away, fearing bad news from home.

"Sarah?" April's voice had answered. "Are you okay?"

"Of course! Why wouldn't I be? Are you okay?"

"Of course I'm okay. But you! You haven't been answering your phone for two days! And what is this romantic interlude you alluded to in your post?" April had pressed.

"I lost my phone. Dropped it in a canal. I'll text you my new number. And, well," she had lowered her voice, turning away from Fokke, "the rest of your question I can't discuss right now."

"Oh my God. You're with the mystery man?!" April had gushed. "Who is he? Where did you meet him? And why on earth are you mentioning it in your post? Have you seen the responses you're getting? You delivered your best post yet—gorgeous footage, insightful and informative about Vicenza and Palladio—but just like me, everyone just wants to know about the guy."

"What? Seriously? My God. I just. I didn't mean to say anything. It just slipped out," Sarah had admitted.

Aware of her hushed tones, Fokke had kissed her on the forehead before going to the balcony to give her privacy.

"So this is your urgent message?" Sarah had chided. "Wanting to know if I've kissed a man?"

"Have you?" April had asked. Her voice had been so crisp it was like she was right there in the room with her and for a moment, Sarah had felt that strange swell of emotion pressing at her tear ducts.

"Oh yes, and a whole lot more," she had let out.

After a scream that nearly blew out Sarah's eardrum, her sister had gone on to praise her actions. "You keep surprising me sis. Good for you! You deserve a travel affair. Is it strange, being with another man after a lifetime with Matthew?"

Sarah had deflected the question, asking April about the vlog stats. It had been clever of her, because April had taken the bait and launched into a detailed description.

After she had ended her call with her sister, she'd wrapped up in her peony pink winter coat and joined Fokke on the balcony. They had ended up talking about their families. She'd told him about her sister April and her twin brothers and he had listened attentively. He had asked her if she missed them, if she was eager to get back. She had answered honestly. Yes, she missed her family, but she wasn't sure where she planned to land—if she would stay on with her grandmother for a while or head back to the U.S. He had taken this in stride, not pushing for more information, and not reading too much into the vague nature of her answer.

As he had spoken of his sister's family, of his parents, it was abundantly clear to her that he had been raised in a loving household. She hadn't mentioned the recent passing of her mother or that her father had passed on when she was only ten years old. Talking about the living felt somehow less intimate and she needed to keep her senses about her.

But when they had lain down together in that large four poster bed, they had been so present in their love making that it seemed like there had never been anyone else but him.

***

Her eyes are open and the morning bells have stopped chiming. His arm is draped over her chest, his naked form nestled against her. As she carefully lifts his arm off of her and slips from the bed, her sister's question comes back to her. *What is it like being with another man after a lifetime with Matthew?*

After drinking a tall glass of water and brushing her teeth she turns on the shower and steps into its steady spray. She indulges by turning on the second shower head. As the water forms a cocoon of warmth around her, she lathers the soap and washes the earthen scent of Fokke and their lovemaking from her body.

In the rays of sober morning light coming through the bathroom window, she finally analyzes her situation. She has been divorced for nine months now. She knows that Matthew has no hold on her despite their eleven years of marriage, yet she feels something uncomfortable pressing in on her. It is neither shame nor guilt, though it angles in that direction. What it is exactly, she cannot say. But what she does know is that everything has changed.

Her time with Fokke feels sacred to her, like a gift from the Almighty; a man so kind and loving who understands her, who she can talk to so easily, who brings out passion in her body and soul. *A gift I don't deserve*, an internal voice says. The thought bothers her, but it is painfully familiar, as if she has known for years that she is undeserving. And then it hits her. This is the narrative voice of her marriage; a voice that stems from a discourse she and Matthew developed over the years that slowly cast her as the one at fault.

This damaged suit of marriage that she wore for over a decade has been removed, but it is still confining her. Like a phantom limb, it is twitching, demanding to be acknowledged—*you will never deserve happiness Sarah*. The feeling rips through her and nausea grips bitterly at her stomach, sadness and doubt transforming into anger. *I am deserving*, she firmly states. The thought rattles around, but refuses to settle.

She tries again. *I deserve happiness.* It lingers above her as if looking for an opening. She has been happy on this trip: Happy alone and now happy with Fokke. What is stopping her from accepting it? Fear? Doubt? The experience of being betrayed? Her dysfunctional relationship with her husband? *A mix of all of these things*, she realizes. She can't rush the process of healing, but she doesn't want to get stuck in the wrong place either. She closes her eyes, envisioning herself open to being in a loving relationship. *I deserve love,* she tries.

"Sorry to disturb you, but I have to pee," Fokke announces as he enters the bathroom.

"Go ahead," she responds over the steamed up shower door, laughter spilling from her. No matter that he has just interrupted a major emotional breakthrough with his need to relieve himself. As she hears his steady pour of liquid and pictures just where it's coming from, a smile forms on her lips. She has not heard a man pee in such close proximity for years. Matthew would have never done such a thing in her presence. Yet there is Fokke on the other side of the shower door performing one of the most basic of human functions. We are humans; animals who must perform their daily acts. And this basic act brings a certain intimacy, makes it, them, more real.

"Can I join you?" he asks when he is finally done.

"Yes, of course," she calls. He stops at the sink to brush his teeth and she watches through the fogged glass as his blurred form comes closer. The door opens, letting a bit of cold air in as he steps inside.

"Good morning beautiful," his deep voice greets her as he comes into focus. Her eyes graze over his strong pectoral muscles, but also the gray hairs mixed in with the blond on his chest, arms and legs; the scars on his knees and left thigh; his manhood at rest, dangling between his legs; the creases at the corner of his eyes when he smiles; his crooked, broad nose that just begs one to ask if he was a fighter in his youth.

She is aware by all the details she can see that the morning light around them is not kind. She pictures herself through his eyes. She knows she is strong and fairly toned, but her body is a far cry from the images gracing the fashion magazines. She has her own set of scars from her adventurous childhood and a lifetime of trail running in Oregon; knows that her skin, though soft and smooth, is no longer that of a teenager. She is covered in freckles that have no rhyme or reason to their patterns. But she does not cover herself. She will not betray her body and its imperfections with such an act. As if reading her thoughts, he moves toward her, bending to kiss the freckles along her neck line.

"Looks like Cassiopeia fell from the sky and landed right here," he murmurs as he traces his fingers along her neck. She squirms, her nipples hardening as his chest presses against hers. He kisses her gently on the lips, the water from the double shower heads washing over them, bathing them in liquid heat. He picks up the soap and washes her body, massaging over her arms, stomach, legs.

"I can't seem to get enough of you," he says. The words reverberate through her body, and she smiles up at him. The sunshine highlights the steely blue of his irises, sharp and intelligent. She sees the aristocratic features of his passport photo intermingled with vulnerability. His eyes search hers, asking a silent question, receiving a silent answer. It is in the silence of their exchange that her earlier missive to herself gains entry; *I do deserve happiness; I do deserve to be loved.* She absorbs what she sees there in his gaze and it washes over her, through her, swirling inside of her deeper and deeper until it finds its mark: a Cupid-style bullseye as he keeps his eyes locked on hers.

The feelings erupting inside her border on pain. She closes her eyes as dizziness envelops her. *What the hell is happening to me?* When she opens them again he is looking at her with a sense of bewilderment bordering on fear. Does he feel it too?

"You okay?" he asks in concern.

"Dizzy. Too hot in here. I need to get out," she responds. He hugs her to him, turning off the shower heads.

"Let me help you out. You're shaking."

She wants to tell him she's fine, but he's right. Her legs are shaking, her heart racing. So she takes his arm as he opens the glass door, holding her steady as he wraps one of the white hotel towels around her.

"I just need to sit down."

"Why don't you get back in bed," he suggests. She dries herself off before climbing under the covers, handing him the damp towel.

"We were up pretty late," she says, playing along with logic.

"Yeah. I didn't let you get much sleep. My fault."

No. She doesn't want to begin a discourse that lays blame, no matter how subtle and well-intentioned. She will learn from the past, move forward. "Our fault," she replies. "You can't take all the credit. But you know? You're right. I need to sleep."

He picks up her silk pajamas that are draped over the velvet upholstered chair by the bed and hands them to her. She slips them on over her naked form and he leans over her, tucking the covers around her before planting a kiss on her forehead.

"I'm going down to the lobby for breakfast. I'll bring something up for you in an hour. Would that work?"

"Yes. An hour would be great."

She watches as he dries himself off and slips on his underwear, his t-shirt. She observes the methodical way he buttons up his striped shirt over the t-shirt and tucks it into his gray linen pants. A man, her man, dressing for the day.

Once he leaves, she pulls further into the covers, trying to sort through the emotions spooling and tangling inside her. *It was just a look paired with a thought,* she thinks. Yet she knows. She is falling. Hard. And she's not sure if he's falling with her. *I can't do this. I'm smarter than that. I need to just go with the flow; develop my European Style Detachment.* She pulls the sheets over her face, blocking the sunshine and struggles against the heaviness of her eyelids until she finally drifts off into a deep sleep.

***

As she stretches awake, she sees him sitting on the balcony reading. On the table is a basket of little Italian breads and fresh fruit. She gets out of bed and splashes water on her face before throwing on a jacket over her pajamas and taking the basket to the balcony.

"What time is it?" she asks.

"Almost noon. Feeling better?"

"Completely. I think I was just tired," she says rubbing her neck.

"No problem. This is a vacation after all. But we've got to get going in half an hour if you want that surprise," he says mischievously.

Half an hour later they are walking east along a side canal. She is trying to figure out where they are going when Fokke greets a gondolier in a sleek black boat with red interior. He helps her into the gondola and they set off.

As they glide through the waters of Venice she remembers how she had longed for him when she took that solo gondola ride just three days ago.

"Is this my surprise?" she asks, leaning into him.

"Not yet." He wraps his arms casually around her shoulders, pulling her against his chest.

"You know, this is enough Fokke. Just this," she gestures around her, before resting her hand back on his. And she means it. It is such a gift to be in his company and to experience him out in the open instead of within the confines of a snowed-in lodge. Although that had its benefits as well.

"Probably," he says. "But I don't know if I'll get to share another birthday week with you. So this is my chance to spoil you."

Sarah shifts slightly in his arms. He can't see her face as she is sitting in front of him, but her shoulders are no longer relaxed.

"Hey," he whispers into her ear. "You okay?"

"I'm fine," she says back, feeling far from it.

The air is crisper as they leave the shelter of the smaller waterway and head into the grand canal. They ride in silence until Sarah makes a game of occasionally pointing out a building and asking him about it. Fokke the storyteller is back. It doesn't matter which building she points to. He seems to know them all personally: their history, former occupants, the century in which they were built.

They enter a smaller canal and the gondolier slows as they approach a rather nondescript shop with stained glass windows.

"We're here," Fokke announces. She reads the sign above the door: Signora Isabella.

As Fokke opens the front door for her, she is greeted by a bouquet of heady scents. The room is filled with little glass vials, cabinets of oils, dried and powdered herbs, roots and spices.

"Is this a parfumerie?" she asks in surprise.

"Yes," he responds, a look of triumph on his face.

A petite young woman with large green eyes and a head full of dark curls steps behind the counter from a back room. "Signor van der Veld!" she greets, extending her hand to Fokke.

Sarah does not miss how this younger woman parts her full lips and raises her perfectly sculpted eyebrows as she looks at him.

"Chiara, che bello rivederti," Fokke says.

"È sempre un piacere," Chiara replies, her eyes dancing in the low lights of the shop.

"Sto cercando una fragranza speciale per la mia amica Sarah Turner." Fokke's gaze shifts to Sarah.

"Piacere, si accomodi Signorina Turner." The woman's fair green eyes land on her and Sarah can't help but stare at the beauty of this younger woman.

"Sarah, this is Signorina Chiara, the daughter of Signora Isabella. She is going to assist you in making a custom perfume."

"Oh, Fokke. This is amazing!" Sarah leans in and kisses him on the cheek. "Where are my manners? Nice to meet you Signorina Chiara," she says, stretching out her hand. Chiara's hand is warm in hers.

"Nice to meet you, Ms. Turner," she returns. "So. Please. Have a seat, you two."

Sarah approaches the stool next to the high table, curious about the tiny vials filled with what must be essential oils. Fokke sits next to her as Chiara explains the scents and combinations. She recognizes many of the flowers and fruits pictured on the bottles, though the words throw her off.

"Aloe I know. But what is Ibisco and gelsomino?" Sarah asks.

"Hibiscus and jasmine," Fokke translates.

Rosa and viola are clear enough. Fruits have their own row, though she cannot imagine that arancio and anguria (orange and watermelon) will make their way into her custom fragrance. There are others she knows, but is surprised by their heady scents: legno di sandalo, mirra, incensos translate to sandalwood, myrrh and frankincense—fragrances older than Jesus.

"This is a personal process. I'll leave you in capable hands," Fokke kisses her on the lips before heading out the front door. It isn't until the two women are alone that Chiara speaks.

"Never brought a woman here before," Chiara informs her. "You must be very special to him."

Sarah brings her hand to her chest, touched by this woman's words. She doesn't bother to explain she's known Fokke for just over a week. Nor does she let her mind dwell on the possibility that Fokke has had custom perfumes made for other women over the years. How else would the shop owners know him by name? She is too excited by the process unfolding before her to let these thoughts get under her skin.

As Signorina Chiara opens the bottles and presents them to her, Sarah learns her sense of smell is far more advanced than she thought. Before long she has a blend that reminds her of a spring evening next to a high mountain lake: pine, moss, pear blossom and jasmine with a clean undertone of spring water. Yet it seems to need something more.

"Try," Chiara suggests. Sarah dabs it onto her wrist. The perfume transforms when it mingles with her skin, as if her own natural scent was the missing ingredient.

"La combinazione perfetta," Chiara concludes. The two women sit in comfortable silence as Sarah lets the intimacy of the moment percolate through the rest of her senses.

The bell jingles as Fokke returns and he smiles at the two women. "Success?" he asks.

"The perfect alchemy," Chiara responds, looking from Sarah to Fokke.

As they head back to the gondola, Sarah is at a loss for words, but she leans against him.

"Thank you," she finally says, her voice rough with emotion.

"You're welcome." He breathes in the fragrance at the edge of her neck. "You smell amazing. It really fits you. Pure yet sensual."

She has never received such a thoughtful, intimate gift. She realizes she has been holding her breath, waiting for something. What? She racks her mind and then senses it in the distance: that cultivated sense of guilt and shame waiting to puncture a hole in her happiness. But it is too far away.

She exhales and breathes in the cool afternoon air as they glide through the water and she leans into the warmth of Fokke's chest, his arms wrapped protectively around her.

"I'm honored to be here with you," he whispers into her ear. His words combined with his warmth blanketed around her are like an antidote, eradicating her cultivated self-doubt. Something clicks open inside of her. The sensation is raw, vulnerable, loving. Her eyes are moist and although she thinks this will finally be the moment when tears spring free out of joy rather than sadness, they still do not come.

It's as if her tear ducts know what is happening in her heart and have capped themselves off by an evolutionary development to counter heartbreak. *The pain stops here,* they proclaim. *We will not let your heart break again.* Ah, if only evolutionary response could develop so quickly.

Chapter 30
Labyrinth

Via Mia is a cozy restaurant deep within the labyrinth of interior streets, far from the tourists and main canals. They are tucked into a corner table next to the fireplace on their second glass of chianti after a sumptuous dinner. The chef, yet another old acquaintance of Fokke's, had made a vegan dish just for Sarah. *Espen's not the only one who can cook vegan,* Fokke had chided.

"So how is it possible that you don't like Venice?" Sarah asks.

"I never said that. It's just that I consider it a bit cliché, over-romanticized. But under current circumstances," he responds, his hand grazing the top of hers, "I'd say I'm experiencing it with new eyes."

"That's good," she sighs happily. "Because it's not cliché for me. It's amazing, sparkling new and extremely old all mixed in one. And after treating me to a custom perfume? I'd say you are the definition of a romantic," she teases.

"Touché. Has your alter-ego posted about Venice?" he asks.

"Several times. You're not one of my followers?" she smiles up at him as her foot touches his under the table.

He viscerally reacts to the contact. He longs to be back in the room, back in bed with her, seeing what else he can discover about this amazing woman. He leans toward her, taking in the delicate pear blossom and jasmine of her new perfume as he whispers in her ear. "I'd need your pseudonym in order to follow you."

"Ah. True. But I'm not ready to hand that over," she whispers back, trailing a gentle kiss along his cheek. "I want my anonymity."

She is relieved to know he isn't one of her followers. Especially after her novice blunder in her vlog a few days ago, mentioning a romantic encounter in Sappada. Even though she didn't use his name, it was just as April had said; her followers responded exuberantly to her news and they want to know more.

Fokke tops off their glasses and makes a toast.

"To doing exactly what we want to be doing."

"Cheers," Sarah responds, clinking her glass to his.

"Have you ever wanted to do something besides school counseling?"

"You asked me that before. I did have a few dreams, though kind of impractical."

"Tell me anyway." His gaze is friendly, open.

"All right. Guess it can't hurt." She plays with the wax that has spilled onto the tablecloth as she talks. "I had this idea for a 'cause café.' I wanted to open a trendy restaurant with delicious vegan cuisine, and a stage for performances." She hasn't talked about this in years, and as the concept comes back to her, she feels a mix of excitement and embarrassment.

"Every month we'd showcase one non-profit—for example, 'Save the Children'. We'd have activities throughout the month, each with a cover fee. At the end of the month, a percentage of the earnings would be donated to that non-profit."

"Beautiful idea," Fokke acknowledges. "It could be great. You could start with one, get the concept dialed in and then create a franchise model."

"You think so?" she laughs. "My ex-husband shot that dream down before I could even formulate it, saying eight out of ten restaurants fail. He said that if I planned to give away a percentage of the profits, my idea was doomed from the beginning. He had a head for finances, so he was probably right." That feeling in the shower, before Fokke joined her is looming again and she sees it—how Matthew's opinions and judgments had filtered through in so many places, slowly eroding her ideas, her dreams, infecting her day-to-day activities.

"He sounds charming," Fokke states sarcastically, noting the tension in Sarah's shoulders as she mentions her ex. "I'm pretty decent with finances and I love the idea. And I know you can cook."

"Yes I can," she acknowledges. "Counseling and cooking. There lies the sum of my talents," she thinks out loud.

"Your talents form a much longer list than that, Sarah," he states. "And do you have the capital to start such a thing?"

"For the first time in my life, yes." She takes a sip of wine, letting the smooth liquid swirl over her tongue before swallowing. She hasn't thought of her former dreams for a long time. Probably a bit more than she can take on if all goes according to plan in Amsterdam, but she's having fun entertaining the idea.

"If you do the research, find the right location and create a thorough business and marketing plan, I bet you could make a success out of it," Fokke says as he leans forward in his chair, taking her right hand in his.

"I could showcase your photography on the walls," she adds. The flicker of candlelight is reflected in his eyes, giving him a slightly dreamy appearance.

"We could open it in Amsterdam, fill it with my chair collection," Fokke continues as he pulls her hand to his lips.

"See? My dream in Sappada was prophetic." She gazes at him, mellowed by the wine as she thinks about the version of "we" that is Fokke and Sarah. In what world could such a we exist?

They get on the topic of her lost cell phone, and how it ended up in the canal. As she recalls the story, she doesn't mention that she was hoping to get a message from him, but shares a simpler version of the epiphany she had about herself: she likes her own company.

"Didn't you like your own company before?" he questions.

"I used to when I was younger. But Matthew, my ex, he had a way of undermining my self-confidence. I don't know how to explain it, but I also let it happen. After eleven years in his shadow . . ." Sarah stops mid-sentence. She might be sharing too much. This man, her temporary lover, doesn't need to know she had a confidence problem. Or perhaps still does. She doesn't realize how much her thoughts are affecting her until she feels his finger brush across her cheek, catching a single tear in its wake.

"You don't deserve all those things he put you through," Fokke's smile is gone.

"I know," she responds, dabbing her face with a napkin. One single tear. *It's a beginning*, she thinks. It won't stay bottled up forever.

Sarah can't put her finger on it, but there's something about his words, as if he knows much more than she's told him in their short time together. Like the way he wasn't at all surprised that she is deathly afraid of the dark; takes it in stride so easily that her husband cheated on her; the way he seemed to intuit she needed space to explore the little record store they came upon yesterday afternoon; knew just where to rub her shoulders last night to alleviate tension she didn't even know she had; seems to have a personal roadmap to her erogenous zones. Or is she just not used to someone paying attention? Someone that kind?

"How do you seem to know so much about me?" she asks, gazing at Fokke in the soft candlelight. Her heart is opening to him so quickly she doesn't think she can stop the process anymore.

Fokke doesn't shoot back a casual answer, but stares at her, his lips drawn into a tight line.

"Well, I don't know that much about you, but there's something I need to tell you."

His voice is deeper than usual.

"What? What do you need to tell me?" A shiver runs up her spine as her mind races. *So it's true! He does know more than he should about me. But how?* Scenarios flood her mind during his moment of silence and she catches her breath. "Do you know Gregory Golder? Did he hire you for this? To be my companion?" She realizes it's an impossible scenario, but at the same time, she wouldn't put it past Gregory to take his gift to her to this level. "Or Matthew? Is this some sort of—"

"God no. Sarah. No one hired me. I don't know your ex or Gregory Golder. It's nothing like that."

"What exactly is it, then?" she asks, holding her breath as fear pierces her.

"I read your diary," he admits, letting out a deep breath.

"What? How much? When?" she gasps.

"A fair bit," he admits as he pushes a hand through his thick hair. "I read it while I was still trying to figure out how to contact you."

"Well, you couldn't have read much, then," she replies carefully, her mind scrambling as she thinks about all of the intimate things she has recorded in the last month. Not to mention the journal entries her therapist asked her to work on during the trip. *Holy crap! God. Please. No.*

"Well, unfortunately—oh, Sarah. Please don't be pissed—I read a lot. It was while I was waiting in the snow on the return trip to the lodge. Before I even met you."

His face wears an expression she has not seen earlier: shame. Damned right he should be ashamed.

"I know so little about you, and you know *everything* about me." She is staring at him like he has morphed back into a stranger; not the gentle, honest, romantic man she thought he was. What can she do with this? Everything is not what it seems. She stands up abruptly and accidentally knocks over her wine glass, which shatters at her feet. The other patrons in the restaurant turn toward them, staring for a moment before continuing their conversations.

"Stay here Sarah. Please. Let's talk this through." His voice is firm.

She wraps her pink wool overcoat around her, grabs her purse.

"I trusted you. I liked you," she says angrily. "I was even beginning to think I . . ." She catches herself just in time, her eyes narrowing. "You've played me like the fool I am, Fokke. I'll make sure your bag is at the front desk."

"No, Sarah. Please. I—"

"No. Just stop!" She cuts him off. She glares at him one last time before she walks away. Fokke gets out his wallet and waves to the waitress, but she's occupied at another table. Sarah is already out the front door, turning left. He throws far too many euros on the table, grabs his coat and heads out after her.

She's fast. He almost misses her disappearing down an alley way between tall apartment buildings as she breaks into a jog. He heads after her.

"Sarah! Please! Come back!" he calls, but she keeps going. He realizes he's going to have to work to keep up with her. He is running now, giving chase as she disappears behind another corner.

The sun has already set. The alleys are narrow, poorly lit, but she keeps going.

"Sarah, stop! This isn't safe!" he calls after her. He sees the flash of her pink scarf in the street light. They are paced about a half block from each other, but she's gaining distance.

"I don't want to chase you!" he yells. But she pushes harder, her arms pumping as she heads over a bridge. *Christ, she's fit*, he thinks as he breaks into a sprint. He is suddenly grateful for all those hours spent on treadmills in luxury hotel gyms across the world, because it means he can keep up with her. He doesn't want to grab her, but doesn't want to lose sight of her either. As he closes the distance, he intentionally stays a few lengths behind her, his footsteps echoing down the stone alleyways. Another ten minutes pass and his legs are growing heavy, his eyes straining against the darkness, but he knows she has to run it out. She's just a few feet in front of him when she finally begins to slow down. He slows as well, keeping the distance between them. He can tell by the way her shoulders are rising and falling that she is shaking, crying. He reaches for her hand, but she pulls away. They walk side by side, both trying to catch their breath.

"I'm sorry," Fokke repeats quietly.

"How could you do this to me?" she asks, not looking at him as they walk. Not tears, he realizes. She is heaving with anger.

"You were a total stranger then. I thought I'd give you your backpack and never see you again," he pants, wiping his forehead. "I didn't know we'd end up here . . . wherever the hell here is," Fokke adds, looking around them. He can't believe it. She's finally done it. He's lost in Venice and can't get his orientation.

"That's no excuse," she responds bitterly, turning toward him. She sees the light of a cigarette burning in the distance behind them. Someone is watching them, witnessing their lover's quarrel. She is suddenly aware of how isolated they are; how quiet it is, save the sound of their own footsteps and breathing. And the darkness. God. She has acted carelessly.

"I know. It's not right. But I'm so glad you left that Matthew asshole, Sarah. That you're free of him. And about your mother . . . my condolences." Fokke is all shadows, his face barely visible in the darkness.

Her imagination jumps into overdrive. She hears something moving behind them, tries to peer into the darkness, but sees nothing.

"God. You know about my mom, the betrayal, about my inner thoughts, my fantasies, my fears."

Fokke flinches, resisting the urge to take her hand and force her to face him.

"Yeah. I do. I know you're working through some doubts. That you're deathly afraid of the dark too, Sarah; even though I don't know why. That's why I had to find you when the lights went off at the lodge. Remember? That's why I gave you space. Didn't push you into anything you didn't want. Because I know what you've been through. Is it so bad what I did?"

Just ahead of them, the grayish white steps of a footbridge loom out of the darkness. Soon they are in the middle of the bridge over a canal, the same sort of bridge on which she had imagined a couple might get engaged.

She finally stops, turning toward him. "You lied to me." Her sweat is cooling quickly on her skin and she shivers.

"I might have kept it to myself, but no. I didn't lie to you. Please, Sarah, tell me there's some way I can make it up to you," he implores.

There is movement again and she sees someone approaching.

"Behind you," she whispers to Fokke, her voice firm. He whirls around, arms up. There are two figures coming at them fast.

"Don't move azzhole. Give me wallet, and you lady, give me purse," says the silhouetted figure closest to Fokke in broken English. The second figure masked in darkness approaches.

"Listen. We'll give you our wallets, but don't move any closer," Fokke responds as he juts his arm into the air in warning, his deep voice menacing yet strangely communicative.

A bright beam of light pierces the darkness, darting into the eyes of the two assailants. Fokke takes advantage of their temporary blindness and punches the man closest to him in the gut before angling another punch into his nose. All hell breaks loose. Sarah hears movement behind her on the footbridge and whirls around to discover a third man. He lunges toward her, but she quickly steps to the side. Her combination of punch, roundhouse kick and cross punch send him yelping to the ground. She spins back around just in time to see Fokke taking a blow to the shoulder, but Fokke kicks forcefully down into the man's knee, which twists into an unnatural position. Fokke pushes him hard and he topples over the other man he has already knocked to the ground. The darkness around them lifts as the moon peeks its half-face over the rooftops.

"Let's get the fuck out of here," Fokke yells to Sarah. But she is coming toward him as one of the three men begins to scramble to his feet.

"Cover your eyes and mouth," she warns Fokke in a whisper as she aims something at the man's face. Fokke covers his face just before the air fills with a nasty pepper smell.

"Merda! Puttana!" The man yells as he raises his hands to his eyes. She sprays another dose on the man at her feet. All three men start coughing and cursing as the pepper spray fills their lungs.

"Now let's get the fuck out of here," Sarah returns in a muffled voice, her scarf over her mouth and eyes. They run into the night, side by side, their steps echoing on the brick pathways which are easier to see in the half moonlight. After they've put a healthy distance between themselves and the three men, they finally slow, panting for breath. They look behind them straining into the silence, but they hear no one. Two streets up they enter the glow of electric light and they are suddenly out of the maze in a more prominent location. The restaurants with their cozy lights and the presence of other people on the street create a sense of safety.

"I think we're okay now," she says, her voice strangely calm given the circumstances as they move into the light. "I'm really sorry I put us in that situation."

"Partially my fault," Fokke admits, thinking of his earlier confession. "But damn. You were amazing back there, Sarah. I wouldn't want to run into you in a dark alley!"

She laughs nervously as the insanity of what just happened catches up with her. "Thanks. I think you're supposed to just hand over your wallet in a situation like that. But I was just so worked up, I couldn't think straight."

"You were thinking plenty straight. Flashlight blinding them, pepper spray. Not to mention kicking the shit out of that one guy."

"I think you're right. My language classes might not have gone so well, but self-defense? I've been practicing for years for a moment like this. And clearly, you know how to fight as well," she remarks.

"Yeah. Comes with the territory of traveling for a living. You've got to know when to negotiate and when to fight." Fokke looks over at her. "And where did you get the pepper spray? It's illegal in most of the countries you've visited."

"How do you know which countries I've . . .oh yeah," she flinches. "But yes. I know it's illegal. That's why I made my own."

"My God. You look so innocent. I had no idea," he shakes his head as he pulls out his cell phone. "I want to figure out where we are, get us back to the hotel."

Sarah can't help glancing over her shoulder a few more times as they plan their route, sticking to the main streets. They see a semi-crowded bar.

"Let's duck in here, Sarah. Get off the street."

They order a large bottle of water, thankful for the warmth and change of scenery. They talk a bit further about the confrontation before dropping into silence. The reason Sarah ran out on him looms over them, spoiling the cozy atmosphere of the bar.

"If this is the end of us, I'm going to seriously rethink the old adage 'honesty is the best policy.'" He untucks his button-down shirt and uses a corner to wipe his face.

"I don't want to punish you for being honest, but I might have a solution," she replies.

"What would that be?"

"You can read me your diary."

"What diary?" he asks, clearly confused.

"The one in your backpack. With Jackie."

"Oh. No. I can't," he retorts.

"Why the hell not?"

The grooves on his forehead, otherwise barely noticeable, wrinkle into furrows of concern. "That diary is old, Sarah. I was a mess. I don't want you to see me that way," he answers slowly.

If it's old, why are you carrying it around Europe? she wonders. Nevertheless, his excuse irritates her. "And what am I? A dream come true?"

Fokke is about to answer in the affirmative, but she's not done.

"Let's see: Divorced, cheated on, alone, mourning my mother, scared of the dark, struggling with my self-confidence. But you know all that, don't you? I can't be anything else in your eyes but a broken person."

Fokke stares at her and gently touches her cheek. "I don't see you that way. I promise you." He is looking her in the eyes, and she is aware of how handsome he is; thinks of how he made love to her just last night. Was that attraction or pity? She takes a sip of water.

"Have you been feeling sorry for me? Is that why you've been so incredibly loving to me?" She is whispering now, quieted by her words.

He leans closer, catching the pear and jasmine scent of her perfume, all the more intoxicating when infused with her sweat. "Don't second guess me, Sarah. Want to know what I think of you?"

"Yeah. I do," she challenges. He places his hands on her waist, facing her in the booth.

"You're intelligent, kind, honest, sexy as hell. I'm totally attracted to you," he begins. Sarah's lips are trembling. "And even though I know you've been through hell and back, may feel vulnerable after all you've been through, you are most beautiful to me because you're a real woman, not afraid to share what's going on inside of you."

She's shared a few things, but he's read so much more. She wants to smack him; to kiss him. "I'm so confused, Fokke. I, I believe you. But you have to make this right."

"How?"

"I'll tell you how. Get your damned journal out of your bag and start reading." She sees it on his face; fear.

"It's not with me. It's in my backpack in the hotel."

"Okay. You've bought some time," she says gently, evoking a smile on his face. "But when we get back to the hotel, you read to me. With a translation."

"Okay," he grunts, as if signing a treaty of surrender. "But promise me, no more running unless we're in our sports clothes out for some exercise. I'd like to walk back to the hotel like a civilized person."

"I promise," she smiles.

As Fokke types in the address of the hotel into his phone, she is almost disappointed. She is cold, scared, vulnerable, exposed, but invigorated. She, Sarah Beth Turner, kicked some ass in a darkened alley way! Right now she wants to be lost with him in the dark, wants the time to process what is going on between them; because even though he has read her diary and it feels like a betrayal, he didn't run. He stayed, came after her. Loved her and spoiled her. She is still mad as hell about the diary, yet she is aware of one, overriding thing: All of the carefully laid plans she has made for her future are shifting before her eyes as she tries to picture a way to make Fokke van der Veld a part of them.

Chapter 31
Journal

It's approaching midnight by the time they finally make it back to the hotel. They are tired from the full day, not to mention the emotional rollercoaster they have been riding, the chase, that crazy encounter with thieves, their exchange on the walk back to the hotel. The last remnants of Sarah's anger wash out of her in the shower, but a promise is a promise. Once Fokke is done with his shower and sitting beside her in his sweats on the bed, she pours them two glasses of wine, sits next to him and nods at his bag.

Reluctantly, he retrieves his journal and sits back down beside her. He thumbs the journal as he clears his throat, but he doesn't open it. As he hesitates, Sarah thinks again of all the personal things she has written in her journal; from little observations and insights, to heart-wrenching sadness about her mother, about her marriage falling apart; the battery of tests she took to make sure she didn't contract any sexually transmitted diseases from the betrayal; how she desperately wants a baby. He's read all of it.

"Start from the beginning, and translate," she orders.

Fokke clears his throat again as he opens the journal.

"Ik ben kapot van binnen," he starts. "En ik weet niet of ik ooit nog heel zal worden." His grip tightens on the journal. "I am broken inside. And I don't know if I will ever be whole again," Fokke translates.

"De wolken dansen in de hemel, en een majestueuze reiger vliegt hoog voorbij; maar ik zie de schoonheid niet. Ik ervaar alleen de pijn van jouw verraad. The clouds dance in the heavens, a majestic reiger um, heron flies overhead, but my eyes are blind to beauty. I experience only your betrayal." He switches to direct translation as he reads. "I think only of the son I wanted, loved, as he grew in your belly. The love I felt for you, in the truth that we conceived him together, with intention. Blessed after six months of trying."

"Stop," Sarah says, putting up her hands. "I'm sorry I asked you."

"No. It's just getting good." There's a darkness to his voice. "We have prepared our home to welcome our son. The midwife says the contractions are close together . . ." Fokke is shaking, his voice breaking. "Come, see your son being born."

Sarah grabs his hand. "I'm so sorry. Stop!" she implores.

Fokke drops the journal, but the story flows out of him. "I held her while she pushed. Helped her bring a child into the world, but not my child." Fokke describes the red-haired, freckled baby that could not possibly be his. How he recognized the features of the Irish neighbor in the baby almost immediately. How Fokke broke at that moment.

"That is so awful," Sarah gasps. "I didn't realize, when you told me before, what exactly you went through." She shakes her head back and forth. "You didn't deserve that." Whatever anger she might have felt toward Fokke earlier this evening, it is nothing compared to what she feels toward this woman named Jackie whom she has never met.

"I know." He rubs the back of his hand over his face. "It's been over a year, Sarah, and I still can't get my head around it. How she could do that to me." Fokke sets his full glass down on the bedside table.

"Did she ever apologize? Explain how it happened, I mean . ."

"I never gave her a chance," Fokke admits. "I shut her off."

"Maybe that's why it's still lingering. You never had closure. Maybe a part of you is still holding on to her," Sarah ventures.

"I haven't loved her for a long time now." He breathes in deeply. Just saying these words seems to clear the air. "But I still have the letters she sent."

"What did they say?" She sets her glass down too, turning toward Fokke to give him her full attention. She realizes the irony of sitting in this fancy hotel talking about his ex. Another reason to detest this woman. But she knows that there are always two sides to a story.

"I don't know. I never read them," he admits uncomfortably.

"But you kept them," she says. "So you're still holding on."

Sarah sees the creases in his forehead deepen.

"Yeah. I think you're right. But I sure as hell would like to move forward, extricate those memories from my mind." Fokke has picked up his journal and is flipping through it rather dejectedly.

"Two wrongs don't make a right. You don't have to read anything else," Sarah apologizes. "I'd rather get to know you naturally, over time." She takes his hand in hers and brings it to her lips.

"Me too, Sarah. Sorry again that I read it. The last thing I want is to be another jerk that breaks your trust." The dogged look on his face tells her he is doing his best to right the situation.

"I'm glad you told me," she realizes out loud. She ponders him, this man she's known just over a week, who is so familiar, yet so mysterious, hidden to her. How he has looked inside her, read her like a novel in her own words. That he wants to be here, even after reading all of that. "I still feel weird about it, but considering you came to stay with me after reading everything; well, you definitely have a strong stomach."

He reaches toward her face, pushing a curl behind her right ear.

"I'm not the type of man to have a love affair with a stranger. But given the circumstances that threw us together, topped with having read your diary . . ." he gazes at her with a resoluteness that makes her feel naked and vulnerable, yet beautiful. "Your words gave me insight into your pain, but also your depth, your kindness, your sense of humor. It broke down my armor," he admits.

She is taken once again by his honesty, realizing that she's not the only one who is vulnerable.

"I'm glad I was able to break down your armor, because you've got a wardrobe of it," she responds. "But I wish there'd been another way."

"It's not just the journal," he confides. "Do you remember that morning I was showing you my travel photos? You got me. You looked at those pictures and it was like you knew my thoughts, my motivations." He is thinking in particular of her comments on the gauchos of Argentina; her insight into those nomadic travelers she has never even met.

"You seem to get me too, Fokke," she responds, her breath short, a bit husky.

As his eyes graze over her, the familiar heat of desire returns to her body. She shivers under his gaze.

"Fokke, can we get under the covers?"

"Yeah. I'm beat after having to chase you all over Venice and fight off bandits," he grins.

"That was pretty crazy. I'm sorry."

"I'm sorry too, but you were amazing, Sarah." Fokke switches off the light and pulls her into his arms. She presses her body against him; a physical admission that she has at least partially forgiven him. They lie in the darkness, neither talking as they get used to the post-fight feel of each other's bodies.

"Fokke," she says into the darkness.

"Hmmm?" he murmurs.

"We have something in common. Both betrayed; both still holding onto it in our own ways. I don't want to be a victim. I don't think you do either. We cannot give them that. Not ever again." Her words are strong, coming from some previously untapped source. "I don't want Jackie or Matthew here in this room with us. Let's throw them in the canal, be done with them. We are far too wonderful to let their negativity pull us down."

Fokke's grip on her tightens. When his words come through the darkness, they are strong and clear, edged with excitement. "That is the best damned idea I've heard all year," Fokke says. He gets out of bed, pulling the covers off of her.

"What are you doing?" she complains as the cold hits her.

"Come here. Stand up," he orders, reaching for her hand.

She rises and stands beside him, curiosity waking her. He opens the window overlooking the canal, a sparkling, slithering creature in the moonlight. He pulls a box of matches out of his backpack.

"Um. This is a non-smoking room," she points out.

"Not planning to smoke anything. Just to perform a much more satisfying act," he says as he retrieves his diary from his backpack.

She watches as he brings the flame to the edge of the well-worn journal.

"You sure about this?" she asks as the pages start to curl from the heat.

"Yeah. I had planned to do this on this trip. I was just waiting for the right moment."

They watch together as the flames lick through the paper.

"Now what?" she asks in alarm as the flames grow larger.

"Damn!"

"Drop it in the canal, quick!"

Fokke is the last person who would throw trash in the canal, but as the flames reach three inches in height, he realizes he hasn't thought this one through. A fire in the hotel room would be just the thing to make this already crazy night even crazier.

Sarah disappears into the bathroom and comes back with two glass cups of water and throws it over the journal. Fokke lets the book drop onto the open windowsill, but the fire is not yet out. He grabs the cups and runs to refill them, dousing the journal a second time and the flames are finally out.

"Feeling better?" she laughs as she looks at the charred remains of his journal.

"Much better. Anything you want to burn?" he asks.

"No. I'm good. I did a lot of burning, ripping and cutting back in Oregon before I left," she admits.

"Really? Like what?"

"Oh. Photos, lingerie he bought me over the years, his credit cards and, well. . . I destroyed his golf clubs."

"Damn, woman. How did you do that?" Fokke asks.

"I have a friend who's a welder. We made a nice sculpture for Matthew out of his TaylorMade clubs flipping the birdie, which I placed in the middle of the front lawn the day before I left for Europe."

Fokke can see the glee in her eyes. "You're brutal. I'm not letting you anywhere near my golf clubs."

"Wait. There is one thing," she realizes. She goes to her pack, and digs to the bottom, pulling out a pair of ugly gray socks.

"Those have special significance?" Fokke laughs. But then he notices the serious look on her face as she unravels the socks. The ring falls onto the floor and bounces, the band of diamonds glinting in the moonlight.

"This," she says. "I was going to sell it, and buy something nice . . . but I hate this ring. It would feel like blood money; you know?"

"Are you sure? I bet that's worth, well . . ."

"About twenty-six grand," she responds, tension in her voice. "Titanium, with a full circle of diamonds. He made sure I knew how much he spent on it."

"And you've been carrying it around Europe with you?" Fokke asks in disbelief.

"Yep." She picks it up and heads toward the window. "For a moment just like this."

"Hold on Sarah. Please. I have a better idea for this ring than hanging out at the bottom of a canal in Venice. Invest in your cause café, or another cause you believe in."

She is leaning out the window, her hand outstretched. The ring is balanced on her open palm, glinting in the moonlight. He watches her, sees the hesitation.

"You're absolutely right," she replies as the palm of her hand closes firmly around the ring. "But that would have felt good." She lets out a deep breath as she drops the ring back into the sock, and tucks it into her backpack. She shivers and Fokke kisses her suddenly, pulling her close.

"Thank you for that. Finally alone," he whispers in her ear. "Just you and me."

"Just you and me," she responds.

He nibbles on her earlobe, whispering a series of words in her ear that make her shiver with excitement. "Unless you're too sleepy," he adds.

"I'm completely awake," she murmurs.

"Good," Fokke responds as he pushes her back on the bed.

She thought she knew what it was like to be ravished by this man, but this time is even more intense, and far more free and intimate. She is lost in her lover, her body and mind opening to his gentle touch. As they make love in the darkness, she does her best to stay in the pleasure and warmth of the present moment and not think of her post-vacation life: a life without travel, adventure, freedom or Fokke van der Veld.

Chapter 32
Proposal

Fokke wakes early and is greeted by the sight of Sarah lying next to him fast asleep. In the last three days in Venice he has learned the contours of her body; has come to know the cadence of her laugh; knows that she is ticklish behind her knees; has discovered multiple ways to bring her to orgasm. Through hours of talking, he has also come to know her hopes and desires, and she, his. He has witnessed her delight in taking in the history of the city around her, her insight into the pulse of the culture, into him. He is tragically aware that his desire to wake up next to her each and every morning to come is born of fantasy.

Today she will move on to Padua. They have decided he will rent a car and drive her there before he flies back to The Netherlands in time for his fraternity class reunion.

He gently takes her hand in his, knowing this small act will not wake her. He contemplates the feelings resonating within him—bliss, desire, contentment—as the sun rises. When the church bells begin to chime, she stirs, her blue eyes opening, bringing him into focus.

"Hey," he says.

"Hey," she responds sleepily, a smile lighting up her face. She stretches before hopping out of bed to use the restroom. He knows she will brush her teeth and hair and drink a tall glass of water before coming back into bed with him; that they will kiss, perhaps make love again, or simply hold each other for a while before starting their last day together.

They haven't talked about the future, besides a rough outline of today, and how nice it would be to meet up in The Netherlands if the timing is right.

She crawls back under the white covers, minty breath and shining curls and cuddles up next to him, holding on tight. His right arm is pinned beneath her head and he bends it, rolling her into him. He takes the opportunity to kiss her. Her eyebrows are bent downward, a sadness on her face that comes, he thinks, from the knowledge that today is their last day together. He kisses her deeply and feels her response, sees her arch a bit toward him. But then she shifts, sits up in bed, her pink camisole falling slightly off her shoulder.

"Fokke, I need to talk to you about something kind of serious," she sighs.

"I'm okay with serious," Fokke says, not sure if it's true.

"Let's sit at the table, have some coffee while we talk," she suggests.

"Ah. It must be serious if it requires coffee," he teases, kissing her forehead.

While the coffee brews, he pulls on a robe over his naked frame and sits down at the table across from her. After she pours them both a cup, she breaks the silence.

"I want to tell you about the Amsterdam appointment. I know you read about it in my journal."

"Great. I've been curious about that. 'On Thursday, November 16th at two o'clock in the afternoon, my life will change forever.' How can I not be curious?" Fokke smiles at her. She sees the kindness there, meant for her.

"There's that photographic memory again," she comments, realizing that this could very well be the last time he smiles at her so warmly. "What I'm about to tell you might upset you, or you might understand it. But, either way, I think you should know so we can explore, um, whether or not we want to take a next step together."

This doesn't sound promising, he thinks. But he nods for her to continue.

She takes in another deep breath, exhaling slowly. "If you recall in my journal, I mentioned that I want a child," she begins, looking at him evenly.

"Yeah," he confirms. He does his best to keep his features even, to hear her out.

"I've wanted a baby for a long time. Matthew and I tried, but we couldn't conceive. Ended up the problem was on his side. Long story short, I just turned thirty-seven as you know, and my window of fertility is closing quickly." She pushes a loose curl behind her ear, which he's come to recognize as a sign of discomfort.

"Go on." His mind is already guessing where this is going.

"I'm going to Amsterdam to visit my grandma, but that's not all." She inhales, as if mustering up the courage to continue. "I'm going to participate in a program offered by the PNC Institute to help single women get pregnant." She looks at him, presumably trying to gauge his reaction.

"Wow. That's not quite what I was expecting you to say, but it makes sense. You're taking action to fulfill one of your greatest desires." He tries to smile at her, but he can't get his facial muscles to cooperate.

"Yes, it's a big deal for me," she states evenly.

"So you're doing an in vitro fertilization program?" Fokke asks. "Seems like a long way to come. They've got that in the U.S." He takes a long slow breath, trying to keep calm.

"No. It's a different program that's in one way, much less invasive. No artificial hormones, no removing my eggs and placing them back in."

"So, what? Sperm donation and a more natural insemination process?" he asks, carefully controlling the rhythm of his voice against the tension forming in his body.

"You seem to know a lot about this," she shifts uncomfortably.

"Well, between trying to get pregnant with Jackie and the fact that my younger sister just went through in vitro, I know a bit about it, yeah." Fokke's discomfort is growing, but he wants to hear her out; support her in her own decisions. He reaches for her hand, feigning an understanding he does not yet feel.

"So, how the PNC program works is that you're paired with a donor and you conceive naturally." The red splotches over her cheeks confirm that he has not misheard her.

"Are you telling me that you're going to have sex, with a stranger . . . to get pregnant?" Fokke asks, his voice eerily calm.

"A stranger; well. Yes and no," she falters. "It will be someone chosen based on a long list of criteria, plus blood analysis to reduce chances of incompatibility."

"Christ," Fokke whispers, pulling his hands from hers. Whatever calm he was holding onto just moments before has given way to anger. "You couldn't have told me this before we slept together? Or at least, before I came here? How could you keep something like this from me?"

Her eyes are big and watery. She is looking at him with something akin to love laced with sadness as he stands up, suddenly uncomfortable with his half-naked state.

"It's not exactly something you share with a stranger or a passing affair."

Fokke flinches at her words.

"I'm telling you now, because you feel like much more than a fling to me, Fokke." She swallows, aware of the stern look on his face. "And, I have a proposal for you."

"What proposal?" he asks, even though he is already mentally packing his bags. *She was never mine. She used me. One last fling before taking the plunge. I'm the fool once again*, he thinks.

"I could cancel my participation in the whole program if you want to be my donor; if you want to get me pregnant." Her eyes are shockingly wide, as if she can't believe she has actually asked him.

The pureness of her suggestion—he the father of her child—fills him with a warmth he thought he would never feel again in this lifetime, perhaps has never felt. But the warmth just as quickly fades as a thousand other thoughts enter his mind. He is locked in silence as he tries to process the tumult inside him.

"Please, Fokke. Say something," she implores.

"I've known you for less than two weeks, Sarah. How can I commit to being the father of your child?"

"I know it's a big question." She folds her arms over her chest uncertainly.

"It's a hell of a question. Especially since you know what I've been through already on this topic." He looks at her, his stern expression penetrating her. "And if I'm ever going to get a woman pregnant, I need to know that she's mine, that we love each other, that we'll raise our child together." His blue eyes transfix her. Freeze her in place.

"I know that about you Fokke," she replies, her gaze steady.

He glances toward the bed where they have made love multiple times in the last three days; where he has come to know her intimately. But this admission of hers has blindsided him, left him reeling. "How can I respond to this?" His confusion is rampant as he listens to conflicting voices within him: He wants to be a father; he doesn't know her; he has fallen in love with her; he's just met her.

"It's way too soon. I get that. I just, I want a child so badly. My clock isn't only ticking, it's winding down. Plus, the longer I wait . . . I want a healthy child." Her effort to control her emotions is no longer successful. She bites her lip as the swell of feelings within her threatens to turn into tears. "Can you just think about it, Fokke?"

He sees her struggling with emotions she cannot handle and her expression disarms him. A part of him wants to comfort her, but he forces himself to keep his hands at his side.

"I can't help you here."

"You could. I've been tracking my temperature, taking the Ph tests. I'm—"

"It's a beautiful idea, Sarah," he exhales heavily. "But it's also naive. We can't jump into that situation. There's a million reasons not to." His words sober him, breaking the spell between them.

"What is a big enough reason not to take a chance in life? On love?" She has finally admitted her feelings; is holding her breath, waiting for his reaction.

The obvious answers come to the forefront: they live in different countries; his travel schedule would make him an absentee dad. But then a bigger, highly charged issue pushes its way to the surface. "And what if we don't conceive? What then? Are you willing to give up your dream of motherhood to be with me?"

Sarah pauses, uncertainty clouding over her.

"No. I didn't think so," he answers his own question. "And then you'd want to go ahead with the program, go have sex with another man to get you pregnant. Do you think that's a scenario I would want to go through?" he asks as he stares into her panicked eyes.

"I would never want to put you through that," she says, her voice shaky. "You're right, I haven't thought it all through." She leans her head into her hands. "I'm sorry, I just, I feel so connected to you Fokke. Like we could work together. Love one another. It seems like a real possibility."

He can't stand it anymore. He has to stop the pain flooding him. Has to push her as far away as possible. He steels himself as he forms the words that will set him free.

"I feel close to you too, Sarah, but this is what a travel fling is like— intense, emotional. It feels very real right now, but in a few weeks, you'll have forgotten all about me." He watches the shift, sees the pain in her eyes as if a part of her is breaking in half.

"Is that how you think of me? As just a travel fling?" she asks.

No, I don't. I feel so much for you, he thinks. But he cannot, and will not put himself in the position of having a woman choose someone else—another donor, a baby—over him. Now that he knows he can't have her, he wants the rest of her to leave as well; leave him to his solitary, screwed up life.

"Yeah," he says. "I've been through this a dozen times. Great connection. Hot sex. Caught up in the moment. But now it's time to move on."

PART THREE: IF ONLY

Chapter 33
Amsterdam

He arrives at his old fraternity house with a sheen of rain on his crisp blue suit, his gray-streaked blond hair a mop of wet curls that give him an unplanned wild look, though he is hardly wild; at least not anymore. The four-story brick building with its old glass windows and wooden doors with brass knockers are just as he remembers. Behind the doors is the entry hall with its worn parquet floors; the living room with stone fireplace situated on the first floor, a wall of windows with spectacular views over the canal. One of the oldest in Amsterdam, his fraternity is tucked away in the trendy Jordaan district. He is the third generation of van der Velds in this fraternity, and although he didn't turn out to be a famous lawyer like his grandfather or father, he is one of the more famous members for far less prestigious reasons.

"Van der Veld! His lordship has finally arrived," Theun Tijman greets him at the entry. Tall and lean like Fokke, Theun has made a name for himself in the brewing industry. And like a good alumnus, supplies the fraternity with beer for their reunions, this year being no exception.

"Good to see you Theun!" Fokke would rather be behind a camera lens quietly observing, but as the one-time president of his fraternity, he's on the other side tonight. He does his best to tolerate his former classmates pulling him in for a selfie, one after the other.

His speech about why their fraternity is the best in The Netherlands is met by deafening applause by the seventy or so men in the room. He is offered a cigar by a scrappy blond kid named Lennart who doesn't seem old enough to be drinking the beer in his hand, let alone hold the position of the current fraternity president. But that's what happens; the older you get, the younger these university students look. Despite the twenty-one-year age difference, he and Lennart have a few things in common: height, charisma and a devilish wit that motivates the men around them.

"Any advice old man?" Lennart smirks as he lights Fokke's cigar.

"Yeah. Don't insult the person from whom you're asking advice," he counters as they pose for a photo together. The glass pitcher with *van der Veld Foundation* taped on its front is already half full with euros and bills, which elicits his first heart-felt smile of the evening. He's genuinely thankful for their contributions, but what truly amazes Fokke is how his old fraternity brothers—those with whom he hasn't kept in contact—treat him like a celebrity because of the travel writing. True; his name is on the guide books, in the in-flight magazines. Yes he's been all over the world. But these aren't the only reasons his brothers, young and middle-aged alike, flock to him. They think he's living the bachelor's dream; has a woman, they say, in every port. He did bed quite a few beauties during his fraternity days and continued this behavior into the first few years of his career, but it's been over a decade since he gave up that part of his persona. Breaking hearts loses its appeal after a while.

"So what's your count?" they ask. "Which nationality is the best in bed?"

Even though they have it all wrong, he laughs along. He knows this is not the time to get pissed off because some drunk old classmates think he's a womanizer. He was president of his fraternity all those years ago for good reason: he knows when to react, when to lay low, when to roll with it and when to set the record straight. And right now, it's about forgetting the worries in his life and bonding with the boys in the most juvenile way—for one long weekend being impossibly young again.

He sees Jan, Peter and Barometer on the far side of the room. His feet trace a familiar path across the old parquet floor beneath the dusty crystal chandelier. They are by a large window, the warbled glass letting the cold into the second floor of the fraternity house. *We need to upgrade those windows to double glazing,* he thinks as he reaches his buddies.

"Top speech there Fokke," Jan says, raising his beer bottle.

"Thanks," Fokke replies, blowing a smoke ring.

"Nice impersonation of your younger self," Barometer adds. "Eloquent, with an air of devilishness. You've still got it."

"Considering you're on a never-ending vacation, seems like you're the envy of every man or man-child in the room," Peter comments.

What irony, Fokke thinks. *Do Peter and Barometer know I envy them? Their loving marriages? Their children?* Fokke shakes his head, the cigar smoke wafting into the air. "That's why we're all here, denying the pending mid-life crisis."

"And you're our denial poster child," Barometer states.

If only he knew how true his words are, Fokke cringes. He can't even think about what he did to Sarah earlier today without a crushing wave of self-loathing.

"Let's get fucked up!" he shouts. Peter, Barometer and Jan can't help but laugh at his sudden outburst. And so the debauchery begins. The four friends, in an alien, yet completely familiar setting, add whiskey shots to the mix. Time blurs, surges forward, slows down. People he hasn't seen in a decade or more merge into the conversation and disappear again. They have polished off an entire bottle of whiskey when Paul Akins heads their way.

"Ah. Finally, a bigger celebrity than you, Fok," Peter blurts out by way of greeting Paul. Just one year younger than Fokke, Paul Akins served as secretary on Fokke's board all those years ago. Now he's a television producer in England, best known for cooking and gardening shows.

"Looks like my four minutes of fame are over. Good to see you Paul," Fokke smiles.

"Likewise, mate. You're just the person I wanted to see." Paul flashes him a commiserating grin.

"I know you're British, but I don't remember you being the type to say *mate*," Fokke banters.

"Wife's Australian. You pick up the strangest speech patterns after being married to an Aussie for fifteen years and raising four boys, all with Australian accents."

"Understandable. So, what can I do for you? Some travel advice?" *More salt for the wound*, he thinks; everybody but he and Jan are apparently married with children.

"More than that. I've got an idea for a show, and you would make the perfect host," Paul claims in a silken voice.

"What do you mean by host?" Fokke inquires.

"You know. The handsome, forty-something man with a European accent traveling around the world, staying in posh, yet undiscovered lodgings, sharing his tips on local cultures and cuisine, visiting the markets of Marrakesh, the temples of Borobudur."

"Doing that already as you know," Fokke returns. He is vaguely aware that the alcohol has subdued his heartache and guilt to a tolerable numbness.

"Yes. But I'm not talking about writing, Fok. Or just a YouTube channel. I'm talking about a whole new level; your own travel program on international television, earning way more cash than the royalties from those books and articles or the adverts on YouTube could possibly bring in. Not to mention fame."

Why is it that these exec-types always think it's about the money and fame? Frankly speaking, Fokke has enough money. His books are still selling and the travel channel he started two years ago is extremely popular. The ad revenue alone is enough for him to live off, should he care to. He's

211

not earning a ton, but he is smart with money and frugal by all accounts—besides his chair collection.

"I've got enough money and fame. What I need in life is love. And everyone knows, money can't buy you love," Fokke states sarcastically, despite the truth in it all.

"Your life is a fucking Beatles song my friend," Jan chants, causing a round of laughter.

"Well. I take it you're no longer with Janie?" Paul inquires.

"Jackie. Nope."

"And no other love in your life?" Paul asks. His friends await his answer with curiosity.

"Only capable of star-crossed love, apparently," Fokke muses darkly, exhaling a cloud of smoke. "Now. Why do you think I'm your guy?"

"I conducted a test with a group of middle-aged housewives, our main demographic. Your photo received the highest scores."

"You're such an asshole. When did I give you permission to do that? Which photo?" Fokke is annoyed, yet curious.

"What does Fokke have to do with your middle-aged housewives?" Peter interrupts. He is thinking about his own wife who regularly watches *Grey's Going Gourmet*, one of Paul's biggest shows featuring a celebrity chef with the muscular build of a professional rugby player.

"The photo on the cover of your travel guide for Vietnam that came out last year," Paul replies to Fokke. "And we're contemplating a new series," he nods at Peter.

"That was a pretty hot photo," Barometer says. "According to Genevieve, my wife," he clarifies.

"Your wife thinks he's hot?" Jan asks. "With that banged up nose and graying hair? Not to mention a bit of girth over those abs."

"They all think you're hot," Paul concurs. "And you do something for the thirty-something second-time-around poppies."

"Women who want to go again in the same night?" Jan again, up to his usual crassness.

"No, Jan. Divorced women looking for a husband, fantasizing about the perfect male with which to reproduce," Paul explains.

Fokke's face drops. Sarah qualifies as a second time around poppy. Was all that desire and connection just a side-effect of my looks? I appeal to her demographic?

"You okay Fok? You look pale." It's Peter this time. The responsible father-figure checking on his friend. "Are you going to puke?"

"I'll be all right. Didn't get much sleep the past few nights," Fokke says as memories of Sarah Beth Turner flood him. Regret pecks at his heart with the tenacity of a mythological bird of prey sent to punish him for his crimes. He obviously isn't drunk enough, he decides.

"Ah. Sleepless nights. We'll have to hear about your doomed love later," Barometer winks.

"Here's my card. Put this in your wallet before you puke. I'm serious Fok. You could be huge. A new stage in your career." Paul is giving him a look that conveys both seriousness and excitement, as if saying to Fokke— *this is your big chance in life. Don't screw it up.*

"Whether or not I'm soft on the eyes, I'm not cut out for television. I'm not going to wear make-up and read any scripted text, get a nose job or do product placement," Fokke raises his eyebrows dismissively. He doesn't like the hard sell. Never has.

"Doesn't work that way. You'll have more editorial control than you think," Paul ensures him. "Though a nose job's not so bad an idea."

This garners a round of laughter from his so-called friends. "So get over your star-crossed lover and give me a call. I'm serious, Fok. You could be the European version of Rick Steves."

"Trying to piss me off, Paul?"

"You know I do my best."

After celebrity Paul makes his exit, Fokke and the guys help themselves to another round of beer. They give a shake of appreciation with their bottles in the direction of their brewer fraternity brother Theun Tijman, who raises his bottle in return.

As his thoughts take another detour toward Venice, Fokke nabs a second bottle of whiskey from behind the bar and declares a drinking competition. Peter, Jan, Barometer and two others sidle up to the bar and the game is afoot.

With Paul out of the picture, young fraternity men start hovering around Fokke again, proposing ridiculous questions: Does he need an assistant on his next trip? Can he mentor them in the art of seducing a woman? He'd like to put an end to these rumors, but what can a man do?

"He just finished seducing an American woman he met in Italy," Jan announces cheerfully, clearly inebriated.

"I've always wanted to do an American girl," a young man says, laughing along with Jan. Fokke has had enough.

"Leave Sarah out of this," he snarls.

Both men pause, staring at Fokke.

"Touchy, touchy," Jan replies good naturedly.

It is clear how these rumors keep circulating; misrepresentation. He turns toward the young man, squaring up to him.

"You want to know about travel writing or want more information about my charity? Give me a call. As far as the Don Juan thing, that's in the past," Fokke states loudly. But the young man only smiles with clear admiration, refusing to let go of the legend. Wisely, he drops a wrinkled ten euro bill into the van der Veld Foundation pitcher on the counter before moving away.

Emotions Fokke has been defiantly suppressing with logic are coming to life through Tijman's generous provisions of beer topped with whiskey shots. And the resulting internal boxing match is getting uglier by the minute. Has he made a mistake saying no to Sarah's proposal? Pushing her away? He could be with her right now, making love to her with the intention of creating a child together. *What a bunch of sentimental crap! She's headed to Amsterdam to fuck a stranger; someone more a stranger to her than you are! She'll get pregnant and be on her way back to America. You know you care about her and she cares about you. She asked you to be that man, and you're the chicken shit asshole that walked away.*

"Fugg that," Fokke says out loud.

"Fuck what?" Barometer asks.

"Nothing," Fokke mumbles, shaking his head.

"I think ish time to head back to the hotel," Peter slurs.

"Yeah. I'm beat. Haven't been up 'til three in the morning since Stephanie was a baby," Barometer states in a crisp, articulate voice, a happy twinkle in his eye.

***

They are walking in the middle of the street, which has very little traffic this time of night, save for other people on foot or cycling past. Moonlight ripples across the canal, reflects in the glass windows of the gabled houses along the Herengracht and Fokke recalls Sarah in the moonlight.

"I'm a total fugg up," he says to no one in particular.

"No you're not, Fok," Peter responds as he walks beside him.

"Greatesht woman I've ever met and I pushed her away," he mumbles. "She was right there, reashing out her hand, and I couldn't get out of the tar pit."

They walk in silence, but Fokke doesn't offer any more words.

"You want'r back? Then go after her," Jan puts in.

"Nope. I don't deshurve her. Must ferget her." Alcohol might have obliterated his ability to speak, but his heart seems rather sober.

"This schmight be a good time to give you this," Peter drunkenly returns. Fokke opens his hand and Peter places a business card into it. "Sheesh very good. Eashy to talk to. Doeshn't push you too hard, but also gets to the point."

"You setting me up with a proshtitute?" Fokke asks belligerently. "Think I can forget Sarah by banging another woman? Do I sheem that fugging shallow to you?" He sways, almost stumbling.

"The card's for a therapist, Fok," Peter chuckles as he reaches out his hand to steady him.

"Don't need a fugging ferapisht," Fokke replies. But he pockets the card anyway.

"The hell you don't," Jan counters in a voice just as slurred as Fokke's as he flanks Fokke's left side, Peter on the right. The three friends weave down the street unevenly as Barometer leads the way.

As they approach the hotel, Fokke contemplates the odd feeling of jealousy he experienced over Barometer's memories of his daughter's infancy. As he broods, another image breaks into his mind; Sarah telling him he is lying about how he feels about her; lying that she is no more than a travel affair; the pleading look she gave him as she all but begged him to contradict her. How he'd stubbornly stuck to his bullshit story until she finally walked out of his life for good.

As he lies face down on the hotel bed in his clothes, his mind throws another punch his way: Thursday, November 16th, 2:00p.m.—a date and time in the not-so-distant future when her life will change forever.

Chapter 34
Descent

The two-hour flight from Rome to Amsterdam is going smoothly. Sarah sips on her tea as she writes an entry in her journal with some ideas for an Alexi post. Her thoughts begin to drift into painful territory and she reaches for the in-flight magazine to distract herself. She mindlessly peruses the luxury watches and jewelry she will never purchase. She turns the page and heat slams through her. There is Fokke, staring off the page with his baby blues directly into hers. Next to his headshot is a short article about the *van der Veld Foundation*. She closes her eyes for a moment, trying to adjust to the shock running through her system, before she continues to read. Her stomach tightens as she reads about his non-profit that helps people in rural communities in Benin and Guatemala by providing access to renewable energy.

In the middle of the article is another photo of Fokke in Benin. He is standing in dusty red soil, earthen huts behind him. He is flanked by smiling African children and adults holding up notebook-sized solar panels attached to lamps and cell phones. His short-sleeved dark blue t-shirt shows off his strong arms and brings out the blue of his eyes.

Of course. Not only is he handsome and smart, he's doing good in the world. *Except when he's ripping my heart out in his spare time. Fuck you, Fokke!* she thinks as she rips the page from the magazine.

She listens to the announcement through the overhead speakers, first in Dutch and then in English. The plane is making its final descent. She puts her chair in the upright position as instructed and slips her journal into her purse. She peers out into the dismal weather, seeing an impenetrable blanket of clouds.

Rain pelts the windows as the plane descends below the cloud line. Neatly organized squares of green fill the landscape. Slowly, Amsterdam, with its mix of picturesque brick buildings and canals in one direction and modern skyscrapers in the other comes into view.

She clears customs and then waits for her backpack to appear on the baggage carousel. Finally, she is heading out the glass doors and into the crowd. Her grandmother Nettie is waiting for her in arrivals. Sarah admires the shock of gray hair streaked with blonde; her grandmother's strong legs; her elegant, yet practical clothes. Nettie waves as she approaches and embraces Sarah with enthusiasm, giving her three kisses, alternating between cheeks.

"Welcome to The Netherlands, Sarah!"

"Thank you Nettie!" Sarah cries. "It's so good to see you!" She hugs her back and the two women take an escalator to the underground train platform, chatting away. Sarah likes the feel of her grandmother's arm linked with hers. She is taken back to earlier times, when she and her grandma would go out on the town, commiserating about the current family or school drama.

"Are you hungry, tired? What should we do first? Want to drop your bag at my flat and go to a museum? I know how you like museums," Nettie asks as she squeezes Sarah's arm.

"Let's go to your flat. I'd love to just have some tea and talk. There'll be plenty of time for museums in the next few weeks."

They catch a train to Amsterdam's central station and then hop on a tram. Sarah marvels at the crowded streets and the bicycle paths packed with cyclists. The tram is also crowded with people of all ages and nationalities. The smell of pot fills the air and she can't tell if it's coming from a teenage girl in a black dress and skull-and-crossbone-patterned tights or the Japanese tourists sitting across from her. Men and women of all colors dressed in business suits stand in the aisle speaking in rapid Dutch while an older middle eastern couple take pictures out the window. The tram drops them near the Jordaan quarter, a pretty neighborhood along the Rozengracht canal, which stretches out of sight in both directions flanked by narrow, uneven streets and rows of three- and four-story canal houses. As they walk along the street, she welcomes the slight drizzle of rain, which seems fitting to her mood.

They walk past ground floor businesses and Nettie stops at a blue door nestled between a restaurant and a cigar shop.

"This is us," she announces, as she places a key in the lock. Sarah gazes upward at the narrow building flanked on both sides by ground floor businesses with two story apartments above. All three share a similar style of gabled roofs, a small sculpture adorning the front of each. The angel above Nettie's apartment causes Sarah to smile. They climb the stairs to an unexpectedly spacious modern apartment. Sarah places her backpack in the room where she will be staying for the coming weeks, freshens up a bit and joins her grandmother at the kitchen table.

Nettie pours her a cup of tea from a red ceramic teapot Sarah recognizes from her grandma's house in America. She glances around the room, looking for other familiar objects to tie this contemporary flat to the rambling farmhouse her grandma and late grandpa had in northern Oregon. But there's no trace of the heavy wooden furniture and glass cabinets that used to display all of the knick-knacks that were part of Sarah's childhood: an entire collection of owl figurines, Navajo baskets and jewelry, her grandfather's seashell collection, the abundance of clashing artwork. Where is all that now?

The walls in Nettie's new flat are taupe, and a single framed photograph—a black and white of a cityscape Sarah believes to be Chicago—hangs on the north-facing wall. Low slung leather and stainless steel chairs sit on either side of a glass reading table decorated with a single pink tulip in a crystal vase next to two art books.

"This flat is very modern Nettie. You wouldn't expect it from the looks of the outside." Or having seen her grandma's tastes while living in America. How can someone change so drastically? But then she thinks of her own house filled with eleven years of accumulated objects and memories from which she simply walked away.

"A pleasant surprise. Isn't it? The exterior is a classic Dutch canal house, dating back to the 1820s. They left that intact, but completely gutted the inside during the renovation. I love the clean lines, the simplicity."

Sarah smiles at her grandmother, nodding her head, while thinking about the owl collection, wondering where it could be. Perhaps Nettie misses her husband and doesn't want reminders to pull her back to those last few painful years of his life before he passed. But what about all of the good years? Don't those require a few bric-a-brac reminders?

"I have so many questions for you Sarah, but where to begin? How is your grand solo adventure?"

"Amazing. Eye opening. Stimulating." *Heartbreaking*, she thinks. "I'm a bit travel worn, to be honest. Ready to stay in one place for a bit."

"Understandable. I'm so proud of you for doing this. You've made some brave steps," Nettie nods at her granddaughter, as if placing an exclamation point on her thoughts. Sarah knows that Nettie is not only referring to her travels, but to her bravery in leaving Matthew and her year sabbatical.

"I couldn't have done it alone. Once Gregory came up with the proposal to fund my trip as a means of getting back at his ex-wife, there was no talking him out of it. I have to say; I enjoyed the idea of Katie fuming, knowing I got the luxury European vacation that he'd promised her. Serves her right of course." Sarah doesn't want to think about Katie and Matthew wrecking two marriages, breaking a circle of friendship, destroying a business partnership, putting themselves before everyone else. She thinks of Matthew as a little speck of waterlogged lint floating in that canal in Venice and her thoughts settle down.

"Not worrying about money made it a whole lot easier, but it's been a big trip, teetering on the verge of overwhelming. But it's changing me for the better, making me stronger." Sarah lets out a sigh. It's so good to talk openly.

"You've always been strong, Sarah. But that marriage faded you. I see a light in your eyes I've missed." Her grandma is beaming at her with an expression that reminds Sarah of her own mother. She feels a lump in her throat, a catch of emotion.

"Thank you, Nettie. But I'm not feeling much light right now."

"What's troubling you?" Nettie questions.

Sarah thinks for a moment. "This next stage, actually. The PNC Institute. If I will conceive. If it will be a healthy baby. That's part of it." Sarah rubs her temples. Her grandmother nods compassionately, her face open, attentive. "But also the idea of raising a child without a partner. Wondering if I should wait. Give myself a chance to meet someone naturally, see where it goes." Her thoughts gravitate once again to the Dutch travel writer she fell for, who opened her heart and then threw her away out of his own fear. Sarah isn't sure she wants to talk about Fokke and what it meant to her, but if anyone can help her sort through her emotions, it's Nettie.

"It might take a while before your heart is ready to open up to someone else, Sarah. You need to heal first." Nettie is holding her tea cup in her hands, a kind look on her round cheeks.

"You're absolutely right, grandma. My heart needs to heal, but . . ." Sarah drifts off.

"But?" Nettie encourages.

"I fell out of love with Matthew quite a while ago," Sarah admits. "I didn't realize it until he betrayed me. I felt hurt, angry, empty. My heart was broken. But not in the sense of having lost the love of my life." Sarah takes a sip of her tea as the pieces fall into place. "But I've discovered something else in the last six weeks." She looks up into her grandma's eyes, pleased to see the acceptance there.

"And what did you discover?"

"I like me. And I don't ever want to lose myself to a man again." Sarah pulls the sides of her Irish cardigan closer to her body, as if it is a shield.

"I like you too. I love you, as a matter of fact. And I don't want you to lose yourself to a man either. But, I wouldn't mind if you found love with a man who honors you for who you are," Nettie says softly.

Sarah feels the pressure in her eyes building. "There's more. Remember the Dutch man? The backpack mix-up?" she sighs.

Nettie observes the heated look on Sarah's face. "Based on your expression, you mixed up a lot more than your backpacks," Nettie states.

"Yeah. We did." She can feel the blush on her cheeks, but not out of embarrassment. She is used to talking candidly to Nettie. "Fokke van der Veld. I loved my time with him."

"Well. That's great. Are you going to see him again?" Nettie inquires.

Sarah takes a sip of her tea. "Nah. It was just a, you know, a travel fling," she tries out. The words sting her, but she keeps her face neutral. "And, considering my next step with the PNC . . ."

Her grandmother nods with understanding. "Did he tell you what he does for a living?" Nettie asks curiously.

"He's a travel writer," she begins. "He's also a talented photographer." *An amazing lover and the man who truly broke my heart.* The idea shocks her. Does she really believe this? How could Fokke have broken something that was already broken? But the idea stays with her.

"Honestly? Travel writing? Van der Veld is a common name. Could be a coincidence, but, just in case." Nettie sets down her tea cup and walks out of the room with a spring to her step. Sarah shifts uncomfortably as Nettie returns with a stack of books. "Is this your Fokke van der Veld?"

Sarah stares at Fokke on the cover of each travel guide, his last name boldly printed across the front. She flips one open, eyeing him in Agra, India, that familiar glint of humor in his eyes. She picks up another and there is Fokke, ten years younger on the cover of *van der Veld's Peru*. His hair is completely blond and there are less wrinkles around his eyes. His body is just a bit more chiseled, but besides that, he looks astonishingly the same.

"I had no idea he wrote to this extent," Sarah sighs again, touching the cover longingly with her fingers. "I wish I could read Dutch."

"They're translated into English, German, French and countless other languages. I'm surprised you haven't heard of him," Nettie remarks as she observes her granddaughter. Sarah is quiet, contemplative, lost in her thoughts.

Seeing him yet again pulls at her. Searing pain shoots toward her tear ducts. *I could have loved this man.* Her heart races at the idea of love. But then she remembers Fokke dismissing her as a travel fling. And despite calling upon her best counseling skills to see if he was just saying this out of fear, he stuck rather convincingly to his story. *If this is love, it is of the unrequited version*, she thinks.

"I really fell for him, Nettie." She gazes at the cover photo, concentrating not to cry. She recalls with humiliation the proposal she made to him, how he came back at her with a whole list of reasons it wouldn't work. "I really mistook what we had together as something bigger. I'm so naive. It was stupid of me to open myself up like that so soon," she says as she pushes the books away from her. "I'm pretty sure he did more damage to my heart in seven days than Matthew in all eleven years."

Thankfully, Nettie doesn't press her with any questions, but simply pulls her into an embrace, holding her until all of the pent up tension she has been holding back comes to a head and breaks free. The sobs wrench her body as the tears finally begin to flow.

When she is all cried out, Nettie slowly releases her.

"Wow, grandma. We skipped all the small talk, didn't we? Aren't you supposed to ask me about April and the twins?"

"How are April and the twins?" Nettie asks as they break into laughter. Sarah blows her nose, and wipes away her tears before giving her grandmother a rundown on her siblings; their successes and trials; how April wants to come for an extended visit if Sarah ends up getting pregnant. When they get on the subject of Annemieke, Sarah's mother, Nettie's daughter, another wave of emotion passes over her.

"You look so much like her darling. Your long blonde curls, your big blue eyes."

"She always dyed her hair brown," Sarah points out.

"I know. But not when she was a girl. She had your gold. She was such a lovely child."

"And a wonderful mother," Sarah adds. "How are you holding up without grandpa?"

Nettie's face softens and her eyes go damp. "I miss him every day, Sarah. He was the love of my life; always will be. But I know he's in a better place."

Sarah wants to know true love like that. As Fokke enters her mind once again, she sighs. *I apparently have a lot to learn before I can recognize true love.* She won't be fooled again.

Chapter 35
San Antonio de Areco

It has been two years since his last trip to Argentina and he still can't believe his luck in getting the annual Gaucho festival assignment in San Antonio de Areco—one of his favorite festivals on the South American continent he has attended only once before. The story concept he pitched to *InDepth Travel* was not only accepted, but comes with generous pay, includes travel costs, his room and board and all fees to attend every aspect of the festival. To his surprise they have also asked him to submit his own photography.

He is fascinated by the diversity of colors, sizes and builds of the hundreds of horses he has seen in the last week and equally in awe of the rough and tumble gauchos who ride them. Nothing better to take his mind off romance than Argentinian cowboys and the distinctive smell of horse sweat.

His first few days in the high-end hacienda doing endless laps in the sparkling swimming pool made the transition from cold Amsterdam to the hot November spring quite pleasant. But it isn't until he moves to the bare-bones hotel farther from the banks of the Areco river that he connects with the culture and emotion all around him.

The nightly "asados," or barbecues over open fires, are festive, the local people friendly and welcoming. The ballads claiming the night air seep into his lungs, pulsing through his blood like a transfusion. If he listens to this pulsing, he has the sensation of having been born in the Pampas, growing up riding the vast open plains.

He feels intensely alive and at the same time detached, as if he is an unbiased observer that can delve into the gaucho culture around him. He recognizes this as the space from which he does his best writing, honing in on the right words to describe the experiences unfolding around him. But it is also a space in which to exercise caution. Otherwise you can be swallowed by it, lost in its depths, which can lead to a case of cultural vertigo. It happened to him in Tibet three years ago and in Java the year before that. The only way to reclaim yourself is to shift back into your own cultural garments, re-enter your own history, and no matter how appealing, cast off the charms of that foreign world.

He nods in appreciation as the half-empty wine glass in his hand is refilled by a young woman who smiles at him shyly. Too much wine and he will lose the prose that will make his travel article stand out from the rest. Caution, balance, while going with the flow.

He hopes he can keep this balance in the next phase of his career. He thinks back to his meeting with Paul the day before his flight to Argentina. Fokke had pitched the idea of doing a travel show that explores the local culture as well as the local environmental issues threatening the culture.

"Environmental issues are trendy right now, but that would be a depressing show," Paul had responded.

"What if you turned it around? First the environmental problem," Fokke began.

"And then what people are doing about it, and what people can do," Paul jumped in, finishing Fokke's thought.

"Bring light to the local heroes while informing people how to contribute during their visit," Fokke added.

"A simple luxury travel show is what I had in mind, but this eco-element. Hmm. Let me ponder it."

Paul Akins hadn't pondered it long. The handsome contract arrived yesterday at Fokke's hotel outlining the concept and terms: A nine-month trial period followed by a three-year contract if the target markets responded favorably to his environmental travel television series. Who knew he could just pitch his dream job to his old buddy Paul and have him fund him to do it? More hours of travel; a lucrative contract that far outweighs what he makes in travel writing, and the chance to make a difference. It's the perfect offer. All he needs to do is sign the contract.

***

He looks across the campfire at a gaucho strumming his guitar, singing slightly out of tune, surrounded by others.

The gaucho is a stoic figure, Fokke notes in his journal, *a nomad disconnected from society except for these rare, festive occasions.* The gaucho pulls a smart phone out from under his poncho and starts texting. Fokke frowns, revising his last line of text.

There is a feeling he can't shake about these gauchos. Despite the cell phone and the camaraderie he is witnessing at the moment, he knows they should be lonely men, considering all the time they spend on the range, in the Pampas, on their own. But there is an air of satisfaction around them, as if they are completely at ease with their nomadic lifestyles—his kindred spirits.

He recognizes the contented look in their eyes as a reflection of himself. He too has been perfectly content with his own company for years of journeying across the world. He eases into this idea, but his shoulders can't quite fully relax into the comparison.

***

The second to last night of the festival, as he sits digesting a gluttonous amount of barbecued meats, a group of young women, girls really, eye him from across the fire. He recognizes the pattern: quick glances followed by hushed whispers and giggling—local girls egging each other on to approach the tall, blue-eyed foreigner. To his surprise it isn't the confident, full-bodied girl in the white dress with plaits of black hair roping down her back that approaches him; but a wispy girl in a jade top embroidered with flowers, shirt tucked into baggy jeans tethered to her thin frame by a large leather belt.

"Hello mister, you enjoying the asado? Having enough to eat?" she asks in a sing-song voice.

"Yes. Thank you," he responds. When his gaze reaches her eyes, she swallows.

"Where you from, mister? America? Europe?" she asks, emboldened by some unknown force. Singapore or Vietnam, South Africa or Argentina, it is all the same; they want to know where he's from, what he does, what he thinks of their country, if he's single.

"The Netherlands," he answers. Her black eyes are deep and mysterious, her youthful skin a glorious earthen shade. Under other circumstances, she could have been a runway model or featured in fashion magazines. He obliges her questions for a few more minutes before letting the conversation taper off. After he politely declines her invitation to join her and her friends for an after-party, she eventually excuses herself and heads back to the safety of her girlfriends.

As the young beauty leaves his side, he wonders why he doesn't have it in him to say yes. A three-word answer to his query boldly jumps to the surface: Sarah Beth Turner.

He feels her presence, sees her dark blue eyes, that sad smile of farewell as he watches her walk away. His eyes smart and he wipes at them. *Smoke from the fire irritating my eyes, making them water*, he justifies as he pushes the thought of her away once again—a technique he has been working hard to refine since that last day in Venice.

The following day he explores the small shop fronts, happening upon a furniture maker. Before he knows it, he has ordered two custom butterfly-style chairs made of tanned saddle leather with hairpin iron frames. On his ninth and final day of watching the festivities, from the Argentinian take on rodeo known as the "jineteada gaucha", the riding games and parades to the nightly musical performances and dancing, Fokke has the sensation of coming down from a high.

It is noon. From his front row seat along the parade route he watches the endless line of horse and riders going by. He realizes the close of the festival also means a return to his real life; a return to the issues that have been pressing for his attention.

A man on his steed corrals a herd of white horses into a tight formation inches from where he is standing. Fokke startles as a horse bucks toward him and he looks up, suddenly catching the dark eyes of the gaucho who brings the horse back under control. There is an unexpected smile on his weathered face as his gaze shifts from Fokke to something just over Fokke's shoulder. Fokke turns, following his gaze and sees the young woman waving to him, witnesses the intimate glance she sends back to the gaucho. There is a flash of recognition; not of what they have in common, but where they differ. It is in this moment that the spell is broken. He is no longer interested in championing the nomadic lifestyle, of being the poster boy of a single man, he realizes with a jolt. Although he has been perfectly happy with his own company for miles of journeying across the world, he wants more. He wants Sarah.

He feels his phone vibrating in his pocket and flips it open. A message from his agent: *You're trending on twitter, pictured with vlogger broadcaster Alexi—an overnight sensation.* He steps away from the crowd, annoyed that someone else is using him for a popularity stunt, but as he clicks onto the link and sees the photo of himself, his arm linked with Sarah's, he stares in disbelief. *Alexi is Sarah's pseudonym for her travel vlog,* he realizes. But who would post a picture of them together? Only someone who recognized them both; who knew about both of their identities.

He leaves the parade and heads back to his hotel room and logs onto his laptop. Within a few seconds he has found Alexi. The latest vlog alone has over 260,000 likes. He scrolls through the recent posts. He selects one with a particularly devastating title and listens to Sarah talk about love and loss in Venice, how she trusted too soon and had her heart broken, a story to warn all females everywhere about the risks of a travel-romance. Although she doesn't mention his name, someone has made the connection and their story is out in the world. But it's the wrong story, he realizes. *I am in love with Sarah Beth Turner and I've made the mistake of a lifetime by letting her go.*

This time, as she enters his mind, she is sitting on a throne over his heart. She's on the inside, and no amount of wall building can protect him now. No coaxing words or rash epithets can dislodge her. And that is how he comes to call Sarah from the South American continent on Tuesday, November 14th in the middle the Gauchos parade. As the phone rings just two days before her life will change forever, he prays with all his heart that he's not too late.

Chapter 36
Hutspot

On Tuesday evening, she and her grandmother prepare a leafy green salad and "hutspot," a hearty Dutch dish Sarah remembers from childhood. A mix of cooked potatoes, carrots and onions all mashed together, hutspot is perfect for a cool evening like tonight. Though she has no connection to this contemporary flat besides Nettie's presence, the familiar flavors of the hutspot combined with the warmth of the food relaxes her, reminding her of home.

Sarah is still reeling from the news her sister April shared with her three days ago. Her Alexi vlog has been redistributed by a few popular vloggers and she is suddenly an overnight sensation. Though her identity has been protected thanks to her sister's IT expertise, she has made a novice's mistake: she posted about her heart break, which has somehow gone viral. At least no one knows who she is, or who broke her heart.

"That framed picture in your room. Who took that?" Nettie asks as she lifts her glass of wine to take a sip.

Sarah stops mid chew, staring at her grandma. "Why do you ask?" she mumbles.

"You look vibrant, vulnerable," Nettie contemplates. "As if the person on the other side of that camera excites you."

Sarah hears the delicate choice of Nettie's words.

"Fokke," she says at long last.

"Oh," Nettie responds, her voice clipped. She has done a bit of undercover work over the past four days, learning more about this man who clearly broke Sarah's heart.

Sarah doesn't pick up on the tension in Nettie's voice as she continues. "He took that picture in Cortina, before we spent another three days together in Venice," Sarah explains. She tells Nettie about their reunion, leaving out many of the more intimate details, and talks about her feelings for Fokke.

"He might have seemed amazing, but he left you in the end, didn't he?" Nettie states.

Sarah cringes at her words, wanting, despite her own pain, to give Fokke a bit more credit. She tries to put herself in his shoes; imagine the reverse situation. *What if Fokke had been a donor at PNC? Was planning to get a stranger pregnant through unprotected sex just weeks after his affair with me? Wouldn't I be upset?*

"Sarah? Are you okay?" Nettie asks, her concern hovering over Sarah like a thundercloud .

"I just wonder . . . if there was any way for Fokke and I to work out."

Nettie recalls what she has learned about Fokke van der Veld through her network: purportedly a woman in every port, perhaps all feeling as broken-hearted as her granddaughter.

"No use contemplating something like that. Especially with your upcoming appointment."

Chapter 37
Travel

Her voice on the line jolts him out of his South American stupor.

Thanks for calling. Apparently, I'm doing something more exciting than answering my phone at the moment, but the least you can do is leave a message. I promise to call you back.

Her tone is friendly, confident. He is disappointed to reach her voicemail, but hearing her voice again confirms his feelings. He can picture her walking beside him, oblivious of the men slowing to gaze at her as she holds his hand. He wonders where she is right now. Amsterdam is seven hours ahead. He glances at his cell phone. 12:37p.m. That makes it 7:37p.m in his home country.

She could be eating dinner, or out for an evening run. *Or on a date with one of her potential partners from the PNC Institute.* He hangs up. As he peers out the window at a cluster of horses grazing in the pasture, he is gravely aware of the solitary life he has chosen for himself, the contract awaiting his signature. But he can't get her out of his mind, and if he doesn't act now, there's no turning back.

He hits re-dial, this time clearing his throat in preparation as he waits for the beep.

"Hi Sarah. It's Fokke. Fokke van der Veld." He pauses, gathering his courage. "I can't stop thinking about you. Please don't go through with your appointment the day after tomorrow. I have a proposal of my own that I'd like to discuss with you in person."

He hangs up, terrified yet relieved. He has spoken his mind. He has asked her to wait.

With close to a terabyte in photos and a notebook full of notes and interviews, Fokke's work in San Antonio de Areco is pretty much done. He foregoes the rest of the parade and the closing ceremonies. He packs quickly, hoping he can get on standby for a flight back to Amsterdam this evening, rather than his scheduled departure on Friday. *Friday, when it will be too late*, he thinks.

***

Through some small miracle aided by a fair amount of pesos distributed into the right hands, he manages to get a seat on an overcrowded bus back to Buenos Aires. The acrid smell of body sweat and cigarettes; the rapid staccato of Spanish and the guarded looks that come his way are a familiar cocktail in his life of travel. He settles into the balance, neither staring at, nor ignoring those around him.

As the energy of the people in the bus slowly settles, he gazes out the window, seeing very little. His thoughts are on the research he did on the PNC Institute before he left for Argentina. The Planned Natural Conception Institute *'creates a place for women to conceive naturally and safely'*. Why should this seem like such a radical idea? Not surprisingly, the institute already has a growing number of participants from around the world. He is both proud of Dutch ingenuity and open-mindedness in this matter, and at the same time extremely perturbed. He doesn't want Sarah near the place.

The miles and miles of open space interspersed with farmland and the occasional outcropping of homes too small to call a town finally give way to larger settlements as they approach the outskirts of Buenos Aires. Fokke takes his time to formulate his plan, and sure enough, he realizes what he wants to do. But he can't pull it off on his own. He flips open his phone once again and hits one of the few speed-dial numbers he's programmed in.

"Fokke! What a pleasant surprise," his mother's voice is breezy and cheerful.

"Hey Ma. How are you?"

"What? What is it?" she asks immediately, hearing something in his voice.

"I'm fine. Don't worry, but I need your help with something." As he explains what he needs, he can almost hear his mother smiling with relief through the phone as she scribbles down the list.

"I have some of these things digitally, but that's a pretty long list! I'll definitely need your sister's help to get half of these scanned in."

"If you could call her and enlist her help, I'd really appreciate it. I need it all emailed to me before my flight takes off, which is in about three hours."

"You're not demanding at all, are you?" she sighs. "And may I ask what you need all of these things for? School counseling positions? Are you considering a career change? And all the photos? Starting a scrap book? A personal blog?"

"You'll know soon enough . . . one way or another," he answers cryptically.

"Okay. Fine. I'll do my best, though the scanner has been giving me trouble lately. Have you decided about that TV show yet?" she asks.

"No. I have until noon on Friday to make my final decision."

"If you're still undecided, that's a sign right there."

"Usually, I'd agree with you. But I'll explain everything when I'm back."

"You need anything else you just call me, darling."

"If I think of anything else before the flight takes off, I will. Thanks Ma."

"And Fokke?"

"Yeah?"

"You sound a bit out of sorts. I know you're a grown man and perfectly capable . . . but please, take care of yourself."

"Don't worry. I will."

He'll have the entire flight to assemble his plan and figure out exactly what he's going to say to Sarah. Only after that—he feels once again the nagging presence of the unsigned contract—can he plan the next phase of his life.

Chapter 38
Morning Jitters

When she awakes on Thursday morning, the day of her appointment, Sarah's mind is racing. She rolls out of bed and reaches for her journal and pen and props herself up with two overstuffed pillows. Her pen races over the paper as she tries to keep up with her thoughts.

I have come to a few conclusions about travel: It can distract you from your worries, allow you to escape by the mere presence of 18th-century canal houses, their stepped gable roofs glinting in the sunlight. Ordinary experiences, like being caught in a downpour in Amsterdam, or entering a small café at sunset in Berlin to get the last cozy table are somehow transformed into the extraordinary. I attribute this to my senses cataloguing the differences in sights, sounds, smells and telling my brain how special it all is, which makes me feel exciting and alive, a part of something bigger.

But travel can also have another effect, acting like a microscope to your soul— forcing you to face your demons, clarify your dreams and hopes. I know from hours of exploring Europe and basking in its history, that I am curious about life in a way I haven' t been before, like I have awoken from a sleep I mistook for real life. I acknowledge that I have a whole lot of fears I need to work through, but I love my newfound freedom. And I love travel.

But I also know that I feel somehow bound to Fokke van der Veld. Our short time together was more than a travel fling— or just a romantic entanglement in an exciting setting. I felt alive in a way I haven't felt in years, yet comfortable, like I could be my entire self in his presence. And this bond I feel leads me to believe that my appointment this afternoon with the PNC Institute is a betrayal to Fokke.

But how can I betray someone who has told me he doesn't want to be in my life? I have to throw him into the canal. Not for dislike. On the contrary, for the very fact that I am in love with him and he is not mine to love.

Sarah puts on her sweats and boots, quietly slips out of her room and walks down the three flights of stairs to the ground floor exit. She steps into the soft morning light, glancing skyward toward the darkening clouds. She shuts the blue door behind her and crosses the brick street to the canal. The photo that Fokke had taken of her, the one that captures her vulnerability and trust is clasped tightly in her hand. She feels none of the anticipatory satisfaction she experienced when she was about to hurl her old wedding ring into that canal in Venice before Fokke had stopped her. Now, as she releases the photo in her fingers, there is only a sense of loss.

That's a shame. I was rooting for him, Sarah. Hoping you'd keep him. Her mother is in a thin summer jacket, much too light for the late autumn weather, her arms frail as she wraps them around her body. Sarah wants to reach out to her, hug her; comfort her, be comforted by her. *Fokke is the one that didn't want to keep me, not the other way around*, she wants to scream at the image in the water.

The choking and belching of a boat engine starts in the distance, the first ripples of its approach breaking the stillness of the water's surface. She stares at the image, which seems to be both her and her mother undulating with the rippling water and she reaches for it, sorry for her hasty decision. She looks around wildly, searching for a branch, something to retrieve the photo as the water presses upon it, pulling it under. But it is too late.

Sarah wanders back over the street to the blue door, opens it with her key and climbs up the staircase to the flat. After a short, hot shower, she opens her bathroom kit and as she reaches for her toothbrush, she notices the turquoise glass perfume bottle. She doesn't dare to remove the lid to release the jasmine and pear blend that embodies the most romantic time of her life. She's tried to throw it away three times over the last few weeks, but she can't bring herself to do it. Sarah transfers the perfume bottle into her purse, wanting this last symbol of Fokke to be with her on this important day.

Her stomach is knotting up by the time she approaches the breakfast table. Nettie gives her beschuit, a terribly dry round toast, and a bottle of 7up. Miraculously it settles her stomach right down.

"Not too late to change your mind," Nettie offers.

"I haven't changed my mind. This is what I want," Sarah says, weighing the words for their honesty as they fall over her ears. Yes, she realizes. This is the option available to her. This is what she wants. But there is still a niggling feeling, a residue of hope.

"You haven't seen my phone, have you?" she asks her grandma.

"When was the last time you remember having it?" Nettie responds, not meeting Sarah's eyes.

"Wednesday afternoon, when I went out for my run."

"Well, it's got to be here somewhere, and if not, there's always that 'locate my phone' app," Nettie suggests. "Everything is trackable."

"Good point. I'll do that when we get back," Sarah responds, impressed with her grandma's phone savvy. When Nettie lived in the U.S., she never had a cell phone. Now she has a cell phone, a laptop and an upscale contemporary flat.

"Do you want me to go with you this afternoon?" Nettie asks, pulling Sarah back to the moment.

"To the entrance, like we discussed. But the rest . . . this is the type of appointment I need to do on my own," Sarah sighs, dropping her face into her hands. Nettie hesitates, sees the struggle and fear wending its way through Sarah's shoulders, her neck. She recalls the longing she saw in her granddaughter's features when she looked at the cover of *van der Veld's Peru*, the outpouring of emotion and despair. A ripple of anger washes over her as she thinks of the heartache this man has bestowed on her sweet granddaughter Sarah.

"Are you sure you're emotionally ready for this, darling?" Nettie gently taps her fingers on Sarah's hands.

"Is anyone ever emotionally ready to have sex with a stranger to try to conceive?" Sarah offers a half-smile.

"This is just the intake interview. I don't think they'd have you just jump right in like that. But just in case, try to keep an open mind. Remember, this is your choice."

"I know, Nettie. I know. And of course you don't start the physical part at the first appointment. It's orientation, signing of contracts. Details like that."

* * *

The Institute is not what she expects. Rather than the clinical white walls and modern furniture she had envisioned, the center is housed in a converted 19th century residence with high ceilings. The lobby, with its warm wooden floors and Persian rugs must have been a living room. Comfortable lounge chairs, couches and a coffee table with baskets of fresh fruit create a welcoming atmosphere.

A woman in jeans and a white silk top with a tablet in her hands greets them.

"You must be Sarah Beth Turner?" she asks like an old friend.

"Yes," Sarah answers, not quite at ease. "And this is Nettie Turner, my grandmother."

"Nice to meet you both and thank you for being right on time. I'm Esther. Mrs. Turner, you can wait here in the lobby. Sarah, please come with me."

Her grandmother gives her a smile of encouragement before taking a seat in the lobby. Sarah follows Esther past a series of closed doors to a little office that must have been a bedroom at one point. Sarah gazes past the desk to the windowsill lined with potted plants, the light green leaves offering cheer against the gray sky.

"I'll need to make a copy of your passport," Esther says.

"Yes. Of course," Sarah responds, handing it over.

"Thank you. Have a seat. These are your intake forms. Take your time filling them out and Mr. Kuipers will be right with you," Esther smiles.

"Mr. Kuipers?" Sarah asks.

"Doctor Kuipers. He will review all of your answers."

"Okay," she answers timidly.

"No reason to be nervous, Sarah. Can I get you a cup of tea? Coffee?"

"No. I'm fine," Sarah responds as Esther leaves the room.

The questions are straightforward, many of which she already answered on the digital forms they sent her back in the U.S. She is annoyed that she has to go through the forms again. She breezes through the questions about her motivation for choosing PNC instead of in vitro fertilization. She is also unfazed by the financial questions, which she knows are designed to ensure that she, as a recipient of the PNC services, will be able to properly care for the resulting child. She has no problem until half way down page three, question number seventy-six.

'When was the last time you had sexual intercourse?' Instead of the "one year" that she so ruefully filled in on her last form, her revised answer gives her pause: *15 days ago.*

'Did you use prophylactics (condoms or other contraceptives / disease preventatives) during your last sexual intercourse?' *Half the time* . . .

'What is your relationship with the person(s) with whom you had intercourse?' *??*

'How long have you known the person(s) with whom you last had sexual intercourse? *One month.*

'Is he or she aware of your potential participation in the PNC Institute's program?' *Unfortunately, yes. That ended our relationship.*

Sarah's hand is shaking. She sets down the form, her eyes going back to the plants on the windowsill. She is studying the slender stem of a deep purple orchid, trying to breathe.

A knock on the door startles her, and she realizes she has been staring out the window for a good ten minutes, lost in thought.

Doctor Kuipers is tall with the requisite blue eyes and blond hair of his countrymen. She stands up nervously.

"Hi Sarah. Sorry to keep you waiting. I'm Doctor Kuipers," he crosses to her, shaking her hand. He sits down behind the smooth wooden desk and motions his long arm toward the chair across from him. She moves into it.

"Nice to meet you," she nods. After a bit of small talk meant to set her at ease, he launches in, describing what he calls the PNC process.

"First the paperwork. We start with an overview of the forms, then have you sign the confidentiality papers. Then you have three sessions with our in-house psychologist. This is a healthy step that has proven instrumental to our clients in preparing them for the next phase, whether that is choosing to opt out of the program, or moving forward. If you choose to move forward, you make the next suggested donation of 2,500 euros, followed by the required second round of blood work."

She knows they have to label all the finances as donations; otherwise they'd have to change their status category from research foundation to house of prostitution. She ignores her observation, and the nagging judgment it conjures in her mind.

"Then it gets interesting," he pauses and gives her a conspiratorial smile. "We go through the list of potential partners based on your specifications. You will have three days to select your top two candidates. We will do additional compatibility tests, based on a combination of blood work and other biological and social indicators, and then we can start the pairing sessions, held here in the center in our mood rooms—a safe, controlled environment. I'll show you the rooms before you leave today." He talks on for a few more minutes, explaining the projected duration of the coupling, based on menstrual cycle, fertility zone and the pheromone response of the partners. She half listens, both intrigued and concerned. Finally, he gets back to the forms.

"Do you have any questions?" he asks.

"I haven't had a chance to finish these forms," she replies.

"That's okay. We'll go over them together."

"But I filled these in online, from America," she protests.

"Yes. Of course. But we need to do them again in person," he explains. "Just in case some of the answers have changed."

His words pierce her. The fear she has been keeping at bay comes back in full force as they start through the questions. She is one of forty-seven recipients they accepted this year; she has sent medical documents attesting to her clean bill of health and has been through a series of online psychological evaluations; has passed every test and made her non-refundable deposit. *Please let my updated answers be okay*, she thinks, *or I will never forgive myself.*

Chapter 39
Homeland

His plane touches down at Schipol Airport at 1:03p.m. He clears customs by 1:18p.m. and is out of the airport print shop by 1:39p.m. He successfully heralds a taxi in the driving rain at 1:44p.m. He keeps his backpack with him in the back seat to save time as he gives the driver the address.

"Hurry," he commands. The windshield wipers are beating at full throttle as the traffic slows. He powers up his cell phone, impatient as it takes a few minutes to recalibrate to his current location. Twelve new messages and not one from Sarah. His hand runs through his hair as he thinks of the scenario he wants to present to her. Will she even talk to him considering the way he dismissed her from his life as a simple fling? Hopefully she knows better; knows that he was just a scared idiot. Fokke looks at his watch. 1:53p.m.

"Can you go any faster?" he asks, fully aware that the traffic is at a standstill. The driver's charcoal eyes meet his in the rearview mirror, and with one flex of his tangled eyebrows the driver dismisses his question as unreasonable.

Fokke glances into the mirror again, seeing his disheveled appearance staring back at him: eyes red from lack of sleep, his too-shiny, unshaven face topped by hair poking out in all directions as if he slept in a haystack rather than the cramped conditions of economy class—not that there was much sleep involved. With all the air miles he has accumulated, he hasn't traveled in economy class in years, and hopes never to have to succumb to such horrid circumstances again. He does his best to tame his hair, remembering a small refreshing wipe that he took from the plane. He can't exactly shave in a taxi or do anything about his bloodshot eyes, but he can clean his face and pat his hair down.

It is 2:34p.m. by the time Fokke arrives in front of the PNC Institute. He pays his fare and steps out into the pouring rain. He rings the bell and a young woman greets him at the door.

"Good afternoon. Do you have an appointment?"

"No."

"I'm sorry, we do not allow any unscheduled visits," the young woman states in a matter-of-fact tone.

"Oh, sorry. I don't have an appointment, but my . . . sister, Sarah Beth Turner does," he says, raising his voice against the door that is slowly closing. "I'm supposed to wait for her outside, but," he motions helplessly toward the rain. "I might have missed her?"

The woman takes mercy on him. "No. No. She's still here. Please, come in," she acquiesces. "May I take your coat?"

So she's gone through with it, he thinks. Once he is inside the entry foyer, he admonishes himself for lying, but at least he knows she's here, that he will have a chance to talk to her.

"Nice that she has such a supportive family. You can wait in the lobby with your grandmother," the young brunette says. "She's just over there."

The only other person in the lobby turns toward him and Fokke instantly sees the similarities between this tall older woman with curly hair and Sarah. As she glares at him, her left eyebrow rises. It is the second time today he has been put in his place by the mere shift of an eyebrow.

"You're a little late, aren't you?" Nettie says cryptically. "And no flowers?"

He feels like he's been thrown into a ring, her words pummeling him with the deftness of a professional boxer.

"I just flew in from Buenos Aires and came straight here. No time for flowers."

"Tea or coffee?" the young woman asks, aware of the tension between these two *relatives*.

"Coffee," Fokke responds cautiously.

"Great. I'll get you a coffee and leave you two to talk," Esther says as she heads toward the coffee machine.

"Thank you," Nettie replies, her eyes not leaving Fokke's. "This ought to be interesting. I can't remember the last time I had a chat with my *grandson*."

Chapter 40
Rabbit Hole

Sarah steps into the lobby and for the second time today, feels like she's fallen down a rabbit hole into an alternate reality: Fokke van der Veld is sitting across from Nettie in the middle of a tense conversation. She pulls herself back against the wall, very much planning to eavesdrop or find another exit out of the building—whichever proves to be the most helpful in keeping her heart from racing even harder.

Their conversation is audible, but besides her own name, which pops up more often than she'd like, she can't understand a word of it. They are speaking Dutch; not the slow Dutch she had listened to on the language CDs at home—which proved utterly useless to her language-challenged ears—but rapid, fluent Dutch. The conversational tone shifts between friendly and professional, fiery and outraged to confiding and back again. She remains flattened against the wall, uselessly eavesdropping for a solid two minutes, until the blood begins to willfully circulate again and she remembers to inhale, bringing oxygen back to her brain. *Why the hell am I hiding?*

"What is going on here grandma? Fokke?" she says as she steps into the room. Her words silence them as they turn guiltily toward her, as if they've been caught planning a bank heist.

"Nothing," they say in unison. They stare at each other, sizing each other up as if getting ready for another round.

"Don't you two nothing me. I've heard you both for the last few minutes."

"Then you know how I feel about you," Fokke implores.

"Don't be so quick there Fokke. This is my granddaughter and you've already broken her heart once. I'm not going to let you do it again. You have no idea what she's been through in the last year."

"He knows quite a bit of it, actually," Sarah admits. Even though Fokke is the last person she wants to see right now, she wants to know why he's here. Better get it over with.

"What are you doing here?" She looks him straight in the eye. As he stares back at her she feels it: connection, desire.

"I just explained that," he replies, staring at her with such longing that she has to concentrate not to walk right to him.

"I'm sure you did, but perhaps you could explain to me instead of my grandma? And preferably in a language I understand?" She crosses her arms at chest height, keeping her distance.

"Of course! She doesn't understand a word of Dutch!" Nettie says suddenly. She and Fokke let out a mutual sigh. What have they been saying about her that they are so relieved she didn't hear?

"Excuse me. Sorry to interrupt, but would you mind carrying on your family reunion at, may I suggest, one of the restaurants just two blocks to the right? The Silver Spoon café is quite nice. We expect another client in just a few minutes." Esther's voice is smooth yet professional. It is clearly not the first time she has had to suggest that clients calm down and move on.

"Yes, of course," Nettie exclaims. She stands, prompting Fokke to stand as well. Sarah, who is a good five feet away, keeps her distance from them both.

"Oh, Sarah. Before you go, there is one more form you need to sign. It will just take a few minutes for me to get the files," Esther says, motioning for Nettie and Fokke to take their seats.

"Okay," Sarah sighs as someone rings at the door.

"Oh. Sorry. I need to get that," Esther remarks. Fokke and Nettie sit back down, glancing at each other uncomfortably as Sarah walks to the desk to wait.

Esther opens the door to a well-dressed man. He is chiseled, handsome, probably in his early thirties. His strong jaw line, slate blue eyes and dark hair put Fokke on guard.

"Nice to see you Damon," the receptionist greets him. "You will be in the blue room today. Can I get you a coffee or tea?"

"Herbal tea, thank you," Damon responds as he removes his rain-spattered overcoat.

Esther returns to the counter, retrieves a glass tea cup and pushes a button on the sleek metal espresso machine. As she sets the steaming cup of hot water with a tea bag on the counter, Damon approaches, standing beside Sarah.

"Now, Sarah, let me get those forms," Esther says as she turns around.

"So you're Sarah," Damon smiles, turning to face her as he stretches his hand politely out to hers.

"Yes . . ." she responds, confusion on her face as she ignores his outstretched hand.

"I'm Damon. It's a pleasure to finally meet you in person. I guess this is the big day." He is impeccably polite, his smile broad, his teeth blindingly white as he nods toward her. Yet she recognizes something in his eyes: subtle desire and curiosity flickering behind that mask of civility.

Esther, who is retrieving a document from a printer glances up suddenly, and for the first time in their short acquaintance, Sarah can see that she is thrown off guard.

"No. Damon. This is not that Sarah," she interrupts. "This is a new intake." She nods curtly toward Damon before shifting her attention to Sarah. "Now. Sarah, if you could just fill out this form."

He thinks I'm his appointment in the blue room, Sarah realizes. She purses her lips into a tight smile, humiliation flooding her body.

Fokke is already on his feet bristling with anger. Nettie reaches for him just in time, her hand tugging firmly on his.

"I have to get out of here," he utters huskily, straining against Nettie's firm grip. "Otherwise, I can't take responsibility for what I might do next." His eyes are on Damon, who is suddenly aware of the breadth of his mistake. Damon nods warily toward Fokke, shrugging his shoulders apologetically before retreating to a chair, picking up the closest magazine and flipping it open.

The man named Damon keeps his slate-blue eyes trained on an article about menstrual cramps, not daring to flip the page until the sexy Sarah and her scary, red-eyed partner are out of the building.

Sarah power walks through the lobby, not bothering to look at her grandmother or Fokke as she reaches the entrance.

"Sarah, please wait for us," Nettie says in her soft but forceful voice that brings Sarah's feet to an unwilling halt.

"We'll leave together. The three of us," Nettie says sternly. "And you two can have that talk."

"We don't have anything to talk about," Sarah replies as Nettie and Fokke catch up to her.

"Yes we do," Fokke states, still not able to catch her eye. He sees her pink winter jacket on the rack. Without thinking, he reaches for it and holds it ready for her. She slips it on, trying to ignore the familiarity of this gesture.

Chapter 41
The Offer

They walk in awkward silence down the rain-drenched street toward the cheerful sign that says Silver Spoon café. As they reach the front door, Fokke holds it open for the two women and follows in after them.

"I'm going to sit over in the corner. Sarah, you just give me a sign when you're ready to go home," Nettie says. She nods at Nettie and she and Fokke take a table by the window.

After they order tea from the young waiter, Sarah notices the dark circles under Fokke's eyes, the backpack by his side. He must have just flown in from Buenos Aires, she realizes.

"So, Fokke. What are we doing here? What do you want to say to me?"

"First off, I'm really sorry how we ended things . . . how I ended things between us," his face is earnest, apologetic. "I made a mistake."

Sarah inhales sharply, nodding.

"Second, I don't want you to go through with the PNC program." He is getting ready to launch the idea he has carefully formulated during a hellish 41-hour trip in economy class with three layovers, but stops as Sarah exhales loudly.

"You've succeeded on that account without even coming here," she says.

Hope bursts forth in his chest. "That's great news, Sarah." He is just about to reach for her hands, but the cloudy look on her face gives him pause.

"That's terrible news, Fokke. I'm on a three-month probation period, had to go through the blood tests all over again to re-establish a base line. Need to undergo psychological assessment. Might even get kicked out of the PNC program, depending on the test results. All because I slept with you."

"What? Why?"

"You can't enter this program if you've had sex with anyone within six months of the intake date. I didn't even think about it, because I had only been with one man the last eleven years—was celibate for close to a year after that—until you," she sighs. "And sleeping with a stranger, especially with how careless we were with prophylactics, is considered 'risky behavior,' which puts my character in question. What kind of woman about to embark on the journey of motherhood would have an illicit affair? Not the right kind."

Fokke swallows hard. This is not what he was expecting at all. "There was nothing illicit about what happened between us, Sarah. And yeah, we could have been more careful, but we both got tested after our exes cheated on us. So we're clean. But if you want to talk about illicit. Hell, the way that man looked at you in the Institute . . ."

"It was hardly illicit, given the circumstances, but yes," she cringes, "it really upset me. I was so fixated on having a baby naturally, that I forgot what naturally means—it's certainly not having sex in a lab with a stranger." She lowers her gaze to the tea cup in her hands.

"Well, I might have a solution." He pauses, watching her. "Please Sarah, look me in the eyes."

She holds firmly onto the cup as she begrudgingly raises her eyes. When she finally holds his gaze, he sees it, the pain he has caused her, the love he feels for her.

"You were not a travel fling. I'm so sorry I said that to you Sarah. It was a total lie."

"Why, then, did you say it? Do you have any idea how painful that was?" She is blinking, clearly trying not to cry, which she manages. He sees something else in her eyes, a hardening, a distancing; the same preservation tactics he tried just two weeks ago. He swallows as his carefully planned proposition abandons him and his heart takes over.

"I want you in my life, Sarah. I want you to move to The Hague, live with me, stay in my house when I'm out on assignment, and I want us to try to make that baby together."

She startles, her hand going to her chest. Fokke interprets the way her head sways gently from left to right to mean no. He plunges forward.

"I'm 100% serious, here. I'm crazy about you, Sarah. I know we've only known each other for a few seconds, as you've said, but the things we shared in Cortina, the things we said in Venice. They went right inside me, passed through all my armor, all the excuses. I might have even fallen in love with you in that short time, and I think you have too? And if we can't conceive, I want us to adopt a baby. Or two or three." He squints, rubbing at his eyes. "And I want us both to follow our dreams."

She can't believe what she's hearing. She wants to believe every word of it, but she exercises caution. She is certainly not going to tell him she loves him, because the last time she half-uttered those words he broke her heart.

Are those tears in his eyes, or is he just seriously jet lagged? she wonders. Rain pelts against the window, darkening the restaurant inside. She gazes at him searchingly, not saying anything. Her continued silence cuts into him.

"Please, Sarah. Say something." He unconsciously wipes his brow with his sleeve.

"I'm amazed by what you've just offered me, the way you feel—it's everything I want— but I'm not sure it's the best thing for us to do anymore."

Fokke grimaces, pulling her hands into his. "What can I do to change your mind?"

His touch reverberates through her and the warmth of his hands encasing hers brings it all back: the idea of love, the connection, the pain, and her words are set free.

"I completely fell for you Fokke. I opened myself to you, trusted you and you told me it was nothing; that I'd get over it. Then you walked out of my life. I felt about this big," she says, pushing her thumb and forefinger together as if holding a grain of sand. "If you can do that to me in nine days, what will it be like later? When my heart is fully invested? If this experiment doesn't work out? I can't, I won't let a man make me feel small like that ever again."

"I'm so sorry I put you through that, but let me be clear, Sarah. I'm not picturing an experiment." He is looking at her so openly, that she feels almost guilty for her doubt.

"Well, I'm glad to hear that, but even so, I need to be able to stand on my own two feet. And I don't want to lose myself again."

Fokke is again surprised by her answer. "Is that a no? You don't want me in your life? Or that we need to take this whole thing a bit more slowly? Because if I remember correctly, you asked me to be the father of your child just over two weeks ago. You said you wanted to have a relationship with me. Did I misunderstand you?"

Sarah is staring at him. "No. You didn't. It's just . . ."

Fokke raises his hand to his chest, massaging between his pectoral muscles.

"You okay?" she asks.

"Yeah." But he's not okay. He is ready to give his heart to this woman and she is not ready for him. He had his moment back in Venice and he blew it. The pain circulates upward, causing shortness of breath.

"Fokke?" she says again, concern on her face.

"It hurts here," he says.

"Shooting pain, or a slow, numbing pain radiating outward?" she asks.

"I'm not having a heart attack if that's what you're thinking." His face is etched with pain, but perhaps of the kind with which she is so recently familiar.

"I'm afraid of losing you before we've even had a chance to start," he admits.

Sarah raises her left hand to her face, covering her mouth.

"I'm still here, Fokke," she answers, lowering her hands to his. "I'm just a heck of a lot more cautious this time around. Just give me a little time to catch up and figure this out; get used to the idea of having you back in my life. Then I can make a decision about the rest." She eyes him with concern, noting how pale he looks.

Between going through multiple time zones during 41 hours of travel and wrenching open his chest and placing his imperfect heart on a platter in front of her, he is about to collapse.

"I can promise that if you are willing to commit to this, that I will commit one hundred and fifty percent. But if you can't, then I need to know soon, very soon."

"How soon?" she asks.

"By tomorrow."

She pulls back, bewildered by his words.

"Fokke, I. Why tomorrow? Why on earth would you give me 24 hours to make such a major life decision?" She hasn't let go of his hand, and he is grateful for this small sign of hope.

"Just like you had a deadline for the PNC Institute, I also have a deadline." He stops for a moment, wiping his brow which is beaded in sweat. "I've been offered a job that will mean traveling much more than I do now. If I take it, I'll barely see you. If I don't take it, I'll see a whole lot more of you. We need the time together to make this work."

Sarah tucks a loose strand of hair behind her ear, aware of the confusion within. "I'm going to need that 24 hours," she answers.

He looks at his watch. "It's actually 20 hours and counting. Contract is due at noon tomorrow."

Sarah shakes her head, amazed how the tables have turned. Now their future is in her hands, including his future employment.

"This job with the deadline. Is this a job you want?" she asks, noting the perspiration on his face.

Fokke leans toward her, lowering his voice. "It's a dream job, Sarah. But I want you more. No one has worked their way into my heart like you have. And believe me, I tried to get rid of you, but I couldn't." He is close enough to kiss. His loving words, combined with the scent of him—even the tired, travel-weary scent of him—makes her heart ache with longing.

"I tried to get rid of you too. I held onto you all this time, but just this morning I threw you in the Singelgracht. But here you are, risen from the canal," Sarah gives him a fragile smile.

Fokke's lips pull into a line. "I'm more resilient than that, but apparently Jackie isn't. She's finally out of my head." Fokke yawns, squishing his eyes closed, then opens them again with what appears to be effort. "Before I go, I've got something for you." He reaches into his backpack and pulls out a binder. She notices how he flinches slightly as he sits back up.

"This is my offer to you. I pulled an all-nighter putting this together on the flight."

"This is rather business-like; don't you think?" she asks.

"Yeah. But you and I, this is serious business. I want your answer in person. Any questions, any questions at all. Come to my house in The Hague. The address is in the binder," he coughs slightly, rubbing at his eyes.

Sarah nods as she takes the report. They make their arrangements and he hugs her fiercely to him, placing a kiss on her forehead.

"I'll call you first thing in the morning. And seriously, get some sleep Fokke. You don't look well."

"Call before that, please. I pray you say yes," he whispers into her ear before he stands to leave. But as he gets to his feet, dizziness engulfs him. He barely catches his balance, landing hard on the chair.

Sarah jumps up, grabbing onto him.

"Fokke! Are you okay?"

"I'm dizzy as hell," he admits. "A bit short of breath."

Sarah presses against him, trying to keep him from falling out of the chair. His hand is back on his chest, rubbing at his pectoral muscles as Nettie approaches.

"Is your vision blurry?" Nettie asks him, and he nods. "Chest pains?" she asks, eliciting a second nod. "I'm calling an ambulance."

As Nettie dials 1-1-2 and reports the situation, Sarah holds onto Fokke. She signals the waiter, asking for water and a cloth. The waiter responds quickly, running back to the kitchen and returning with a white bar towel and a glass of water.

Sarah dips the towel in the water, and wipes his brow off gently.

"You're going to be alright, Fokke. I think you're just exhausted," she says with determination. "How long have you been traveling?"

"Left Argentina Tuesday night and I've been traveling ever since, 'til I got here. About forty hours if you count the layovers in Los Angeles and New York," he grimaces.

"Did you sleep at all that entire time?"

"Maybe a few minutes here and there." He blinks his eyes heavily at the mere mention of sleep. "This tightness in my chest . . ."

She thinks quickly. "Try coughing, Fokke. It's supposed to help with your heart, just in case." He starts coughing, but each cough makes his chest hurt even more. They hear the sounds of a siren getting closer.

This can't be happening! she thinks. *What should I ask him in case he loses consciousness?* "Do you have any conditions I should tell the doctor about? High blood pressure? Any medication?" she asks.

"No. Nothing like that," he breathes out, his brow beading up again. She dips the cloth in the water, and brushes it across his forehead.

"Did you do anything out of the ordinary, besides traveling forty hours straight?"

"Fell in love with you," he replies.

"Come on Fokke. Be serious," she reprimands as her stomach tightens.

"I am," he coughs. "That is extraordinary."

"Who should I call, Fokke? Your sister? Your parents?" she presses.

"My mom Anne. She's listed as Ma in my phone and my sister Frouckje. My phone is in the top right pocket of my backpack." He takes in a deep breath and grimaces in pain. "It hurts to talk."

"Shh. Save your energy," she returns, intertwining her fingers with his.

"Stay with me, Sarah," he says suddenly.

"Of course," she responds.

The paramedics come in the door and Sarah shares everything she can with them. They check his blood pressure, pulse and temperature while asking him his name, age and where he lives. Although he struggles, he answers coherently.

"The fact that you can still talk is a good sign, Fokke. But your blood pressure and temperature are both high. We're going to take you to the hospital."

"Are you family?" they ask Sarah. She is about to say no, but Fokke nods.

"She can travel with you."

As the paramedics load Fokke into the back of the ambulance, Nettie opens up her purse and retrieves Sarah's phone. Sarah glances at her in confusion.

"I'll explain later," Nettie says as Sarah climbs into the ambulance. "I'll meet you at the hospital."

Chapter 42
Hospital

In the ambulance, Sarah calls Fokke's mother first and explains the situation, giving her the name of the hospital and her own cell phone number. She calls his sister but gets voicemail, which prompts her to send a text.

When they arrive, Fokke is taken to the emergency wing and Sarah hands over his insurance card and identification as Fokke instructed. Alone in the waiting room, she closes her eyes, aware of the panic trying to set in. Regardless of whether or not they end up together, she is certain of two things. She is in love with this man and she desperately wants him to be okay. She closes her eyes, creating space within before praying. *Please, Lord. Let Fokke survive this. Please let him have a long life. And if there is a way, Lord, please let me be part of it.*

Twenty minutes later, Fokke is wheeled back out the door in a portable hospital bed. He is wrapped in a gown, electrodes taped to his chest.

Sarah stands up quickly and moves toward him.

"Are you Sarah?" the nurse asks.

"Yes."

"We're transferring him to cardiology on the fourth floor. You can come with us in the elevator."

Sarah reaches for his hand, the one without the thin needle and tube connecting him to an intravenous drip.

"How are you doing, Fokke?" she asks quietly.

"My chest still hurts, but looks like I'm not having a heart attack. That's the good news at least. But they want to run more tests."

Sarah keeps her eyes on his, her face calm and reassuring as they travel upward in the large metal elevator. The doors open, and the nurse wheels the bed down the hall.

As the nurse sets him up in his room, Sarah sits out of the way, but close enough so he can see her. She watches as the nurse adjusts Fokke's intravenous drip before hooking him up to an EKG machine. Another ten minutes pass before an energetic young woman enters the room and introduces herself as Doctor Eshuis, greeting Fokke and then Sarah. She looks through the reports before proceeding.

"How are you feeling, Mr. van der Veld?"

"Please. Call me Fokke. Not so good. Chest is tight. I feel dizzy, a bit foggy."

"Your partner reported that you traveled for 41 hours straight? Is that right?"

"Yeah," Fokke grunts.

"And did you get any sleep during that time?"

"Not really."

"When was the last time you slept, Fokke?"

"A few days ago," he admits.

"And what has your water intake been like over the last few days?"

Fokke thinks. Usually he drinks water throughout the day, but he's been pounding more coffee than water.

"Low," he admits. "I know better than that."

"Have you been under any stress lately? Emotional or physical?"

Fokke glances at Sarah. "Emotional."

Doctor Eshuis takes on a stern expression far beyond her years as she begins a lecture.

"Prolonged periods without sleep can put your body under severe stress, bordering on exhaustion, which can be quite dangerous. Combine that with extended time in a pressurized airplane cabin crossing multiple time zones, dehydration and heightened emotional stress and you are putting more pressure on the human body than it's designed for." She taps at his chart. "I want to keep you overnight for further observation and I'm going to run a few more tests to address this chest pain you are feeling." She makes some more notes on his chart.

"But it appears that what we are dealing with here is a case of exhaustion and dehydration. The first step is to give you a sedative which will ensure that you get a thorough night's sleep. We've also set you up with intravenous fluids to rehydrate your body. And, Fokke van der Veld. I don't care if you're writing a travel article for King Willem Alexander himself. No international flights for at least two weeks."

Fokke starts to protest, but Sarah cuts him off.

"We understand," she confirms.

Fokke smiles weakly.

A nurse enters the room with two pink pills in a little paper holder.

"This is a non-benzodiazepine hypnotic," explains Doctor Eshuis. "It will ensure that you sleep through the night."

Fokke takes the two pills without a fight.

"We'll give you two a chance to talk before Fokke falls asleep," the doctor smiles. "And please, no stressful or stimulating topics," she reminds them.

Finally alone with Fokke, she pulls her chair toward him, taking his hand. "You really scared me."

"Scared myself," he murmurs.

"Why didn't you sleep?" she asks gently, stroking his cheek.

"You," he says, his voice getting softer. "I had to get to you on time, before . . ."

"Shh, Fokke. It's okay. But maybe you could call next time. Much easier."

"I did call you; three times. Didn't you get my messages? Please read the binder. Please choose me."

"I will read it," she promises. "Just as soon as you're asleep."

The pills begin to take affect almost immediately and he yawns deeply, blinking his eyes.

"You're the ember in the ashes." His voice is getting drowsy. "Need more kindling. Have to keep it going," he whispers as his eyes close. "Ik hou van je, Sarah."

Although she must guess his meaning in likening her to an ember in the ashes, his Dutch words are for once, perfectly clear. *Ik hou van je.* Her mother and grandmother have uttered these words to her on countless occasions. *Ik hou van je. I love you.*

She knows, without question, that she loves him back, but she cannot, will not say these words to him until she is absolutely sure she knows what it means.

Chapter 43
Input

Sarah holds his hand until she is certain he is asleep. An hour has passed since they entered the hospital and it is the first moment she's felt any sense of calm. She settles into the chair beside him, pulling the binder out of her bag. Page one is a table of contents:

Why you should forgive my sorry ass and give us another chance
Why we work together
Why you should move to The Hague to live with me
Beautiful photos to sway you
Why I would make a great father
Contract

She goes over the headings, smiling in amusement. She reaches gently for his hand before continuing to read, the binder balanced on her lap.

"Excuse me?"

Sarah looks up from the binder to see a woman in her late sixties or early seventies standing by the door. Her light blue eyes, and the slight tilt of her nose are familiar.

"Mrs. van der Veld?" Sarah questions as she releases Fokke's hand.

"Yes. You must be Sarah. Thank you for calling me. We came as soon as we could. Is he okay?" she whispers as she crosses the room, standing next to the bed.

"Yes. He's just sleeping now. The doctor thinks it's a case of sheer exhaustion, but they ran a lot of tests to make sure it wasn't his heart. He was having chest pain earlier today." She looks at her former lover sleeping peacefully, an I.V. inserted into his left arm, electrodes strapped to his chest. She doesn't want to leave Fokke's side, but she knows his mother has priority. Sarah stands, placing the binder back in her bag.

"Please, Mrs. van der Veld. Have a seat."

Fokke's mother sits, placing her hand gently over Fokke's. Sarah sees the pain in her kind face and her heart goes out to her. She herself only knows one side of Fokke, but Sarah knows what a close relationship Fokke has with his mother. His mother has known him through every phase of his life. She can only imagine this kind of love.

"He's such a good boy," his mother says.

"Yes he is. I'll leave you two alone," Sarah offers, which elicits a thankful nod from his mother, her eyes brimming with tears.

Sarah steps into the waiting area to discover that most of the seats are taken. At least three men look up at her, but she doesn't notice. Her eyes are on Nettie.

"Grandma," she says, her voice lowered.

"Hi darling. How is Fokke doing?" Nettie asks with concern.

"He's going to be okay. It seems to be a case of sheer exhaustion and dehydration, but they'll keep him overnight to run some more tests just to be sure."

"Oh thank goodness," Nettie sighs.

"Now. Explain what you were doing with my cell phone," Sarah demands.

Nettie lets out a reluctant sigh. "I hid it from you," she admits. "He called you several times, begging you not to go through with your appointment. He broke your heart once Sarah. I didn't want him to do it again."

Sarah takes in this information, thinking how Fokke ran himself ragged traveling to her, preparing a binder of information to convince her of his feelings, how his health might not have been compromised had it happened in a simple phone call. She takes a deep breath, channeling years of counseling experience to stay calm.

"I don't appreciate what you did, Nettie. I had no idea you could be so meddlesome." She exhales heavily.

"I'm sorry. It's not right, but I'm afraid there's more. Something you should know."

Sarah nods at her grandmother, taking another breath to steady her already fraught nerves.

"I did a bit of research over the past few days on your 'Fokke van der Veld, world traveler.' Let me just say that it's not very promising where women are concerned."

"What do you mean?" Sarah asks.

"According to my source, he has a woman in every port. He's a career heartbreaker!" Nettie says quite loudly.

Sarah tries to take in this information. Could it be true? Is she just the latest of a series of women who have fallen for Fokke, only to be pushed away? Although his parting words in Venice might support this theory, the majority of his actions would suggest otherwise. Plus, a career heartbreaker wouldn't travel across the world to beg her not to go through with the program; or create a binder like the one in her bag; or offer to father her children. She is sure of it. But . . .

"Who told you this?" she asks, doing her best to remain calm.

"A woman in my bridge club. Her friend's cousin's grandson is . . ."

"That's three times removed, Nettie! That sounds like gossip more than—"

"Just hear me out Sarah. This source is in the same fraternity as Fokke and he was just at a reunion with him."

That niggling doubt gains hold as Nettie's eyes focus on hers. "Fokke just attended a reunion, right before he left for Argentina," Sarah confirms. "Well. Go on!"

"He heard Fokke bragging about an American woman he'd seduced in Italy," Nettie announces, sorrow creasing her face. "I'm so sorry honey."

Sarah flinches like she's been slapped. *Is this how Fokke describes me? A conquest? A story to share with the guys? Is this the part of him I don't know?* She recognizes the pain, the feeling of smallness all over again as it crawls inside her, sucking at her confidence.

"You were right to protect me Nettie. I am like a moth to the flame when it comes to Fokke, and he just about reeled me back in. Let's get out of here before I get burned to the core."

A good looking bald man sitting in the waiting room stands suddenly.

"Sarah! Please wait!" he says.

"Do I know you?" Sarah asks.

"No. I'm Jan van Buuren, a friend of Fokke's, and that rumor is simply not true. I was on that reunion trip with Fokke in Italy, and at that fraternity party afterwards. I'm the one who blurted out that Fokke had an affair with an American woman. He about bit my head off."

"So you were just blatantly listening to our conversation?" Nettie intervenes. "And what on earth are you doing here?"

"You were talking rather loudly," another man interrupts. "Hi. I'm Jan Taalman. Fokke's brother-in-law. I can vouch for Fokke too. He is not a womanizer. Far from it. He's a solid guy. Thanks for getting him here safely and taking care of him. His mother called us both as soon as she got the news."

"Anyone else want to chime in?" Sarah asks the people in the waiting room, dramatically waving her hand like a talk show host. The mix of men and women glance at her uncomfortably, but a distinguished looking older man in a crisp gray suit with unmistakable Fokke-like cheekbones and jaw nods at her.

"I'm Jaap van der Veld. Fokke's father. My son had his wild days when he was younger, but he's a gentleman. I can vouch for him. Thanks for getting him to the hospital. I am indebted to you." He smiles at Sarah before picking his paper back up.

"Please sit back down," Jan suggests. "I have some things to share with you." Nettie and Sarah take their seats again as he continues. "Fokke fell for you during that snow storm, Sarah. You were all he could talk about afterwards. And about his reputation, let me explain."

"Yes. Why don't you," Nettie pushes.

"Because Fokke's a world traveler and one of our more famous fraternity members, we like to hold a certain . . . wild image of him, if you know what I mean. Even though he's a loyal friend, works hard and we come out in great numbers for his annual fundraiser for his charity, that's not what we talk about. That 'woman in every port?' 'Fokke the heartbreaker?' We've been promoting that image for the last twenty years, and refuse to let it go, no matter how upstanding a life Fokke leads."

Sarah sits unsteadily, as if she's just stepped off a g-force rollercoaster ride at a run-down amusement park.

"Can I get you a glass of water?" Fokke's brother-in-law asks. She nods. Are the Dutch always this invasive? She'd pictured them stand-offish, like they were described in her Going Dutch guidebook, not meddlesome eavesdroppers. Although she has to admit; Jan's explanation is helping a great deal in calming her down.

As she sips the water, the other Jan, the brother-in-law, can't help but make a comment.

"I have to say. After all that happened, I'm surprised he fell for another American woman."

Sarah almost chokes on her water. "Was Jackie American?" she asks.

Half of the waiting room nods.

"It's a big country," Sarah replies defensively. "We're not all self-serving, deceptive liars like Jackie!" She shakes her hands in the air. "Listen, I've enjoyed this group counseling session, but it's now officially over. I'll be back first thing tomorrow morning for visiting hours. Jan?"

"Yes?" they both answer.

"Not fraternity brother Jan, but brother-in-law, Jan. I'll give you my number. Would you call me if there's any change in Fokke's condition?"

"Absolutely."

"And fraternity brother Jan. Thank you for speaking up. I'm glad to have two sides to that story." She slings her bag over her shoulder.

"There's always two sides. Nice meeting you, Sarah."

"And Mr. van der Veld," she continues. "Fokke has a deadline at noon tomorrow for that mystery job. If you are truly indebted to me, then don't let him make that decision until he and I have had a chance to talk in person."

"Yes ma'am," he dutifully responds. Nettie is staring silently at Sarah, her eyebrows raised.

"And Nettie. I'd like to find a hotel here next to the hospital. I have to make a decision about the next phase of my life before 12:00p.m. tomorrow, and I want to be here when he wakes up."

Sarah exits the waiting room without looking back.

"Impressive," Jan van Buuren says.

"Indeed," Nettie concurs.

Chapter 44
The Binder

Sarah drapes her coat across the bed and closes the curtains of the hotel room. Finally alone, she strips down to her underwear and raises her hands above her head, breathing in to begin her yoga practice. She shifts into a sun salutation, then glides effortlessly into a downward dog. She works her way through a series of poses her body knows by heart, sweating out the stress she has accumulated in her body over the last six hours. After a quick shower, she dresses and takes the elevator down to the hotel gift store. She purchases a white silk pajama set and 'I love Amsterdam' underwear before heading to the restaurant.

She is ravenous and orders vegetarian spaghetti with bread and a green salad, accompanied by an ample glass of chardonnay. She eats in comfortable silence among all the business travelers, lost in her thoughts. She has one more glass of chardonnay for good measure before heading back to her room.

Finally, she is calm enough to read the binder Fokke has prepared for her.

The title *Why you should forgive my sorry ass and give us another chance* puts an amused smile on her face. As she reads through his plea for forgiveness, her amusement gives way to heartache. He describes in depth how hard he fell for her, how scared he was of his feelings for her and how he believed it was better to push her away then to risk his heart. In Argentina, he realized it was too late. She already had his heart and he had to do whatever it took to give them a chance.

She flips open to *Why I would make a great father*, and his world is opened up to her. There are photos of him holding his nieces and nephews when they were babies, playing with them when they were toddlers, at different events, on their first day of kindergarten, junior high; scanned-in thank-you letters for his gifts and postcards from around the world. There are pictures of him with families in third-world countries, copies of articles about solar energy programs he has helped fund in Benin and Guatemala through his non-profit foundation. She thinks back to the page she ripped from the in-flight magazine on her way to The Netherlands.

The next page, a black and white medical report, is in stark contrast to the loving photos and articles about his charity projects. She has no idea what it means until she sees that it is from a urology office just days after their last encounter in Italy. Sperm condition: normal. Sperm count, normal.

You are a very thorough Mr. van der Veld, she thinks.

Why we work together manages to push tears right to the edge of her tear ducts, but she focuses to keep them in check. His explanation shows that he has observed her keenly in their short time together, is aware of the nuances of her character, her moods; knows what drives her.

His description of the physical passion between them makes her warm up from deep within. This section ends with four characteristics he believes they have in common: compassion, kindness, respect, joy.

She goes to section four: *Why you should move to The Hague to live with me*.

The man can write. His description of The Hague makes her want to move there even before she gets to the photos. The pictures of The Hague's downtown, with it's gorgeous old European squares surrounded by restaurant terraces are enchanting, inviting. She gazes at Fokke's photos of The Binnenhof, a grand series of brick buildings built in the 13th century which house the offices of the Prime Minister of The Netherlands among other important government positions, she learns by the captions. He has included photos of gorgeous old churches from both the outside and inside, and shots of the North Sea, which lies on the edge of an unpronounceable town called Scheveningen, just 3 kilometers from the city center.

But once she comes to the photos of his house in a neighborhood called Benoordenhout, she has a strange sensation of déjà vu. The passageways, the play of light through the kitchen windows, the worn wooden floors, the mix of contemporary furnishings with classical architecture in the living room, the manicured garden. She knows this house, does she not? She has certainly seen it before.

She flips the page to discover two print-outs of restaurants for sale. One is situated along a canal and Fokke has written the words "Cause Café" above it. She can't help but laugh at the burst of excitement that juts through her. On the next page are two job listings: guidance counselor at the American School of The Hague and academic advisor for Leiden University. Although these listings don't spark her interest as much as the restaurants, it's clear he has thought this through. As she approaches the last section, she is envisioning a romantic, fairytale life with Fokke van der Veld at her side. *The contract ought to sober me up*, she thinks.

Our Contract. The page is blank. She turns it over, discovering two words written in black ink: *Call me.*

Can't call you when you're sound asleep in a hospital bed, she sighs. Could all of the feelings she has for Fokke be situational? Conjured up by the extraordinary circumstances in which they met? Amplified by the romantic nature of their entanglement and the idea of him being in danger? But the sadness she has been feeling in his absence is undeniable. And his carefully crafted proposal of why they should be together seems perfectly plausible. There must be a hitch; some reason it can't work out. Because life is never that simple. Perhaps after a good night's sleep her mind will find holes in his proposal and in her own feelings. Tomorrow morning she will have more clarity.

Chapter 45
News

Sarah awakens from a dreamless sleep to the gentle chiming of her phone.

"Hello. This is Sarah."

"Hi, Sarah. It's Fokke."

"Fokke. You're awake! How are you feeling?"

"Like a new man. Slept fourteen hours straight," he sighs. "Did I wake you?"

"Yes. But it's so nice hearing your voice." She pictures him in his hospital gown, hooked up to all those monitors, and her heart seizes. "Are they going to let you out of the hospital today, or are they running more tests?"

"They monitored me all night and they already ran a board of tests this morning. My heart's in good condition, blood pressure's back to normal. They're going to release me at 9:30 this morning. Where are you?"

"I'm across the street in the Ibis hotel. And I'd like to talk to you in person, about everything."

"Okay. That's so good to hear. I think. So here's the thing. I want you to meet me at my house."

"Well. Like I just said, I'm just across the street," she says gently. "Your house is in The Hague."

"I know. But, it's important to me. You need the whole picture, Sarah. Before we talk any further."

"Okay," she acquiesces as she hears the slight plea in his voice.

"Great. I'll pick you up at ten o'clock. Will that work?"

"Are you fit to drive?" Sarah inquires.

"No. But my parents will bring us."

She swallows hard. "Okay. I'll be in the lobby at 10:00."

She hangs up the phone, and lies back down, rubbing her eyes. Trapped in a car with his parents for an hour? This ought to be interesting. According to the clock on the wall it's only 7:45a.m. and she could use a bit more sleep. She sets her alarm for 9:00a.m. and dozes off.

She is nestled into that space just before you slip into dreams when the phone rings again.

"Hello? Sarah speaking," she answers.

"Hello Sarah. This is Doctor Kuipers from the PNC Institute."

"Good morning," she responds, looking at the clock on the wall. It's 8:04a.m.

"Sorry if I woke you, but I have some good news for you that just couldn't wait."

"Oh? I could use some good news," she yawns.

"Are you sitting down?" he asks.

"Lying down as a matter-of-fact."

"The results from your blood work and urine analysis have been processed. You're pregnant, Sarah."

She sits up quickly in bed. "I am? Oh my God!"

"Is that a happy 'Oh my God?'"

"Yes. Yes. Thank you for letting me know."

"It's the least I could do. We know how disappointed you were about yesterday and we thought this news might make up for it."

"Thank you! It most certainly does," Sarah replies.

"I take it you won't be needing our services any longer."

"No I won't," she answers.

"Your blood work is excellent. You're a very healthy woman. I have faith it will go well. But start on prenatal vitamins right away and continue for the following 10 weeks."

"I started on the prenatal vitamins as part of prepping for the PNC program. Thank you so much!"

"Well, in this particular case, we're not to thank, but I wish you success on your journey to motherhood. And Sarah; considering you've paid your deposit and first donation, you could take advantage of our counseling services during your stay in The Netherlands. We have excellent programs on eating right as a vegan during pregnancy, staying fit, understanding the stages of fetal development and preparing yourself emotionally."

"I just might take you up on that. Thank you so much for calling."

Sarah hangs up the phone and elation pours through her. *I'm pregnant! With Fokke's child!* Despite that box of condoms Fokke had in his backpack, their use of prophylactics was laughable—somewhere around fifty percent. That other fifty percent of their love making turned out to be fruitful, very fruitful.

"I am going to be a mother!" she announces to the empty room. She springs out of bed, excitement filling her body from head to toe. But as the minutes tick by, she is aware of other emotions and thoughts coming into play. *I've known Fokke for a heartbeat. I know he'll be happy about this news, our future child, but what if our parenting styles are totally different? What if I want to raise our child in Bend, Oregon, in a natural environment, not in his multicultural city by the sea—even though it seems intriguing. What does he think of Montessori education? He was in a fraternity, after all. Maybe he's totally traditional. Oh my God! I've been doing ab crunches like there's no tomorrow and I had two glasses of wine last night! What if I've already compromised the baby somehow? Will I still be able to run?*

Chapter 46
Road Trip

She has a little over an hour before she will see him. After a short shower, she puts on her new I-love-Amsterdam underwear and her clothing from yesterday and heads to the hotel restaurant. She makes a point of eating a hearty breakfast before Fokke and his parents arrive.

Will Fokke be excited with her news? Or will it overwhelm him? Does the rule of no stimulating conversations still apply now that he's had a good night's sleep? These are the questions plaguing her when Fokke appears at the entrance of the hotel.

She drinks him in. His eyes are clear again, his face shaven and he's dressed in loose jeans, a dark green button-down shirt and hiking boots. He looks healthy, vibrant.

"Hi." The half-formed smile on his face pulls at her.

"I'm so glad to see you're feeling better, Fokke." She wraps her arms around him, leaning her head on his chest.

"Thank you. God you feel good. I've missed you so much. Have you been through my presentation?" he asks. She feels his voice vibrating through his chest and she wants to stay there, wrapped in his arms.

"Yes, all thirty pages of it," she responds, gazing up at him.

"And?" He looks down into her face. She can see anxiety creasing his brow, fear of what her answer might be.

A sleek gray Peugeot town car waiting in the round-about honks once and Fokke glares at the car impatiently.

"That's our ride. Come on. Where's your suitcase?" he asks, looking around.

"I came here directly from the hospital, after you fell asleep," she answers. "Just my purse and this binder," she responds playfully. He kisses her again on the forehead before taking her hand and leading her to the car.

"My parents can be a bit, well, you'll see. Don't let it get to you," he warns just before opening the door for her.

"What is that supposed to mean?" she whispers, but he just smiles at her and motions her into the vehicle. She lowers herself into the rear passenger seat and both of Fokke's parents greet her at once.

"We met briefly yesterday evening," Anne says. "I can't thank you enough for taking care of our Fokke."

"Oh. Well. I didn't really do that much," she says graciously. "Just got him to the hospital."

"Well, we're grateful," Jaap adds. Fokke slides into the other seat behind his mother, where there is much more leg room and reaches for Sarah's hand.

"So tell us how you two met, Sarah," Jaap demands.

"Oh, well, Fokke didn't tell you?" she dodges.

"He says you stole his backpack," his father announces.

"I'm pretty sure he stole mine first," Sarah returns as a smile breaks out across her face.

"Regardless, we had to both travel back to the same ski lodge to exchange bags," Fokke adds.

"And by the time I arrived, there was a public transportation strike," Sarah continues. They slowly roll out the story, cutting each other off, filling in details where the other has come up short and everyone is laughing. His parents are jovial, friendly. They talk a bit about her travels, where she's from, the weather. It all seems friendly and harmless and Sarah begins to relax a bit.

"What are your intentions with my son?" Anne asks suddenly.

"My intentions?" Sarah responds. She glances at Fokke, asking for help, but he simply wiggles his eyebrows at her.

"Now Anne, I don't think that's an appropriate question," Jaap interferes.

"It most certainly is," Anne counters.

"Not when they've clearly only known each other for a few weeks," Fokke's father goes on.

"We only knew each other for a few weeks when I knew I wanted to be with you for the rest of my life. A woman knows!"

"Not all women process their emotions the same way," Jaap counters.

"And how would you know that?" Anne returns.

It's as if Fokke and Sarah are not even in the back seat. His parents' debate morphs into a polite argument the two had over breakfast that clearly needs a second round. Fokke asks Sarah about the rest of her travels in Italy and the two conversations spin along in two entirely different orbits until they approach The Hague.

Sarah gazes out the window, amazed how skyscrapers give way to the old city center with tall brick buildings and canals. Fokke points out different buildings, sharing strange facts and stories. She tries to get a sense of the driving rules as they come to a busy intersection with cyclists, pedestrians and a long red and black tram that clearly seems to have the right-of-way over all other traffic.

They leave the city center and pass by a large open space called Malieveld. It's the size of several football fields and Fokke informs her it is used for carnivals, concerts and protests. They eventually head into a tree-lined street with rows of tall homes on both sides. Jaap stops in front of a three-story brick flat with a second floor balcony and a peaked facade.

"Here you are," Jaap announces like a taxi driver.

"Thank you for the ride. It was nice meeting you both," Sarah says as she steps from the car. Fokke's father and mother both step out of the car and give their son a hug and three kisses on the cheek before approaching Sarah.

She thinks the encounter is over. But then his mother gently takes her elbow, steering her just out of hearing distance from the men.

"My son seems to care a great deal about you in a very short time. Whatever your intentions, I want you to be honest with him, Sarah. He needs honesty in his life." The cool look in Anne's eyes reminds her of Fokke's passport photo: determined, aristocratic. She is not a woman to be trifled with. But then again, neither is Sarah.

"I am always honest, Mrs. van der Veld," she counters.

Chapter 47
Loose Ends

As his parents head off in their car, Fokke stands before his front door, his backpack resting on the stoop as he retrieves his keys.

"I'm sorry about that. My mom can be a bit . . ."

"Protective," Sarah answers. "I suppose that is a good quality."

"Yeah. If I was five. Now it's merely weird and inappropriate."

"You might have a point there," she concedes.

"So, Sarah. Welcome to my home," he says, opening the door. She crosses the threshold, her boots echoing on the light wood floors. The sun is shining for the first time since she's arrived in The Netherlands and she looks around the house, once again experiencing a strange sense of déjà vu. It's warm inside but she wraps her arms around herself.

"Are you cold?"

"No. I'm. I can't explain it, Fokke. But I feel like I've been here before."

"This house has been in the van der Veld family for generations," Fokke explains. "So unless you've visited some of my relatives at some point in your life . . ."

"It's my first time in The Netherlands."

She spins around, taking in the hallway. She stares at the blue and white tiles plastered into the wall every few feet with newfound certainty. She has seen this hallway.

"Want a quick tour?" he asks.

"I'd love a tour, but let's talk first."

"Okay. We'll sit in the back. I'll set some tea for us."

He leads her to the living room and offers her a seat on one of the worn leather chairs separated by a small table in front of an unlit fireplace. Sunlight pours through the wall of windows facing the garden. White bookcases filled to the brim span the opposite wall. A wrap-around couch and a handful of well-placed reading lamps furnish the rest of the room. Besides a sparse collection of sea shells lining the windowsill, the room is minimally decorated. She explores the book titles as he works in the kitchen. She looks out to the garden, taking in the beautifully manicured expanse of grass edged with little walking paths, small hedges and flowering trees. A large hole to the right of the garden catches her by surprise until she remembers that strange conversation with Fokke's neighbor way back when . . . a boom has fallen. A tree has fallen.

Fokke enters the living room with a tray loaded with a teapot, two glass cups and cookies on a small plate. She sits in one of the two arm chairs and is overcome with the strange sensation of finally coming home. She ignores the feeling and turns her focus on Fokke.

"I hate to get right down to business, but I have a deadline in an hour," Fokke announces. "So please. I need to know what you think of my proposal." He adds a half-teaspoon of sugar to her tea, just the way she likes it. "Ask me anything."

He sits down across from her, his legs stretched out casually in front of him as if he is trying to create the impression of being relaxed. But she sees the crease in his brow, the way he fights bringing his hand up to run through his hair.

She looks at the clock; 10:55a.m. No time like the present. "We've known each other for a very short time Fokke, but I think I . . . have deep feelings for you, and if I'm not mistaken, you think you are quite fond of me too," she carefully proceeds.

"I don't think. I know," he states.

"But that's just it. How can we feel this way so quickly? I mean, I get it that you dismissed me as a fling to push me away—which was quite effective—but who's to say all this passion and connection we feel for one another isn't just a passing phase? What if we go for it, start a family and then . . . we don't really have that much in common after all?"

Fokke listens to her every word, his clear blue eyes watching her. "Believe me. I've thought about that," he answers. "For the entire time we were apart. I almost convinced myself that this wasn't real, but a kind of infatuation. Or wishful thinking. But it's not. I really want to be with you. I know it's crazy. Early. But I just know. I love you."

Sarah releases a breath she didn't know she was holding. Just yesterday, in his drug-induced state, he had told her he loved her, had described her as an ember. But now he is fully awake, professing his love for her all over again. She clears her throat.

"God. I feel that. Right now. Sitting next to you. It's like you're breathing love toward me." She blinks her eyes rapidly, aware of the emotion pushing upward.

"Next question?" Fokke asks, a slow smile forming on his lips.

"Tell me about the dream job with the pending deadline."

"It's a travel show on British Television. But thanks to you, it's not just a travel show, but an environmental travel show."

"What do you mean, thanks to me?" she wonders.

"It was you who got me thinking about my dream job—hosting my own show as a travel guide where I bring to light the real environmental issues threatening these rare cultural spots around the world. And giving people a way to do something about it while they are on their adventures."

"That's the perfect job for you Fokke! But how did this come up?"

"Long story short? An old fraternity friend who's now an accomplished producer asked me to be the host for their up and coming travel show on television. I added the environmental aspect and he agreed."

"You're an excellent tour guide. And this would really fulfill you."

"Yeah. Thanks. I think I'd be a natural. And I'd triple my income while helping address environmental and social problems I've seen over the last 20 years."

"So what's there to discuss?" she asks quietly. "You should definitely go for it."

"I can't start a relationship and this job at the same time. I have to choose."

"Are you saying you'd give up your dream job to play house with me?" she asks.

"In a heartbeat," Fokke replies earnestly.

"Why?" She studies his composure, looking for any signs of doubt.

"You're the career change I want, Sarah. To have your love in my life. Your children."

She feels her heart palpitating, feels the joy seeping into her every pore, but the career counselor in her sees the conflict.

"But there must be a way to do both . . ." she hesitates. "We could compromise. Somehow make it work. Otherwise you'd end up regretting us, regretting—"

"I'd be home about one weekend a month, Sarah; if that. You have to be present to be in a relationship. Especially if we're trying to start a family. Believe me. I've tried the long distance approach and it didn't work out. I'm not willing to do that with you." He squeezes her hand, pulls her toward him. "The way I see it, there's romantic love ruled by emotion and attraction—and thank God we have that kind of love in spades. And then there's the love of long term, daily life together that requires compromise, debate, communication, sacrifice—and you have to work at that kind of love. I want both kinds of love with you, Sarah."

She smiles at him, clearly not believing her luck in finding this extraordinary man who can actually talk about different kinds of love.

"And you're absolutely sure you want this? You're not suffering from some sort of post-hospital duress?" she asks.

"No darling. I know what I want," he responds. "And it's you."

She has all the information she needs.

"If that's the case, then I have something to tell you."

"Okay." His confidence is growing.

"Your heart is healthy, correct?" she asks, just to be sure.

"Yes."

"Your sperm are healthy too," she smiles.

"Liked that touch, did you?" Fokke winks, thinking she's referring to the urology report he included in the binder.

"Yes. But I know firsthand how healthy they are." She can't keep her secret any longer. "We're pregnant!"

"What? We are?"

"Yes! Just a few weeks as you can imagine. But yes. We're pregnant."

Fokke jumps up and pulls her from the chair into an embrace. "And you want to be with me?" His lips are close to hers as he looks down into her eyes.

"Yes! I really do," she swallows. There. She's said it. Or half of it.

"Even if you weren't pregnant?" he asks.

"Still yes."

"So you're mine!" he smiles victoriously. But his elation fades as she recoils from his words.

"I'm not a possession. I'm my own person. I . . . care about you deeply Fokke, but I'm not getting married. I'm not going to be a housewife or be a—"

"Sarah, breathe! I'm not Bluebeard. I'm not going to lock you away in a closet," he tells her, rubbing her shoulders. "I'm going to give you all the space you need. I'm going to love and honor you. Support your dreams. And you, mine. Yes?"

"Yes," she sighs. "Sorry."

"That's why the contract page is blank. We write that together. We create our own rules."

"God. You know me so well! Better than I know myself. How do you do it?" She shifts in his arms, knowing she is on the verge of something tremendous and it scares her.

"That's what love does. It opens the other to you."

"In theory," she responds.

"In practice," he replies. "And by the way, it's a good thing you don't want to marry me because I'm apparently already married to someone else," Fokke stares at her heatedly.

"What?" She struggles in his arms, trying to get free. "You better be freaking kidding me Fokke!"

A part of him wants to draw it out, tease her, but he's not a complete idiot. "My publicist called me this morning. Seems my ratings have gone up since word got out I'm secretly married to the latest sensation, travel vlogger Alexi."

"Oh my goodness!" Sarah laughs out loud. "You're married to my alter ego. That's handy. I have to say, I was jealous there for a minute."

"Alexi and I are trending on Instagram and Twitter," he adds. "Who put us together is still a mystery."

"Do they know who I really am?"

"No. Not yet. But you don't have your wig on, so they could figure it out. You know, your alter ego could make a career out of travel," Fokke comments as he lowers his arms, securing them around her waist.

She has been thinking the same thing, especially since her sister has been sending her reports on the rising statistics, along with the offers from multiple companies for paid sponsorships.

"Maybe. But what I really want is to finish the project of lighting candles in every cathedral I can visit until the baby is born, or I can't travel anymore." She breaks from his grip. "Give me that house tour, would you?"

"Yeah." He shakes his head back and forth. "Christ, Sarah. I'm going to be a father for real this time. With the right woman by my side."

He leads her through the house, but keeps talking. "You know, we might be able to work that cathedral tour out. Visiting the cathedrals of Europe, you and I together."

"That would be amazing!" Sarah responds.

They walk down the hallway toward the kitchen. Sunlight pours through the windows onto the granite countertops.

"But back to the environmental show," Sarah begins. "Maybe you—"

"I'm not going to be away from you in the far reaches of the earth when you're going through this pregnancy," Fokke interrupts her. "I want to be by your side." He grabs her hand and pulls it to his lips and gives it a quick, possessive kiss before letting it go again. "We can work on something environmental locally," Fokke suggests. "Maybe I could even write the scripts for the television show instead of being the guide. I could also put more time into my Foundation. God knows I need to. But you and our baby come first."

She wants to hug him fiercely, profess her love. Instead, she gently rubs her hand across the granite, gazing around the kitchen as she forms her thoughts.

"I want that too. But I want my space, Fokke. I'm serious. I have to hold onto me."

Fokke raises his eyebrows. *This is not a conversation he's had before. Usually, women want more commitment, not less. Usually, they say I love you first.* He leans against the opposite counter.

"How about this. You move in with me, share my house, my bed." He crosses his arms, gazing at her. "You can convert the attic into your own private space, so you have something that's just for you. The extra bedroom upstairs can be the baby's room. We travel together. We'll probably have to set up a legal partner-contract so you can stay in The Netherlands, but we won't do anything rash, like get married." *Fokke hopes he has chosen words that will appeal to her senses without scaring her away.*

Fifteen seconds pass as she contemplates; thirty seconds.

"Sarah, I—"

"Okay," she says.

"Okay? You'll move in? The whole thing?"

"Yes. We're already having a baby together. So yes. Let's do it," she simply answers.

He pulls her into his embrace and kisses her fully on the lips. He sees the way she melts into him, but he reminds himself to slow down; give her the room she needs.

"You have just made me a very happy man, Sarah. I promise I won't push you. You'll have space. And we have a bit of nature here too. I know you've said nature is important to you. There's the Haagse Bos just five blocks from here. It's an urban forest; nothing like what you're used to in Oregon, but there are plenty of trees, birds, rabbits even."

"Rabbits. Is that your version of nature?" she teases good-naturedly.

"And you like gardening, yes? Organic and local vegetables? The climate's not the best, but you can convert a section of the backyard into a garden if you want. Considering that giant tree fell, there's more light and space for a garden now. Or, you can get a subscription to the urban garden. Did you know The Hague has the largest urban garden in Europe?"

"Urban garden? Isn't that a contradiction?" she replies, smiling at his enthusiasm and his clear desire to pepper her with information to make her happy. And boy is she happy.

"This urban garden is exceptional. It's on the rooftop of a former office complex. An expansive greenhouse with organic vegetables and they raise tilapia. I know you don't eat fish. But, they use the fish excrement as fertilizer for the plants. Can't get more local than that. And then we have a huge outdoor fruit and vegetable market on the other side of town five days a week. It's not all organic, but . . ."

But she's not listening. She is looking at a framed picture on the wall next to the kitchen clock. It's a two-page spread from Design & Style magazine when the house was featured in a write-up about The Hague architecture a few years ago.

"Oh my God," she mumbles.

"What?" he asks. "What's wrong?"

"That picture."

"What about it?"

"If I'm not mistaken, that very picture is on my vision board, Fokke. The one I made six months after Matthew and I signed the papers; two months before I bought my ticket to Europe. My ideal home. I cut it out of an old architecture magazine. This is just totally bizarre," she stammers, her hands bound together as if she's about to pray.

"Or destiny screaming at you," he muses.

"I'll tell you what destiny is screaming at me right now." She leans into him, kissing him on the mouth. The words she wants to say are just on the tip of her tongue, but she can't get them out. Instead, she hugs him fiercely to her. He hugs her back, breathing in the crisp mountain lake scent of her, laced with jasmine.

"You're still wearing your perfume."

"Of course I am." Sarah shifts, pushing away from him slightly, as if in torment. She hasn't worn the custom fragrance since their parting words in Venice; until today.

Fokke has an idea of what's going on, and he does his best to hide the joy trying to push to the surface, just in case he's got it all wrong.

"So someone at the hotel in Italy knew who we were," she says, changing the subject.

"And I think I know who," Fokke replies as he tucks a curl behind her right ear. "Celeste, the French woman."

"Why on earth would she post something like that?" Sarah wonders. She could get lost in this man for years to come.

"To throw us together," Fokke explains, looking into her eyes. She falters at his gaze, those aristocratic light blue eyes laced with love. Her knees grow weak.

"But as far as she knew, we were together. Happily . . . married . . . newlyweds." She almost whispers these last words, not taking her eyes off of him.

His hands are on the small of her back, his strong arms on either side of her. "She knew we weren't married, Sarah. She saw it from the beginning. But I was thinking, since the world already thinks we're married . . ."

"I'm not getting married again," she cuts him off.

"No need to. We could just pretend, carry on the charade you started back in Italy."

"Be a fake husband and wife but secretly love each other," Sarah says, her voice strained.

"Are you saying you love me?" Fokke stills.

"Yes, Fokke. I think I love you." For the first time, he sees tears in her eyes break free and she is doing nothing to stop them. "I know I love you. All right?" she murmurs.

"About damned time you admitted it," Fokke whispers. He holds her as she melts into him, tears flowing and he feels his love, in wave after wave, being returned to him.

When she is all cried out, he kisses her forehead, wiping at the corners of his own eyes, gentle laughter coming from his chest.

"Glad we got that out of the way," she says, wiping away her tears, her smile radiant.

"Yeah. Me too. Now, my fake wife, who really loves me. I'd like to show you the rest of our home."

ABOUT THE AUTHOR

 Kristin Anderson is an American living in The Netherlands who is passionate about travel, the environment, literature and romance. *The Things We Said in Venice* is her second novel with a sequel in the works. If you enjoyed this book, you might be interested in Kristin's debut novel *Green*, an eco-romance released in 2013.

www.authorkristinanderson.com

www.facebook.com/AuthorKristinAnderson

www.twitter.com/AuthorKristin

Before you go: If you enjoyed *The Things We Said in Venice*, please help others discover this novel by telling a friend and sharing a review on Goodreads as well as Amazon in your respective country.

CPSIA information can be obtained
at www.ICGtesting.com
Printed in the USA
FSHW01n1056090718
50300FS